SEAN
Eddie
and
ME

*a Novel
by*

PAUL LEGER

First published by Red Press, 2015
Reprinted edition, 2021
info@redpress.co.za
www.redpress.co.za

© Paul Leger, 2015
All rights reserved. No part of this publication may be reproduced, stored in any retrieval system, or transmitted in any form or by any means, whether in part or whole, without written permission of the publisher.

ISBN 978-0-620-57556-0

Editor: Claire Strombeck
Cover design: Caitlin Truman-Baker
Typesetting & layout: Matthew Covarr
Printed & bound by: Pinetown Printers, Pinetown

In memory of Peter and Robert

ONE

Kia? You want my honest opinion? Typical Jap crap. Second and fourth set way too close together. The same goes for the clutch and brake. And less power than a Singer sewing-machine. No wonder I can't get the hang of it. I'm a chip off the old man. Always going for the cheaper option and then regretting it.

Anyway, I better concentrate before I end up in some township, because that's the last thing I need right now. I'm trying to remember what the Avis guy said. Take a left when you get to the fork outside the airport, then carry on towards the city until you see the N1 south. Or was it a right at the fork? Great start. Not even out of the carpark and already I'm lost.

Only once I'm on the N1 do I start to unwind a bit. I don't know why I was so nervy in the first place. But that's just me. Being a Sunday afternoon, the road is quieter than a morgue. A few long-haul trucks, a couple of cars, a taxi or two, nothing much. The rest of the country must be farting under the covers after their Sunday lunch.

At least I have the road to myself for a change. It gives me a chance to think about things. Nowadays I never get a chance to think about anything, what with Jen and the kids, and the company helping itself to its pound of flesh. I don't even have time to piss anymore, never mind think.

There's not a cloud in the sky, only this hazy pale blue. Brown veld stretches in every direction, broken here and there by scraggly thorn trees and overhead pylons and telephone lines. Everything looks worse in winter. Like an old photo with the colour washed from it. I don't understand how anyone can live here. I don't know how I could have lived here.

Off the N1 the road becomes narrow and potholed. I'm soon trailing this massive flatbed that's drifting over the white line and going eighty. I bet the guy bought his licence. That's how it is nowadays. I gear the Jap toaster down to third, press my foot to the floor and crawl past without landing in the veld.

The N18 turn-off pops up ahead. I keep straight. At this rate I'm going to get there way too early. And that's taking it slow. I feel naar just thinking about it. There's nothing worse than arriving somewhere on a Sunday, unless it's in the dark. Especially a place you don't want to be.

Two hours later the town looms up ahead; it's too late to yank the handbrake and do a U-turn. First up is the prison. Not as I remember it. It's twice the size and wrapped in razor wire. No wonder the woman on the phone said the town doesn't get many tourists. A few guys in orange are hanging around the open quad area, looking bored out of their minds.

A hundred meters further down the road *Huis Sonskyn vir* ~~Swart~~ *Bejaardes* is still open for business. If it wasn't for the sign you would reckon it's part of the prison next door.

The Monopoly mine houses on the opposite side are still there and uglier than ever, now that the jacarandas once shading them have been mowed down. So called 'aliens'.

As I lean the Kia into Sand River circle it seems as if I've never been away. Like past and present have collapsed into one, and everything in between suddenly doesn't count for much.

I hardly recognise the Vegas. It's still standing, but only just. The red and white neon sign that flashed twenty-four seven is gone and that green grass that saw how many packets of slap chips drowned in Aromat is a parking lot selling dodgy second-hand cars. I keep driving.

Like the woman on the phone told me, I take a right into Voortrekker, then a left into De La Rey, then another left into Retief, where I find the hotel. All this time I've been imagining this posh new spot called the Jacaranda, meantime it's the old Doringboom dressed up in a fancy new name.

I pull into the half-empty parking ground and find a place near the entrance. I squeeze out of the car. My back hasn't felt this stiff in ages. By the looks of it they've given the hotel a facelift. It could be worse. It's got two stars, whatever that means, apart from an excuse to charge you more. There was nothing else listed on the internet. Besides, I only booked for one night.

I take my overnight bag from the boot and make sure all the doors are locked. You can't trust anyone these days. Not even in small towns.

The woman behind the reception isn't bad looking, in that Afrikaner sort of way. Nice skin, big bones, shiny brown hair going down to her shoulders. She's also friendly, which makes a nice change. I appreciate that. A good-looking woman that's also friendly, that is. A black guy in a red jacket and black pants from the Ark appears from nowhere and takes my bag from me. I follow him up the stairs to Room 104. That's the same number as our house in Durbanville. If I was Jen I would believe it meant something. An omen or something like that. But I'm not Jen.

The old guy is also friendly and polite. Too polite. He's been working here eighteen years, lugging suitcases up and down the stairs. While he fiddles with the key in the door, I'm calculating how many suitcases. Let's say ten a day. Times three-hundred-

and-sixty-five. You get the picture.

I give him a tip, five rand in coins. It's all the loose change I have. But it must be more than he earns in a week because he genuinely seems to appreciate it; you would swear I've given him a Christmas bonus. I tell him I'm not his *baas*, but it goes in one ear and out the other. Like I always maintain, this so-called new South Africa is a bullshit story. Except in the cities, nothing has changed. The same old thing in a different wrapper. That's why I'll never bring Jen and the kids to a place like this.

I lock the door and check out the room. I've long since lost count of all the hotels I've stayed at. That's the price you pay for being in sales. I go around the room opening the cupboards, turning on the hot- and cold-water taps, checking under the bed for dust, testing the mattress, sniffing the bedspread and spare blanket in the cupboard – that type of thing. It's called a ritual. I can't relax until I know what I'm dealing with.

I'm feeling it a bit now. It feels like I've been on the road all day. I don't know what the rush was about. I lie down on the bed and kick off my Crocs. Don't care what anyone says, they're still the best shoes in the world.

They probably haven't replaced the mattress since the Doringboom days; it's way too soft and sags in the middle. There's a long crack on the ceiling, running from one side of the room to the other – I bet caused by an earth tremor from the mines. People don't believe it when you tell them you grew up on an anthill, with these million and one black ants in mining helmets drilling holes miles under you.

Someone has tried to fix the crack, but they've done a hash job of it. You can't just slap on Polyfilla. With these things you have to get to the root of the problem. You can't just cover over the surface and think it will go away. Nine times out of ten you'll have to start from scratch again.

The room has a TV, one of those massive dinosaurs from way back when. Talk about a blast from the past – Barlow-Vision. Because it doesn't have a remote – remotes weren't even invented in the Seventies – I have to sit up and lean forward on the edge of the bed to flick channels. I don't know why I bother; there's nothing to watch on a Sunday, besides Bible bashers getting their rocks off. Nobody must tell me who and what to believe. I turn the sound right down and sit there thinking what to do until dinner.

I should try get in touch with Eddie. He's been living with his mom all these years – that's according to Simon. I wonder if he still looks the same. He probably wouldn't even know who I am; that's how long it's been. Maybe I'll stick to my gameplan and leave it for another time.

This crack on the roof is bugging me. If it were up to me I wouldn't just cover it up with Polyfilla. First, you've got to chip away the plaster around the crack until there's a clean groove. Then you cover the groove with forty-millimetre joinery tape. And only then do you smooth it over with Polyfilla and give it a good sanding with a hundred-and-eighty-grit. Once I'm finished with it you won't know there was a crack there in the first place.

I should give Jen a quick call, let her know I got here safe, make sure everything is okay and tell her to lock the Trellidoor. She's a complete hippie when it comes to S&S – Safety and Security. If I didn't insist she carry a cellphone with our emergency numbers punched in she wouldn't bother. I once asked her what she would do if she broke down on the N2 at night. She just shrugged her shoulders and said some airy-fairy nonsense about karma. That's Jen for you. I would cut my own throat for her, but she's still living in the '70s.

I dig out my cellphone from my jacket and check if there are any messages from her. Nothing. Probably still being faxed through. I hit 'Theron Home', and then hit 'Cancel' before it even starts ringing on the other side. I'll call her later, after suicide hour and the kids have gone to bed. I check my watch again – 15:10. Still three hours to kill before dinner. I get up and fill a glass of water from the bathroom, then dig out the Rennies from my toiletry bag. I down three of them and lie on the bed again. Before I know it I'm staring at the crack, fighting off this heavy lump of dread I've had from the moment I stepped off the plane.

TWO

"You're a psycho, you know that?"

"Check who's talking? I'm just keen, that's all."

"'Just keen', he says. Only psychos go fishing at sparrow's fart. To think I could still be dossing at Club Duvet."

"Ag, it's not that early."

"What? The sun hasn't even poked its head over the mine dump yet? Yikes!"

"What?"

"Almost saw my arse. This path is slimy as all hell."

"Chips with that rod, won't you. You almost saw my eye. At this rate I'm going to walk out here a blind man."

"And me in a wheelchair."

So, with this fine mist hanging over the river and about fifty degrees colder down here than up on the bridge and us talking non-stop crap, we work our way to the water's edge. I swear, I wouldn't want to be here alone, even during the day. With the willow trees on the other side appearing and disappearing like dangly skeletons in the mist it could be something out of a horror movie. I stick to Sean's back as we trek along the path running next to the river.

"Seriously, Nick, you're going to take my eye out," says Sean after I've jabbed him in the back for the fifteenth time.

"Sorry."

"Don't mention it."

It's a bit of a schlep to get to our spot, a soft patch of green grass spread under a huge ancient willow that's jam-packed with weaver-bird nests. It takes forever and a day to get there, at least fifteen minutes from the bridge, but it's always worth it in the end because nobody else comes here. It's just Sean, me, the weaver-birds and the brown moody river.

We chuck our haversacks onto the dewy grass and begin to organise ourselves for some serious fishing. More like Sean organises himself for some serious fishing, while I lay out the flask and sandwiches and . . . I start patting my pockets. Sean must spot the seriously worried look on my face.

"What's wrong?"

"I forgot my lighter."

"You're bullshitting?"

"I'm serious."

"So now what we going to do?"

"I dunno. I'm such a loskop."

"That's no lie."

"Up yours too."

"Maybe later."

"Think I should go back?"

"Are you nuts?"

"Shit, I can't believe it!"

Sean casually carries on sorting out his stuff, like it's no big deal.

"By the way . . ." he says, his back to me, threading his line.

"What?"

"Maybe if you ask nicely, you can use the matches in my tackle box."

You would swear Sean has just saved my life, I'm so grateful. We spread the groundsheet on the grass and I find the matches and arrange them next to our unopened box of Dunhills, with our flask and lunchtin alongside them. Things have to be just so before I can get going. It's not like there's any rush and it's not that I'm really that big into fishing. Not like some guys. They go into panic mode soon as they smell the water. Sean falls into that category. He's big time into fishing. Always has been.

"I wonder if I should use a number two or four hook? What you reckon, Seanie?"

"Maybe try the four. With this mist the bass might be biting."

I screw on the coffee grinder tight and proper. Not like the last time we were here when I almost tossed my reel into the water, together with the rest of the rod.

"I reckon today's the day, Seanie. You watch, I'm going to catch the biggest mother you've ever seen."

And I pick up my rod and start going through the motions of hooking a fish the size of a marlin. Slipping and sliding across the grass, the marlin drags me towards the water. I dig my feet hard into the ground and fight it and slowly reel it to shore. As it reaches the riverbank I pull out the Okapi and stab it in the throat, then collapse on the grass and have a heart attack. By this time Sean's killing himself.

"You're such a doos," he says, shaking his head, but wiping his eyes at the same time.

"That's why you like me. Birds of a feather and all that."

"Ja, true. But sometimes I wonder."

I look at my watch. It's almost eight and the sun is at long last breaking through the mist.

"How about a good luck smoke before we start?"

Now Sean looks at his watch. "If you're keen, I'm keen. You can do the honours."

So I squat down on the groundsheet and unwrap the Dunhills and flick open the box and carefully lift off the gold paper. The last thing we need now is our pack of twenties to land up in the water. I lift the box up to Sean's nose.

"Like flippin' mother's milk," he says.

It's my turn next to take a sniff.

"Nothing like it, hey? I still maintain Dunhill is the best brand in the world."

"You're probably right."

"Of course I'm right. You first," I say, offering him the box.

"No, you first. You paid for them."

"Okay, if you insist," I say in this stuffy English-gentleman accent and help myself.

When we have both settled down and are ready, I light Sean's for him and then mine. It's the ritual. I close my eyes, suck the smoke deep into my lungs, hold it there for a bit and then slowly let it out through my nose. There's nothing better than that first drag. Especially when the guy I'm sharing it with is Sean and we are standing on the misty banks of the Sand. Sean blows a smoke ring into the air and we watch it float away slowly and dissolve into the grey.

"Mother's milk," he says, and soaks up the earth's oxygen with the next drag. We stand next to each other, looking at the river, neither of us saying much. You don't need to say much in moments like this. Sean finishes his first and flicks the butt into the water.

"You want the last drag?" I offer.

"No, you enjoy it."

After I've sucked mine to the bone I also flick it into the river and watch it bob up and down, hoping a fish will go for it. Sean yawns and scratches his balls like he's got crabs or something.

"This is the life, hey. What more can a man want?"

I don't answer, because right now I can't think of anything.

As I said, when Sean and me go fishing I do more messing around than actual fishing. But eventually I get my act together and my line into the water. Sean's already tackled up and trying his luck higher up, which means I get the spot under the willow.

I don't know how long Sean and me have been coming to the river. It must be since we were still in nappies. Okay, I'm exaggerating but that's how long it feels. Compared to Sean I hardly ever catch anything. Not even a barbel. But it's not only about catching fish. It's hard to explain, but there's more to it than that. Only Sean and me understand that.

Once my line's at the right tension and my rod at the right angle, I settle into the gnarly trunk of Old Faithful – that's what we call her, the old willow tree – and stare out over the water, taking in the early morning: the sun burning up the last of the mist, the weaver birds having it out above my head, the gentle slap-slap of water against the muddy bank, the smell of morning grass, the bubbles popping on the surface.

Stupid thoughts start popping in my own head. Like, I start wondering what's been the biggest and oldest fish ever in the Sand River. And are the bubbles on the water just crabs or some other underwater creature we don't know about? Or maybe it's just the mud farting. And were the black things in that Bata shoebox really Swapo ears, or just biltong? And is it true that Luke Scheepers cut them all off or is it just another of Eddie's stories? And about all the stuff we're planning for the holidays, the veld camp and the fête and my birthday that's coming up soon. And whether my uncle's going to make it. Dumb thoughts, floating in and out of my head, as I lie there waiting for a nibble.

The time passes. The sun climbs higher and higher and I slide lower and lower, until I'm on my back staring up at the sky, watching this small cloud changing shape, from a dog into a bird, then into a tadpole, then into a fat dog turd.

"Had any luck?" asks Sean from somewhere way above. It feels like he hasn't been gone for five minutes.

"I just lost a huge motherfucker," I say, blinking my eyes in the bright light and yawning.

"Like flippin' hell you did. We wouldn't hear the end of it, even if a guppy nibbled your bait."

"What about you?"

"Nothing much either. Just a few small ones."

"Where they?"

"Threw them back."

"Are you kidding me?"

"No."

"Oh."

And so we go on, back and forth, until the sun burns a hole in the top of our heads and Sean decides to try for barbel lower down where the water's more muddy, and I decide to stay put. While Sean crawls around in the mud and I park off with my hat over my face, I'm thinking it's lucky no-one's around when Sean and me go fishing; they would think we're nuts.

By the time we've packed up and hiked for miles back to our bikes chained together up at the bridge my shirt is sticking to my back and my face feels as if someone's smeared Deep Heat over it. It's one of those typical Free State days, when it's so hot everything stops moving. Even the insects and leaves on the trees. Everything. It's so hot that breathing is a mission. It's one of those days where you just want to sit on the stoep and stare.

"Looks like someone's moving in," says Sean, after we've crawled to the top of Voortrekker and taken the turn into Van der Stel. A truck with a double trailer is parked outside the old mine manager's house. Van's Household Movers is splashed in yellow down the side.

"About time someone moved in," I say. "The place has been standing empty for yonks."

It's true. Ever since the mine built a new mansion for the mine manager, with a tennis court and a sauna and all, hardly anybody's been living here.

Sean pulls up ahead under the Syringa tree. I pull over next to him and we stand there catching air over our handlebars. It's a real mission getting back from the river, especially when you have to carry a rod and heavy haversack at the same time. I feel like I've got a Checkers bag over my head. Five black guys in blue overalls are hauling a piano up the driveway. It must weigh a ton-and-a-half.

"Definitely not Morkel's," says Sean, pointing with his rod to the furniture on the grass.

"Or Russel's. I wonder who's moving in."

"Larnies. Check that Beemer in the driveway. You know what that thing must have cost?"

"How much?"

"Big bucks. Minimum sixty grand. Can't see from here but if it's the 735i, even more than that. I wouldn't mind getting behind the wheel of that thing."

"You can buy a bladdy house with sixty grand."

"You're telling me. You can buy your own tropical island with sixty grand. These okes earn a wack. And for doing nothing."

"You reckon?"

Definitely. All they do is sit behind a desk all day telling their skivvies what to do. My old man says they don't even bother going underground."

"Is it? If that's the case I'm going to study to be a mine manager."

"Ja, me too. That's if I ever get my matric.

"Of course you will. It's Eddie who won't."

"That's true. Hell, but it's hot," Sean says for the hundredth time today. "How about we hit the pool this arvie?"

"What a ques."

As we pull away from under the half-shade of the Syringa, the five black guys in overalls start hauling the piano up the stairs to the front door.

THREE

Thwack! The first blob lands on Angelo's back. He pretends not to notice. Then a second cruise missile collides with the back of his hairy thigh. Angelo smears the gob off with the corner of his towel, but he's not even done when an orange missile comes flying in from the other side and lands on his arm. He's under serious gob attack.

"Come on, please guys," says Angelo, spinning round on his blubbery arms, trying to catch us in the act. By the innocent look on our faces you would think we're all angels. Angelo pulls up a handful of grass and wipes the gob off his arm, watching Eddie at the same time.

"What you looking at me like that for?" says Eddie.

"I know it was you, Eddie. Don't do it, man. You know I hate it."

"Do what? I'm not doing anything," says Eddie, all innocent-like.

"You're the only one who's drinking Fanta," says Angelo.

"No, I'm not."

"Yes, Porra, don't accuse someone for something they didn't do," chirps Gavin Joubert from across the way; I can see his Fanta hidden behind his back.

While the three of them argue, I prepare for the next attack, mixing Creme Soda with gob in my mouth. The longer you mix it, the thicker and stringier it gets. While Angelo is looking in the direction of the Joubert brothers I fill my hand with a fat glob and flick it in Angelo's direction. It whacks him between the shoulder blades. Angelo swings round like a wounded bull, but by the time he gets to me I'm looking the other way. Eddie and the Joubert brothers pack up laughing. Like that book we did in class, *Lord of the Flies*, Angelo is our very own Piggy. There are some people in this world who bring out the worst in other people. Angelo is one of those.

"Hey, I reckon Angelo's had enough," says Sean, looking at Eddie and me.

"Ja, master, if you insist," says Eddie, and flicks his spitball into the grass.

Angelo stands up and waddles over to the pool, his thighs scraping like sandpaper and Gavin and Chris chirping "oink, oink, oink" all the way. He jumps in and triggers a tidal wave. From across the way Gavin burbs a loud Fanta burp that goes on for about ten seconds.

"I bet I can do it longer than that," says Eddie, and downs the rest of his Fanta.

"Prove it," says Gavin.

Eddie sucks in some more air, filling his lungs, building up the pressure, which is the way you must do it. He looks around to make sure we are watching and then lets rip with this long slow burp, controlling it all the way, stretching it out for as long as possible. It goes on for about an hour and he's blue in the face by the time he's squeezed the last drop of air from his lungs.

"Beat that, china," says Eddie, real chuffed with himself. Gavin's impressed even if he pretends not to be.

"Buy me a Grape Fanta and I bet I'll beat you," says Gavin.

"Like hell. You can buy your own Fanta," says Eddie. "You try, Nick," he says, because I'm the only one who still has some Creme Soda left.

"Okes, get a load of that," says Sean, before I have a chance to beat Eddie's record.

"Where, what?" I say.

"On the high board."

Like a bunch of meercats we twist our heads to where Sean's looking. A tall tanned guy with bleached streaks in his hair is balancing on the edge of the high diving board, bouncing slowly up and down. He's wearing one of those black Speedo things that I wouldn't be caught dead in. Not even if you paid me a million bucks.

"The oke's quite built, hey," says Gavin.

"What are you, a moffie or something?" says Eddie.

"Your mother's a moffie," says Gavin. "Hey, Angelo, maybe you and that guy are related?"

Angelo throws Gavin a zap sign. Gavin's right; the guy is built. Not in a chunky body-builder sort of way, but with these seriously defined arms and chest and abs. He must be a swimmer or something. He carries on bouncing, like he's in no rush, testing the diving board, his eyes closed. You would swear he actually enjoys being up there. I'm not kidding, it's the same as jumping off a ten-storey building. Whoever designed it must have been crazy or mixed up their feet with their metres. We're not the only ones watching. It's like everyone at the pool is waiting to see what he's going to do next. The way he takes his time it's like he knows people are watching.

"I bet he chickens out," says Chris.

"I bet he doesn't," I say.

"We'll bet you a Grape Fanta he does," says Gavin.

"He'll jump, but there's no ways he'll dive," says Eddie. Eddie's right for a change. I've never seen anyone go head first.

The guy has stopped bouncing. He looks over the edge, making sure the coast is clear. That, or having second thoughts. He turns around, his back to the pool.

"I told you he's going to chicken out!" says Gavin. "You okes owe us a Grape Fanta."

"I don't remember shaking on it. Did any of you see me shake on it?"

The tall tanned guy now shifts his feet until he's balancing on the balls right at the edge.

"No ways," says Sean. "The oke is psycho. He's going for it backwards."

I swear, everyone on the grass is now watching this guy. He lifts his arms straight in front of him, goes still for a second or two, then bounces once, twice, three times, and launches himself off the board, twists his body in mid-air and hits the water like an arrow.

"Holy Moses!" says Sean for all of us.

"Windgat," says Eddie.

I'm seriously impressed. We watch as he comes to the surface and swims towards our side of the pool and pushes himself straight out of the water, arms like pistons.

"Who owes who a Grape Fanta?" I say to Gavin, who has gone back to his spot under the tree.

"We didn't shake on it."

"Lekker one!" Eddie shouts across to the guy as he's walking across the grass. He looks back at us.

"Thanks, dude," he says and heads towards the shower.

"You're such a doos, Eddie."

"What? I just said lekker one."

"You don't even know the guy."

"So?"

"Never mind," I say. You can't argue with Eddie.

Eventually we turn back to our towels. Sean wipes his kuif from his eyes.

"Maybe I should shave it all off, go GI for the hols. What you reckon, Nick?"

"If not, why not?"

Sean sniffs his fingers. "I can't believe it, I've had a goof and I still smell like curry."

I smell my fingers. I can't smell anything. "What we doing tonight?"

"I dunno. What you want to do?"

"Dunno, but I can think about it. You coming out with us, Eddie?

"Can't."

"Why?"

"Luke's back from the border. He's taking us to Vegas."

The way Eddie says it you would swear he's going to a five-star restaurant, not a greasy old roadhouse.

"What about you Angelo?" says Sean. "What are you up to?"

"Ja, right, Daniels," chirps Gavin from across the way, like he's listening in to every word of our conversation. "Didn't you know? Angelo's got a hot date tonight. Not so, Angie boy?"

And we all pack up. Except for Sean.

FOUR

As per usual I'm way late for supper because my dad's already behind his *Citizen* and Simon's busy sucking up the last of his spag bol. No lies, Simon has worms. I grab the chair next to my mom, where there's a covered plate waiting for me.

"Don't slurp, Simey," my mom says. For once he listens, but then, typical, leans over towards my heaped plate.

"Can I have some of yours, Nick?"

"No."

"Why not – you said you don't like mince?"

"Since when?"

"Since forever... Since those burgers mom bought that time."

"That was different, dummie. I said I don't like horsemeat. Pass the tomato sauce."

"Please, no name-calling. I hope you wore Blockout?" My mom's pet subject. The way she carries on you would think the sun gives you cancer or something.

"Ja, don't call me names, beetroot face," says my brother. For a ten-year-old he's cheeky as anything.

"Beetroot face. Can't you come up with something better than that?"

"Enough!" says my dad, finally looking up from his newspaper. I don't know why he insists on reading at the table. My mom should make a scene but she doesn't.

The table goes quiet for a few seconds, until Simon makes a grab for my bread-roll, but this time I'm ready for him and grab it at the same time. He manages to tear off a corner and you would swear by the look on his face that he has won the jackpot or something. He's a total pain. Before I can snatch it back he's stuffing it into his face like there's no tomorrow.

"Arsehole," I whisper to him from behind my hand.

"Mom, Nick called me arsehole." My mom looks at Simon, then at me, not sure who to believe. I help her by putting on my surprised and innocent look.

"What are you talking about, Simon? I said rascal."

Simon sticks out a purple Kool-Aid tongue – he's addicted to the stuff – but I ignore him and begin stuffing my face with spag bol. I've hardly eaten a thing all day.

My dad slaps his newspaper down. "Didn't you hear? I said enough of that. Bloody hell." He proceeds to fold his newspaper into a neat square, then into a smaller square, and then into a smaller one still. "So, what have you been up to?"

"Nothing much," I say, and carry on eating.

"Nothing much what?"

"Went fishing with Sean. The whole arvie at the pool. The usual."

"Please don't talk with your mouth full," says my mom. "And it's afternoon, not arvie."

"Sorry," I say, my mouth still crammed with spaghetti. Simon giggles at this. My mom gives him a look, even though she's trying not to smile. My dad's look shuts Simon up. I wipe my mouth across the back of my hand and make the mistake of sniffing.

"Besides a cold, what else did you catch?"

"That's so corny."

"Well?"

"Well, what?"

"Did you catch anything?"

"No, Dad, I didn't catch anything."

My dad gives up on me and decides to interrogate Simon instead.

"And you, Simey, what did you get up to today?"

"I didn't go fishing, Dad. And I didn't catch anything, Dad." And we all laugh at this, although it's not funny. Even my dad smiles. It's just the way Simon says things sometimes. Like I said, he's real cheeky for his age.

After supper my dad and Simon head straight for the Barlow-Vision, while my mom washes up in the kitchen. Sean hasn't phoned yet so I have no choice but to stick around. We are only allowed to switch on the TV after supper – another of my dad's ridiculous rules. He's got this thing about spending quality time together; it makes no diffs that the best times in our house are when the TV's on. It wouldn't be so bad if my dad didn't hog it twenty-four seven. Because he's so full on into sport and news I don't get to watch anything. And then when there's a rugby match or something so-called important happening in the world we all have to play dead.

As the blue clock counts down to seven we settle down on the couch, Simon on one side of my mom, me on the other. It's the same every night. My dad has his own TV chair, a fancy plastic-leather La-Z-Boy thing with a gear lever on the side. My mom can't stand the thing – not that my dad cares. I can't remember exactly, but she said something about zero aesthetic value when he lugged it home from an auction sale one Saturday morning. He had this chuffed smile on his face like he had scored the bargain of the century. I think it's pretty hot, what with the gears and the drinks tray that swings out.

"Zip it, guys," says my dad as the news comes on. My dad

worries he's missing out on life if he doesn't watch Adrian Steed every night. For him the world doesn't exist unless you see it on the news. Lately there's been a lot of political stuff on, which I haven't really been following, but basically PW Botha made a big speech that got my dad hot under the collar. While Adrian interviews some black guy in a suit and tie, Simon is wagging his finger like an idiot. "And now they decide they want to negotiate. No wonder we're heading up shite creek without an oar. Am I right, or am I right?"

My mom looks up from her book. Like me, she's not really into this political stuff, although I think she's clued up in her own way.

"I suppose you can't rush into these things. They must know what they're doing. I'm sure there's plenty progress going on behind the scenes."

"Oh, please, Isabel. Don't give me that. You call sitting down to tea and scones in some banana republic progress? Meanwhile back at the ranch they're going k-a-f-f-i-r in the townships and we're talking State of Emergency. They're a bunch of effing imbeciles, the whole lot of them."

My dad can really carry on sometimes. You would swear he's a politician and not a mine engineer.

"Not in front of the children, Eugene."

"What's a effing imbecile?" asks Simon.

"Don't worry, Simey. It's nothing. Your dad's just getting a bit worked up."

"A bit worked up? Is that what you call it? You watch what the rand is going to do now. It's heading one way and I'm telling you, it's not up."

The phone rings and Simon leaps up and sprints out of the room to get it, slipping and sliding in his pyjamas two sizes too big for him as he takes the corner into the passage. A second later he's back, shouting his head off.

"It's for you, Nick!"

"Who is it?"

"A girl." And he starts giggling and leaps back on the couch.

"Idiot."

"Drop the volume, Simon," says my dad.

I get up and walk to the phone; for some reason my heart is beating. Simon is bullshitting, but you never quite know with him – maybe it is a girl. I pick up the phone. It's Sean. All excited like.

"You want to go to the drive-in?" He doesn't even wait for my answer. "I can pick you up in fifteen."

"How will we get there?"

"I've lent my boet's car for the night."

"Borrowed," I say.

"That's what I said. Anyway . . ."

"You said 'lent'. The word is borrowed." I'm like a teacher sometimes. I just do it to get on people's nerves.

"Who cares a rat's arse – lent, borrow, stolen, what's the diffs, my brother's given me his cabbie for the night. You want to go to the drive-in or don't you?"

"What's showing?"

"Some Clint Eastwood movie. It will be good."

"It looks like it's going to rain," I say, playing really hard to get.

"Who cares, it will clear up. It always does. Okay, how about we pick you up in a couple of minutes?"

"Okay. Who's we?"

But Sean's put the phone down. He's like that sometimes. Totally out of control.

23

The red Fiat idling in the driveway was a complete wreck when Russel bought it. Russel is Sean's eldest brother. But you would never say so; about the car, that is. It's still a wreck inside, but he's done a brilliant job so far fixing up the engine and spray-painting it red. When the engine starts it sounds just like a stock car.

Before I even get to the car I see why Sean was out of control on the phone: there's a girl sitting next to him. I take a deep breath, pull open the back door and climb in. The car stinks of Brut and girl's apple perfume.

"Howzit," I say.

Sean clicks on the light. "Howzit, Nick. Nick, Adele, Adele, Nick."

"How's it going, Nick?" says Adele, in a nice Afrikaans accent. She reaches over and shakes my hand. Her fingernails are long and painted bright red. Her skin is brown, her teeth white, her eyes quite close together, but not badly so. Her hands are cool and soft.

"Don't worry, he's not as bad as he looks," says Sean. "Deep down he's actually quite a decent oke."

"Stuff you," I say, and try slap the back of Sean's head, but he ducks.

Sean, me and Adele hit it off like a house on fire. Sean cranks up his new Dire Straits, until the Fiat's crappy speakers begin to vibrate, and we are singing and messing around before we even get to the Lighthouse. Sean has a bottle of Old Brown that he passes around the car. Every time it reaches Adele she takes a small sip, but doesn't miss her turn. I like that. There's a tug on my jeans when Mark Knopfler belts out, "Money for nothin' and chicks for free". I look up to catch Sean winking at me in the mirror. I wink back and take another sip from the OBs. To think if it wasn't for Sean I would still be sitting on the couch staring at PW's wagging finger and listening to my dad gaaning on.

While we're waiting in the queue for our tickets, Adele tells me she lives up the road from Sean and that Sean's mom knows her mom from the mine tennis club and that's how they met. Every few seconds she looks across at Sean like he's the best thing since sliced bread. And with his elbow hanging out the window and his puffy white shirt Sean must think he's Don Johnson.

The Lighthouse has been around forever and a day and I'm still clueless why they called it that in the first place; there's nothing but dusty mielie fields and mine dumps for miles around and the nearest ocean is Durban, more than four-hundred kilos away.

Like I told Sean on the phone, it's a bad night for drive-in because it starts coming down the second after we've bought our tickets. It's only drizzle, but enough to blur the screen. Sean drives round and round until he thinks we've found the perfect spot. And then he goes back and forwards over the hump until we find the perfect angle. Of course, we are just messing around for Adele's benefit.

"More back," I say, stuffing a handful of popcorn into my mouth.

"Like this?" Sean moves a few inches forward.

"No, more back."

"Is that okay?"

"Close . . . Just a few inches to the front again."

"Better?"

"No, too far. Try again." Sean drops the clutch and the Fiat stalls and we crack up, including Adele. The car next to us must think we are total imbeciles.

For our troubles we end up with a dodgy speaker and have to repeat the exercise from scratch and this time it's not so funny because the trailers have already started. Sean fiddles with the new speaker, but the sound's still coming from inside an empty tin of baked beans – that's because half the people drive off with the things still attached to their car. The Fiat's window winder is broken so I have to climb out and do the necessary; while I push the window up, Sean holds onto the speaker.

Eventually we sort things out and settle back to watch the film. All I know about *Death Wish II* is that Charles Bronson is in it – not Clint Eastwood. Not that I really care either way. It's just good to be here in Russel's old Fiat. Some of the cosiness I'm feeling is Old Brown cosiness, but it's also that cosiness you get when you're with someone you actually like being with. If it was Angelo or Eddie or one of the other guys I would probably feel the odd one out, but it's not like that with Sean. It's him and me first and only then the rest of the world.

"We must come see *Rocky III* next. My boet says it's excellent."

"Who, Russel?"

"No, Gary. He saw it in Joburg just after he klaared out. What you think, Adele? You want to see Rocky with me?"

Adele lets out this giggle and shifts up close to him.

"I want to see *Officer and a Gentleman*."

"That's a chick flick. But we'll see them both."

I shove a fistful of popcorn into my mouth and pass the box back over the seat. Sean manoeuvres his arm behind Adele's shoulder.

Five minutes into the main feature the sky farts and all hell breaks loose: cars hooting, flashing their lights, revving, that type of thing. It's the same every time and all included in the price of a Lighthouse ticket. A few minutes later the rain cuts back to a drizzle and calm returns. Sean and Adele have lost interest in what's happening on the screen and have sunk lower into the front seat and started whispering who knows what to each other. This means I get to eat the rest of the popcorn. I try concentrate on the film, but it's not so easy, what with the misty windscreen and the tinny sound and the whispering coming from the front and Adele's long brown hair hanging over the seat, touching my knee. Before I know it my own film is playing out in my head, with Adele's shiny hair and tanned hands and long red nails digging into the main actor. Meanwhile, somewhere up in front, Charles Bronson is beating the crap out of a hairy greaseball.

We have to get Adele home by eleven; it's a miracle her dad let her go out in the first place. He sounds like a prize doos, all controlling-like and into this happy-clappy stuff that's become the latest fashion in this town. Adele's house is one of those face-brick Monopoly houses that just about every person in this town lives in.

Sean parks around the corner. He climbs out and goes round to Adele's side and opens the door for her. If you didn't know him you would think he's playing the real gentleman. Meanwhile, back at the ranch, the Fiat's passenger door doesn't open from the inside.

"We better move it, Del, you're going to miss your bedtime." Sean is looking worried at his watch. It's already way past eleven.

"Lekker meeting you, Nick," says Adele. She leans over the seat and kisses me full on the lips.

"Lekker meeting you too," I say. Blabber more like it.

I watch Sean walk Adele up the driveway, the wetness of her

soft lips still warm on my lips. To kill time I eat the last dregs of popcorn – those hard burnt bits that leave a shit taste and that you always regret eating. Ten hours later the driver's door swings open.

"What happened?"

"Nothing much," says Sean, playing all hard to get.

"Nothing much, what?"

"You really want to know?"

"Would I ask if I didn't?"

Sean sticks his middle finger out to me. "Smell."

"Don't lie."

"Don't you want to smell? I should be charging you."

So I lean forward and take a sniff. "Smells like bladdy popcorn." I slap his hand away.

"Got ya! Zilch happened; her old toppie was waiting on the stoep in his dressing gown and stokies. But I swear, Nick, I was this close."

All the way home, Sean can't wait to blab on about Adele. Not that he says anything. To be honest, we haven't had much experience with girls. The only woman I've been out with is Sarah Bosch and that was our standard five farewell party, which lasted about four hours. So Adele is quite a big thing. With Sean's bad leg and all it's an even bigger thing for him.

Sean cuts the engine at the bottom of our driveway and we sit there a while listening to the rain banging on the roof. He flips the Dire Straits tape back to side one and adjusts the volume. It must be the hundredth time we've listened to it. Not that I mind. He takes a glug from the Old Brown.

"So what you think?"

"About what?" I say. I've got this thing about pretending to play clueless. I can't help myself.

"About Adele, moegoe. What do you think of her?"

"She's okay." Of course, I'm lying. The truth is, she's hot, but I'm not giving in that easy.

"Okay's arse, says Sean. "Here, have some more of the OBs. It will help you think straight."

While I'm busy taking a swig Sean jabs me in the ribs, sending a spray of sherry over my jeans.

"Seriously, what you think of her?"

"She's hot. I would give it to her any day."

"You would give it to Angelo's sister."

"That's true. Seriously though, she's a lekker chick."

"You really think so?

"Ja. What I can't understand is why she wants to go out with someone like you. That part I don't get."

"It's all about charm. I'll give you a lesson sometime."

"Charm se gat."

"Jissus, but her parents are another story. You must see them, they're these total verkramptes. Everything is God this and God that."

"Worse than Vernon Stevens?"

"Much worse."

"In that case, I'll meet them in heaven. When are you seeing her again?"

"Dunno. It's a whole thing getting her out of the house but maybe I'll try ask her to come with us to the pool sometime. I reckon she looks tit in a bikini. What you think?"

"Ja, I also reckon she looks tit in a bikini."

"I meant about inviting her to the pool, idiot."

"Ja, ja, I know what you meant. Great idea."

"I'll do that. Maybe I'll give it a day or two first. What you think?"

"Whatever, Seanie. Your choice. So, how was that movie?"

"Not bad. What I saw of it."

"Here we go again. You're full of shit."

"I know. But we must definitely organise to see the new *Rocky* when it shows at Phoenix."

"That will be in ten years time," I say.

"Twenty, more like it."

The Old Brown goes back and forth until we're sucking at the last drops from the bottle. The rain cuts back to a slow drum solo. Sean carries on non-stop about Adele. "Brothers in Arms" plays for the two-hundredth time. We play noughts and crosses on the misted-up windscreen and I win four games in a row. Between all of this going on I'm wishing I could stop time. Because if I could, I would stop it right here, with Sean and me in his brother's crappy old Fiat.

FIVE

Four thirty-five. Still ages until supper. Still no sms from Jen.

To kill the time I start sorting through my stuff. Rule number one of the road: unless you're a bergie, don't live out of a suitcase. Not that there's much to unpack. One copy *Weekend Argus*, two pairs blue socks, two white Jockeys, one pyjama pants, vest, one spare shirt in case I'm caught out – you go for a takeaway and the tomato sauce lid comes off. Then what? Toilet bag with toothbrush, razor, Gillette shaving cream (way cheaper than gel and as good), Old Spice on a rope (birthday prezzie from Jen) that I keep in a bankie so it doesn't drip all over the place – ask me, I know every trick in the book. Toothpaste? The last time I brushed the old tusks was crack of dawn. It has to be in here somewhere . . . What I'll do is visit Eddie once I've straightened my head and had a clean-up. No point sitting here all day. Maybe I packed it in one of the side pockets? I try them all. Nothing. And then I see it clear as day. Lying on the shower floor at home, next to Jen's 2-in-1. I can't believe it. I'm such a moegoe. Now what am I going to do? I'll go crazy if I can't brush my teeth. And where do you buy toothpaste on a late Sunday afternoon in a place like this?

Now everything feels disorganised again, like I'm losing control. I knew this was all a bad idea. I should never have come back, should have left sleeping dogs lie, just get on with life like everybody else does. If I hadn't been an idiot and decided to go ahead with it I would be at home with Jen and the kids, on our way to the Spur for the Sunday rib special, me and Jen alone afterwards, listening to music. That's what I would be doing. Spending quality time with my family.

To get my mind off things I start flipping through the *Weekend Argus*. Nothing but missing kids, politics and bus crashes. Malema and Zuma and bodies scattered across the N1. But on page three there's a story I've been following, about this couple that's been going on the rampage. It's been all over the TV lately; even *Special Assignment* did something on them. *Special Assignment* is what you call genuine investigative reporting. Not like that Deborah Patta and her *Third Degree*. This couple is one of those Bonnie and Clyde sorts, hitchhiking around the country and robbing people. Except, they're doing it SA-style, tying up their victims and then slitting their throats. They've been on the run for weeks now and the cops still haven't caught them. They've murdered at least eight people so far. There's an identikit photo of the couple – apparently they hitched a lift with this guy from Pretoria, cut his throat and left him for dead in a veld in the middle of nowhere. But he managed to crawl to a nearby farmhouse. The girl in the photo looks young and innocent and quite good looking, in a secretarial college sort of way. But the guy, Jacobus Gerhardus Barnard, he fits the picture to a T – a psycho with acne-scarred skin burnt black by the sun and a scraggly beard. Who would give this guy a lift, anyway? Asking for it, if you want my opinion.

Bennie Hafejee gets all philosophical and intellectual-like towards the end: "*Is this a case of nature versus nurture? Are some individuals simply born evil?*" You asking me, Bennie? Born evil. No question. It doesn't matter if you're Jacobus Gerhardus, Adriaan Vlok, Eugene de Kok, or . . . Michael Dempsey. It's in the genes from word go. Everything that comes after that is just the icing on the poisoned cake.

"Police caution that if spotted do not approach the suspects, as they are considered highly dangerous."

Still can't bladdy believe I forgot the toothpaste.

SIX

I've hardly had a chance to brush my teeth when my dad starts hooting in the driveway. He's forever on a schedule, worrying we are going to be late for this and that. My mom says that's what comes from having German blood. Lucky I don't suffer from the same thing.

"Come on, for God's sake, we're going to be late," says Simon, imitating my dad as we climb into the car.

Nobody says much the whole way to church. I feel like one of those sheep you see on the way to the abattoir. The parking area is almost full when we arrive and most of the people are inside already, which sends my dad into serious panic mode.

"Why the hell can't we ever be on time? Is it too much to ask, Isabel? That's all I'm saying, okay?"

My dad says it like it's my mom's fault but meanwhile he's the one who got back late from his run. He's battling to park the Cressida in this tiny space crammed between Mrs Coetzee's blue Corolla and the fishpond, which makes things worse. It's one of those old 1970s models with no power steering. He's sweating like a pig by the time we are parked.

It makes no difference we are late – my dad still insists on sitting as close as he can to the front, which means we have to walk past thousands of people. We slide in next to Mr and Mrs Jacobson and their daughter, Amelia, who would be quite hot if it wasn't for her teeth. Father Dominic is still organising his things at the altar so my mom gets chatting to the neighbours. I look around and spot Eddie and his old lady sitting right near the back. Luke's not with them; church must be the last thing you are interested in when you come back from the border. Eddie's wearing his usual Sunday-best mustard-green polo-neck shirt that his mom got from a jumble sale. He spots me, checks to make sure no-one's looking, then throws me a zap sign.

Mrs Daniels is here but there's no sign of Sean or Russel, unless they're upstairs sitting with the blacks like they sometimes do, just for the hell of it. Packed into the front row, Angelo and his family make up a solid wall of flesh. If you add them all together, the Constantinoples must weigh at least a ton. Then there's the usual crowd, most of them old types who come for the free tea and biscuits afterwards, and a few others I've never seen before. That's how it is in a mining town – people coming and going all the time.

Father Dominic has heaps on his mind today; his sermon carries on and on. My mind is elsewhere and I only catch a few stompies, like how we must judge people by their actions and not their skin colour, which is true if you stop and think about it. My dad must be the only person in the church who understands Father's sermons. It's not just the accent; Father

Dominic is way too intellectual for this town.

Simon is picking away at this huge scab on his knee, from when he fell on the school quad just before we broke up last week. The edges are already brown and dry, but the middle is pink and mushy underneath. It's one of those things you don't want to look at, but you can't help yourself. I'm watching to see what happens when he gets to the wet pink part. But when he breaks off a chunk of scab and starts nibbling it, like it's a Big Korn Bite, I can't take it anymore.

"You're disgusting," I whisper in his ear. I must have whispered it too loud because Mrs Coetzee swivels round in her mauve dress that's way too tight under the armpits and gives us a funny look. Simon shifts up the bench and presses against my mom. The look she gives him, you would swear he's an angel.

I actually feel quite sorry for Father; it must be a lonely job being a priest in this dump. It's like the shepherd and his flock come from different planets. I bet he never knew what he was in for when he came here in the first place. If he did there's no ways he would have left Holland. It must have been the same for those missionaries who came to Africa to convert the primitive tribes. If I was them I wouldn't have bothered.

I'm so into my own thoughts I hardly notice Simon tugging at my shirt.

"Move, Nick, I wanna get past."

I block his way with my knee.

"Please, Nick, I have to pee," he says urgently. Mrs Coetzee spins round again, just about setting the nylon of her mauve dress on fire. My dad leans across my mom and gives Simon's thigh a serious pinch that turns his eyes all watery. I decide to let Simon pass because there's no ways I want him peeing and bawling all over me.

There's still no sign of Sean during communion so I give up waiting for him and join the queue. We are now on the home stretch and I'm not the only one who starts feeling a lot better. It's like communion gives you a shot of new energy. Suddenly everyone is in a good mood. You can check it by the way people start packing away their books, sitting up straighter and looking around them.

All that's left are the announcements, which are sort of enjoyable. The fête is the main thing on the list, so Mrs Andrews, who is one of the main organisers, stands up and says we can use her garage for second-hand clothing and other donations, as long as nobody uses it as a dumping ground for their rubbish. Father Dominic then runs through this long list of sick people that we must pray for, including my uncle. He also has a message from Mr Stevens about the youth group he's trying to get going, and which I've been roped into. And then it's the usual farewells and welcomes. Like I said, people are always coming and going in this place.

"May we wish Jimmy and Joyce Gordon the best of luck in their travels. We will be thinking of you as you settle into your new life in Witbank. *Bon voyage*, as they say in French." Mrs Gordon goes red in the face and Mr Gordon nods like there's no tomorrow. "And last, but not least, a big welcome to the new members in our parish, Vanessa and uhmm . . . Malcolm Dempsey, who have joined us all the way from Johannesburg. We wish you a long and happy stay in our town."

Like a bunch of meercats a hundred heads turn and gawk at the new people. They must have come in late because I didn't notice them earlier. They are a tanned and fit-looking couple. Their son is as tall as his dad, with the same wavy blond hair and tanned face. His mom's also quite tall, with red lipstick, dangly earrings and shiny black hair scraped back. For some reason the guy looks familiar. And then it hits me that he's the same guy we saw at the pool in his Speedo. He looks about seventeen, maybe even older, with these broad shoulders. Before you know it, everybody and their dog, Eddie and his old lady included, want to shake hands with them. It's all way embarrassing, if you ask me.

Mass ends with the usual tea and biscuits outside; as I said before, it's the only reason some people come to church. You would swear we are living in some concentration camp because there's a stampede to get to the tea table and those who were sitting at the back and got out first are already tucking in like there's no tomorrow. Eddie's right in there. I elbow my way through to him and grab a handful of biscuits while there are still some left. We work our way along the table towards Mrs Cummings and the coffee. The pot is so huge the old fogies can't lift it by themselves so Mrs Cummings has to pour for them, making small talk the whole time. We will die of thirst by the time she gets to us.

Eddie and me take our coffee and biscuits and work our way out of the stampede to the fishpond, away from the grown-ups and screaming kids. I spot Simon on the other side, acting the clown with the De Freitas twins. Nearby my dad is having a heavy intellectual conversation with Father Dominic, nodding his head up and down like one of those toy dogs on the back window of the car. My mom is standing next to them sipping her tea with her pinkie sticking out. She could have been a movie star in one of those Italian films she's so into. The new people in town are chatting to the Gordons, telling them about life in the Transvaal. Their son is sitting on a bench, flicking pebbles into the water.

"Boring or what, hey?" says Eddie through a mouthful of Lemon Cream.

"What's boring?"

"Church. What else?"

"Ja, I suppose so."

"'I suppose so', he says. I saw you. You were half-asleep."

"Bullshit. I just had a big night, that's all."

"Doing what?"

"Sean and me went to the Lighthouse. You missed out big time."

"And?"

"And Sean's boet lent him his car."

"And?"

"And he had a chick with him. A hottie. Her name's Adele."

"And?" says Eddie, like he hasn't heard me.

"And we shared a bottle of Old Brown between us."

"And?"

"And what? That's it."

"And I bet you went home and trekked draad over Adele."

Eddie packs up at this, spraying bits of Lemon Cream into the fishpond.

"I thought I was sick," I say, even though it's true what Eddie says. Adele's way hot.

We stand and watch the goldfish fight over the crumbs of floating Lemon Cream. Eddie breaks off a bigger chunk and tosses it into the water. Loads more fish head their way and in no time there's a mad swirling of water as the fish fight it out.

"Like hungry piranhas, aren't they?"

Eddie and me look up. The new guy is standing behind us, also watching the goldfish.

"What's a piranha?" says Eddie, like a total idiot.

"A man-eating fish. Not much bigger than those there. But lethal. You find them in the Amazon."

"Oh," says Eddie. I keep staring at the water, not saying anything.

"They can strip a cow to the bone in four minutes flat. And a full-grown man in about half that time. In their case, maybe a bit longer," he says, pointing to Angelo and his sister across the way. Eddie and me laugh at that. The new guy comes closer. He's wearing Old Spice.

"Ja, right," says Eddie. "There's no ways a tiny fish like that can do what you're saying."

"Of course they can," I say.

"How do you know, Nick?"

"No, in a way your friend's right," says the new guy. "On their own, piranhas are pretty harmless and won't do much damage. But imagine a few hundred of them attacking you at the same time."

Eddie and me think about this for a while. It makes sense.

"Ja, I suppose so," Eddie says, but I can tell he's not convinced. That's Eddie for you. He always has to be otherwise. The goldfish have devoured the last crumbs of Lemon Cream and we have nothing more to toss.

"By the way, I'm Michael," the new guy says, and puts out his hand. Eddie wipes his hand on his jeans and shakes the guy's hand.

"I'm Eddie Scheepers. You from Joburg?"

"Most of my life, yes."

"I'm Nick," I say, and shake Michael's hand. He has a strong grip. The thick bracelet on his wrist is probably real gold. "We saw you at the pool yesterday."

"Is that right? I don't remember seeing you guys."

"After you dived off the high board. We were lying on the grass . . ."

"Of course, now I remember."

"Ja, where did you learn to dive like that?" asks Eddie on my behalf.

"I had a few lessons here and there."

"Like hell you had a few lessons."

Michael's dad is now waving at us from the other side of the pond.

"Your old man's calling you."

"Coming!" Michael shouts across to him. "Right, boys, looks like I've got to go, but I'm sure I'll catch you around sometime." He turns to Eddie. "By the way, nice shirt." He winks at me and walks off to join his parents.

"Nice guy," I say.

"You reckon so?"

"Ja, don't you?"

"Stuck up type, if you ask me. But who cares anyway, I must go park a coil."

While Eddie heads off to the bogs I watch Michael and his mom and dad walk to their car. The same gold BMW Sean and me saw parked in the driveway of the old mine manager's house. They're about to drive off when the door opens and Michael hops out and jogs back to where I'm still standing waiting for Eddie.

"You forget something?"

"No. I was just thinking, Nick. If you aren't doing anything, maybe you want to come round to my place sometime?"

"Ja, that will be great. Like when?"

"I don't know. Anytime . . . Like, what are you doing this evening?"

"Nothing much, I guess."

"Great, so why don't you come round?"

"Could do that. What time?"

"Seven good? Let me explain how you to get to our house . . ."

"I already know. It's that big place on Van der Stel."

"That's the one. How did you know?"

"I saw your dad's car in the driveway."

"You're pretty sharp. Fantasimo, all sorted then. I'll spot you later, Nick."

"Ja, spot you later."

As Michael heads off Eddie arrives back, still pulling at his zip.

"What were you okes talking about?"

"Ag, nothing much. He wanted to know where you bought your shirt from."

"You serious?"

"Do I look serious? He invited me to his place tonight."

"What did you say?"

"What a question. I'm keen to check it out. It's the old mine manager's house."

"What about me?"

"What about you?"

"Can I also come?"

"He didn't say."

"Meaning I can or I can't?"

"I don't know, Eddie. Why don't you go ask him yourself?"

"Stuff it. I'm busy, anyway. Shit, there's the doos! I was wondering where he got to."

"Who?"

"Sean!"

Eddie shouts it across the church pond, like we're at a taxi rank. Sean makes his way to us along the thin line of bricks running between the church and the pond.

"Howzit, okes." He looks seriously chuffed with himself.

"Where the hell have you been?"

"Guess."

"We give up."

"Playing Asteroids at the Galaxy."

"You weren't at church?"

"I was, but only at the beginning. You guys must join me next time. It's a jol."

And Sean starts laying out the instruction manual how to get out of church without anyone smelling a rat. 1. Sit with the blacks upstairs. 2. Pretend you need to go park a coil. 3. Climb through the toilet window. 4. Hop the fence at the back of the church. 5. What if Pious the church caretaker spots you? Doesn't matter, because what's an ancient madala like him going to say? 6. The big one: Make sure your watch is set right and you're back upstairs with the blacks before church ends.

SEVEN

What with the glass roof and the heated swimming pool in the middle the old mine manager's house must have cost a mint to build. Not that I've ever been inside to see for myself. Come to think of it, I can't say I know anybody who has.

I get there spot-on seven and hang around outside the gate in case Michael thinks I'm too keen. The Dempseys don't mess around because the garden boy has already climbed in, with the lawn freshly cut and the edges straightened with a spade. The garden is as big as our rugby field at school and has heaps of roses and three palm trees and a fountain with an angel squirting water from its mouth. The driveway is even lit up with small lights buried in the ground, running from the gate all the way to the front door.

Five minutes past seven I walk my bike up the driveway and park it against this Roman pillar thing next to the front door. It's a massive carved number with brass handles and a knocker. The mine must have got it from a German castle. I knock and wait. The house is even bigger and grander than what you see from the road. I knock again, but still there's no answer. Now I start worrying I got the day wrong.

"Hey, Nicolas!"

At first I can't make out where the voice is coming from, until I spot Michael sitting in the shadow of the veranda, with his feet up on a table, reading a book. He must have been there the whole time. He puts the book down and walks over.

"How are you doing?" Michael says, shaking my hand. He

must have just come out of the shower or the pool because his blonde hair is still wet and slicked back. He's wearing those Island Style long white pants and a black short-sleeve shirt with a crocodile badge. A thin gold chain hangs from his neck. And here I am in my old cut-off jeans and Bob Marley T-shirt.

"Where's your friend?"

"Who, Eddie? I didn't know he was invited . . ."

"Of course he was. I thought you knew that?"

"I wasn't sure."

"No problem, it's not a train smash. So . . ."

"How you guys settling into your new place?"

"Not bad, not bad. Still sorting out a couple of things, but slowly getting there."

"Like what things?"

"The usual. Pool thermostat playing up. Still waiting for half our stuff to arrive. That type of thing."

I nod, as if I know exactly what Michael's talking about.

"So what did you get up to the rest of the day?"

"Ag, nothing much. Hung around at home most of the day. You said you guys are from Joburg?"

"Yes and no," says Michael, pushing his hair back.

"What you mean?"

"How do I put it? Okay, what I mean is I go to school there, but because of my dad's job we move around quite a bit. So I can't really say where I come from."

"What does your dad do?"

"He's a management consultant."

"Is that like an accountant or something?"

"Something like that. He sorts out other people's messes."

"My dad's a mine engineer."

"Good for him."

"Where did you live before you came here?"

"More like, where didn't we live? Let me think . . ." Again, Michael runs his fingers through his wet hair. "Last stop was Durban. Before that, mainly Joburg. Oh, and we spend a month or two in London every year.

"East London?"

"No, London London," he laughs. "You know? Royal family, Lady Di, guy with the big ears, London?"

"I was just joking," I say, my face suddenly hot.

"Talking of which. Why does Charles have a blue dick?"

"I dunno. Maybe because he's royalty?"

"Nice one, but no. Because he dipped it in Di."

"That's funny."

"I thought so too. What about you? You been living here all your life?"

"No, I was born in Pietermaritzburg." I don't bother telling him we moved here when I was two years old. "But with all the moving around, how do you go to school?"

"I'm a boarder. At St Andrews in Northcliff. You probably haven't heard of it."

"I think I have."

We carry on making small talk at the front door, taking in the garden and the tennis court and the view: the red roofs of the mine houses below, the open scratchy veld after that, the thick bush and thorn trees along the river. Seeing it from up here makes it looks nicer than it actually is.

"Hey, let's head in," Michael says.

I follow Michael into the house.

"I've never been inside your place before."

"We've only been here a few days. But I know what you mean. Never ever?"

"Well, except when they were still busy building it. But that was years ago. I was still a lightie."

"It's a bit OTT, though I think you'll be impressed."

Michael leads the way down the wide passage, through the hotel kitchen and into the lounge, pointing out this and that along the way as if it's all nothing. Meanwhile the place is a palace. He adjusts the lights in the lounge and points to the couch.

"Make yourself at home. Listen, I was about to have a beer. You keen for one?" Michael says it casually, like he's offering me Oros.

"Your toppies don't mind?"

Michael laughs. "Hey, don't worry about them. They've gone out for supper."

"Okay, why not? A beer would be great," I say, also trying to sound casual.

"Castle or Amstel? That's all we've got, I'm afraid."

"I don't mind. Anything."

"Choose one."

"Okay, Amstel."

"Good choice."

While Michael fetches the beers I check out the lounge. I swear, Sean would cream himself on the spot. It's fitted wall-to-wall with hi-fis and thin speakers and graphic equalisers and a big TV. Next to the TV is a shelf packed with videos. The other side of the room is crammed floor-to-ceiling with books. They're not the books and magazines you normally find in people's houses, like *Readers Digest* and DIY books and old encyclopaedias that some travelling salesmen conned your parents into buying. There is a huge couch in front of the TV and a coffee table with a glass top. The couch is made of real leather, kudu or something like that, not the imitation leather you get on lounge suites at Russel's. Instead of the usual posters and prints from CNA, genuine paintings are hanging on the walls. My mom would go mad for this type of art. Come to think of it, she would go mad for the whole house.

"Anything grab your fancy?" says Michael, from behind me. He hands me the beer, which he's poured into a long thin glass. I've never drunk beer out of a glass before.

"Thanks. Seriously, where did you get all these videos from?" I'm not exaggerating – there must be at least fifty.

"Here and there. You can pick them up really cheap overseas, especially in the East."

"It sounds like you've been all over the place."

The only person I know who has been overseas is Martin Smith, and that was to Mauritius, which doesn't really count.

"That's no lie. Cheers," says Michael and holds his glass up and waits for me to do the same. We clink glasses. "I'm really glad you could make it."

"Ja, no, thanks for inviting me."

We both take a gulp, then stand around inspecting Michael's video collection.

"I've got an idea, Nick. If you are keen, that is?

"What's the idea?"

"The idea is you select something for us to watch and I'll phone for pizza."

"Ja, I'm keen for that. But don't you want to choose? You must have watched them all."

"Hardly. Besides, I want to see what you're into."

So while Michael gets on the phone to Napoli's, I fry my brain trying to decide. Half the movies I haven't even heard of, but eventually I decide on this movie called *Deliverance*, mainly because I like the cover. I bet Michael has seen it, but already I can tell he's one of those guys that is so polite he doesn't let on.

I reach over and help myself to another slice of salami and pineapple.

"They're not bad, hey?" says Michael. "Are you keen for another beer? I'm having one."

Before I can say yes or no Michael has hit pause and gone to fetch two more beers from the fridge. This time he doesn't bother with glasses.

"By the way, excellent choice of movie, Nicolas," says Michael, hitting the remote.

"You think so? I bet you've seen it ten times already."

"Not true. Anyway, I could watch *Deliverance* a hundred times and never be bored."

I'm chuffed because it ends up being a good movie. It's about these guys who go on a fishing trip in the backwoods of America and get stalked by psycho hillbillies. It's quite hectic in parts.

Michael cranks up the volume. "Concentrate now, the best scene is coming up."

One of the guys is called Bobby and he's like Angelo – fat and slow and useless. He has no chance against this hillbilly psycho who's got his buddy tied up against a tree and is getting ready to take Bobby up the bum. "Squeal like a pig, fatty. Classic line or what, hey?" While Bobby crawls around the forest starkers, Michael is leaning forward on the couch and chewing his lip like it's the first time he's watching the movie.

He grips my knee when Lewis, the leader of the expedition, takes the hillbilly out with his crossbow. "Whoa! Now that's what you call the perfect execution. What you say, buddy?"

Michael turns the volume down and lies back on the couch.

"That must rank as one of the ten best films ever made. Right up there with *Clockwork Orange.*

"What's *Clockwork Orange?*"

"Seriously, you don't know *Clockwork Orange?*"

"No, don't think so."

"Man, where've you been? If you like *Deliverance*, then you've got to see *Clockwork Orange*. It's classic. Maybe I can organise a copy from one of my buddies in Joburg."

"That will be kief, thanks. Talking of clocks, I better make like donkey shit."

"Like donkey shit?"

"And hit the road."

"I must remember that one. There's no rush."

I sit down again.

"So what are you guys into?"

"What you mean?"

"I mean you and your buddies. What do you do in this place?"

"I don't know. We're into lots of different stuff."

"I know that. But like what?"

"Where do you want me to start? Okay, we go fishing often, or we hang out at the pool or at each other's house or someplace else. And music, I'm into music."

"What type of music?"

"Just about anything. Even the old stuff."

"Maybe that explains why you seem different to the other guys here. Maybe you're a rock star in the making."

"You think so? I'm actually planning to start my own band one day . . ."

"I've never been fishing."

"Not even on the Vaal?"

"Not even on the Vaal. I once had a goldfish that ended up down the toilet. That's about as much as I know about fish."

"You knew a lot about piranhas."

"Something I read. You must take me fishing with you sometime."

"You would probably find it boring."

"Why do you say that?"

"I mean, you sit around most of the time doing nothing. I hardly ever catch anything."

"But when you do it must be a blast?"

"Ja, that's for sure. It's even quite exciting when you get a take."

"What's a take?"

"When a fish has a serious go at your bait."

"Sounds like fun. So that's what you and Eddie do. You go fishing?"

"No, it's mainly Sean and me. Eddie's not really into fishing."

"What's Eddie into?

"If it has something to do with military and war and guns, Eddie's into it. His brother is a Recce."

"Interesting. Tell me if I'm wrong, but Eddie doesn't look the brightest. And Sean? Who is Sean?"

"Sean's my other friend. We've known each other since I was this high. But actually, Eddie's not as dumb as–"

"And Sean's into fishing?"

"Big time. He's got his junior colours."

"Didn't know you can get colours in fishing. What else is Sean into?"

"A whole lot of stuff. His family had a farm in Rhodesia so he's really good with his hands and outdoor stuff."

"A when-we."

"What you mean a when-we?"

"When we were in Rhodesia. Never mind. Why do you say he's good with his hands?"

"Okay, for instance, you can give him a broken engine or something electrical and he will be able to fix it. And he can build just about anything."

"Like what?"

"You name it. For example, from scratch he built this full-on sound-to-light system for his bedroom."

"Is there anything Sean can't do?"

"Not really. Except if it involves hardcore running."

"Why is that?"

"Because of his leg. He was born with something wrong with it."

"By the sounds of it, Sean's your best buddy?"

"Ja, I guess you could definitely say that. Him and Eddie. We've known each other forever."

I look at my watch. It's almost midnight.

"And girls?"

"What about them?"

"Like, have you got a girlfriend?"

"Ag, nothing really at the moment. And you?"

"Also nothing at the moment. I've got better things to do."

"Ja, me too."

"So, what are the killer plans for the holidays?"

"No plans. We've got a veld camp but nothing much else is happening."

"What's a veld camp?"

"Ag, one of those youth cadet things. Shit, I better get going, Michael. My toppies will think I've been kidnapped or something. But thanks a lot, it's been really great."

"No problem," says Michael, standing up and stretching. He walks with me to the door. "We must do it again soon. It's been fun."

Michael waits until I'm on my bike and I have my jacket zipped up. As I hit the bottom of his driveway and swing a right home he's still standing under the light at the front door.

EIGHT

As I take the next turn left into Dingaan I'm wondering if the years have done to Eddie what the falling gold price has done to this town.

There it is, straight ahead. Eddie's old house. The grass doesn't look like it's been cut in years and the school bus shelter that used to be on the corner is gone, but the house has hardly changed. It's the same old depressing face-brick mine house, with the same ugly metal windows and ugly green pillars on the stoep, and the cracked cement driveway.

I stop a little way up the road and cut the engine. Apart from two women gabbing under a tree in their Zionist best, the street is deserted.

Simon said the place had gone to the dogs; he didn't say it was this bad. He didn't say it's become a ghost town. The wall across the way, that's where Eddie and Sean and me used to duck behind and puff on his dad's Lexington stompies; any second now I'm expecting a small head to pop up to check if the coast is clear.

I take a deep breath and climb out of the Kia and walk back towards the house. The women under the tree stop gabbing as I walk past.

"Molweni," I say, forgetting they speak Sotho here, not Xhosa.

"Molo boetie," says one of the women.

I have to lift the front gate to open it. Nothing's changed. It was hanging to one side then and it's hanging to one side now. I walk slowly up the driveway and notice the garage door is half-open. I bend down to take a look. There's a car parked inside. A yellow XR-6. Eddie still lives here.

The sound of metal banging metal is coming from behind the garage. I lift the roller-door and duck inside, then squeeze past the XR-6 to the door at the back. It doesn't budge when I try the handle.

"Edward!" More metal hammering. "Eddie!" This time much louder.

The hammering holds up for a second, followed by something falling over and then, "Fok!" Eddie Scheepers. Already I'm thinking this was a bad idea. That I should have left sleeping dogs lie. The door unlocks from the other side and a moment later a grease monkey in a blue overall is blocking the light.

"Fuck me! What the hell are you doing here?" Eddie is genuinely happy to see me. "Shit, Nick, sorry I can't shake your hand," he says, wiping his hands on his filthy overall.

"Not a problem," I say, slapping him on the shoulder, careful not to hit the oil patch. "Hell, it's been a long time, Eddie? How is it going? You look good, man."

Eddie actually looks like shit. Much older than a guy of his age should look. His hair, or what's left of it, is grey – the only colour is from the grease flecks. His skin is a Joburg roadmap of creases and lines. And his eyes, there's something different about Eddie's eyes.

"Great, man, great." Eddie's smiling like a lunatic. Not such a good thing because his teeth are a mess. Probably from all the crap that's gone into his mouth. "Shit, man, but it's good to see you, Nick. How long you back for?"

"Only a day or so."

"A day! Are you out of your tree?"

"That's the only leave I could take," I lie. "So what are you busy with here?" Pieces of metal and car parts and other scrap are lying all over the place, but I can't work out for what.

"Ag, nothing much. No ways only a day."

And he punches me on the shoulder and I punch him back. Eddie seems genuinely excited to see me and I think I feel the same way. But I'm already having second thoughts, especially when he says we must go for a little drink for old times' sake. I heard a drink with Eddie is never just a drink. But what did I expect? That Eddie would put the kettle on and we would sit down for a cup of tea?

"Ja, sure, let's go for a drink. It will be good to catch up."

"Excellent, man. I'll go get cleaned up."

Eddie doesn't invite me in. As I watch him disappear inside and slam the kitchen door behind him I'm thinking what's the worst that can happen?

I decide to wait in the car while Edward gets cleaned up. Twenty minutes later I'm still sitting here. To be honest I don't really mind because the Jap crap has a decent radio and I'm happy tuning into the different stations. Half of them I haven't heard in years, so it's a trip down memory lane. Radio Oranje is playing the same tunes they were playing half a century ago. It's probably even the same DJ. Merv Kotze - the name rings a bell. Short for Mervyn, I bet. Judging by the gravel in his throat, he's been around forever and a day. Like all the other DJs in this province, he's into this Tracy Chapman woman. It's the third time I've heard her today.

The passenger door rips open and Eddie jumps in.

"Right, my china, let's hit the road!"

Nobody has called me his china for at least ten years. It's a word straight out of the Ark. I don't say anything, but Eddie also looks like he's come out of the Ark. His hair is plastered back David Beckham skate-style - short in front, long at the back. The worst of it is that Eddie's going bald in the front, plus he's wearing this imitation brown leather jacket, with a V-neck jersey underneath. I'm already feeling embarrassed going out with him in public although he's probably the height of fashion in this place.

"Cool wheels," he says, drumming on the dashboard. "So, where we going, china?" You would swear he's just got out of jail.

"I dunno. You tell me.

"Let's do Players."

"Players. What's that?"

"My new drinking hole. Next to the old Turbo, china.

"Don't tell me Turbo is still going?"

"No ways. Long dead in its moer. Ever since Mandela's brothers took over and moved into the empty mine houses.

Come on, start this thing up, we're going to miss happy hour. Fok, but it's good to see you, Nick."

"It's good to see you too, Eddie."

I don't realise how bad Eddie needs a drink until we arrive at Players. The building alongside, what used to be the Turbo, is now an off-sales.

Players is a total dive and I can't believe Eddie's brought me here. It's a shebeen, not a pub. I'm about to tell him we should go somewhere else, but I've already ticked off the options in my head. There aren't any, except the Jacaranda Hotel ladies' bar. And there's no ways I want to land up with Eddie there. Besides, it's too late; Eddie is out the car before I've even switched off the engine and he's heading up the path like a kid out of control.

"Come china, you're still as slow as ever. Don't you want a drink, or what?"

What can I do but follow Eddie, thinking I could be sitting at the Jacaranda enjoying a civilised drink on my own. I follow Eddie inside. It's like stepping into a cave and it takes me a few seconds to get used to the dark. Luckily, it's still too early for the Sunday boozers. Like a fly to a turd, Eddie heads straight to the bar. Master of his kingdom, he slaps the counter.

"Basil! Two double rum and Cokes for me and my long lost friend here."

He doesn't even ask if I drink rum and Coke. Because Eddie drinks rum and Coke the whole world must drink rum and Coke. What the hell, I'll go along with him for the ride, but I've already decided in my mind it's going to be one drink and then we are out of here.

"Let me get this one, Eddie," I say. I don't need to insist because Eddie's quite happy for me to pay. The drinks arrive and I notice Eddie's hand shakes when he pours his Coke.

Some of it spills onto the bar counter.

"Here's to my old buddy. Good to see you, Nick."

"Cheers, Eddie. Good to see you too," I say for the tenth time, but I actually mean it. It is good to see him again. I think. After all, we grew up together. "It's been a long time, Eddie."

"Too long, china. You should come back to visit more often."

You would think Eddie's come out of the Sahara. He's downed half his glass before I've even had a chance to top mine up with Coke.

"So why have you taken so long to come back?" Eddie's question catches me unawares.

"To visit you. Why else?"

"Ja, right. After how many years?" Eddie says it like an accusation.

"I'm just kidding, Eddie. I grew up here, remember. I wanted to see for myself what's become of the place. No other reason."

"You've taken your flippin' time about it." Eddie's mouth is laughing but not his eyes. "And?"

"And what?"

"And what you think?"

"About what?"

"This place."

"It's a shithole."

"Ag, it's not so bad. You guys from the city are just soft. This is the real Africa, china."

"Maybe. Anyway, I was only kidding. Another one for you, Eddie?" I've hardly touched my drink and he's already finished his.

"What a question. Basil! Same again, but this time skip the Coke. Ja, make it a double. If not, why not, hey?"

And so the afternoon goes. Eddie boozes it up like there's no tomorrow. He must think I'm a charity because I pay for most of them. We make small talk about this and that, but it's hard going. We don't get around to talking about anything that matters, about what happened to him in Angola. I don't know why, we just can't get there. By the sounds of it Eddie's been doing nothing ever since, except maybe the odd job here and there. I push the peanuts away and ask him about his mom. She's got emphysema and spends most of her time between the armchair and her bed, according to Eddie. He tells me Simon visited them when he was out here. His mom still has the stuffed koala bear that he gave her. It sits on top of the TV at the end of the bed.

Eddie doesn't bother asking me any questions. He doesn't ask me what I've been up to all these years. I want him to ask, but he doesn't. Most of the time he stares into his glass, or at the black chick and her skinny white boyfriend in the corner. The guy looks old enough to be her father. She's wearing this short skirt and keeps crossing her fat thighs, uncrossing them, crossing them, uncrossing them. A cock-teaser if ever there was one.

An hour drags by and the bar begins to fill up, which means it's time to hit the road; you don't want to be in a place called Players when the shit hits the fan. It always does in places like this, even on a Sunday. I look at my watch and act surprised.

"Shit, Eddie, I must go!" Eddie looks all hurt, like I'm dragging him away from his own birthday party. "Sorry man, I've got an early start tomorrow."

"Come on, Nick, one more for the road. The party hasn't even started. Besides, we haven't seen each other in years."

I'm already on my feet. "Sorry Eddie, you can stay, but I have to go. You understand?"

"Suit yourself," he slurs. Now I'm feeling guilty for going.

"Listen, have another drink on me." I place a twenty on the counter and he instantly looks much happier. "Maybe I'll swing by your place early tomorrow? My plane only leaves at four." I know I'm lying because right now I don't know if I could handle seeing Eddie so soon again. It's not his fault; he is what he is. I am what I am. Or what I've become. Eddie doesn't budge from his barstool. We shake hands. It's as if he wants to say something, but at the last second changes his mind. "It was good seeing you again, Eddie. We'll talk soon. I promise."

"Ja, china, good seeing you too." Eddie looks past me, at the black chick crossing and uncrossing her legs.

I head towards the door.

"Nick!" I stop. Turn. Wait. "Ag, forget it. Give me a call sometime." Eddie turns back to the bar.

As I walk away from Eddie and into the fading light outside, I realise what it is about Eddie's eyes. The crazy spark is gone.

NINE

Sean's mom is so busy scrubbing the stoep stairs she doesn't hear me come up behind her. It's one of those seriously embarrassing moments because her dress is rukked up high and I can see all the way up, from the blue veins behind her knees to the soft fleshy inside of her thighs. It's hard not to look. I'm deciding whether I should do a U-turn when Mrs Daniels sixth-senses me standing there at the bottom of the steps. She jolts up and straightens her dress like she knows I've been checking her out. Like I said, it's one of those seriously embarrassing moments.

"Geez, Nick, but you gave me a skrik and a half. I almost jumped out of my skin."

"Sorry. Is Sean here?"

"Ja, I think so. Geez, but you're looking nice and tanned, hey. You enjoying the hols?" It's clear as day where Sean and his family get their friendliness from.

"So far, so good. Is Sean round the back?"

"I think so, but you can go check. How's your mom and dad doing?"

"Okay, thanks."

"You must tell them I say hi, okay?"

"I will."

I squeeze past Mrs Daniels and her bucket of Handy Andy. Cleaning is a fulltime career for her because she doesn't have a maid. Crazy. I head through the house, sneaking past Sean's dad, who as usual is glued to the TV with his pack of Benson & Hedges next to him, into the kitchen and out the back door.

Russel's Fiat is parked on the grass, his bare feet poking out from underneath. The soles of his feet are black; no wonder Sean's mom has to clean non-stop. Russel is hammering away at something under the car. The Fiat's radio is tuned into Radio Oranje. I don't bother stopping to say howzit; he wouldn't hear me anyway he's making such a racket.

The *Pomp Paleis* as Sean calls it is actually the ex-maid's room. Before I even get to the door I can hear his huffing and puffing. Ever since Sean saw this programme on bodybuilding he's become obsessed. Like he gets obsessed with anything he's into. I reckon bodybuilding is just an excuse for guys to check themselves out in the mirror, though I wouldn't mind looking ripped like you see in the magazines.

Sean spots me and points to the chair with his nose, then carries on. There's a pile of *Muscle & Fitness* stacked next to his bed, which Sean and me have read front to back and back again, and there's a bench press in the corner with a heap of rusty weights, which Sean got second-hand from the pawn shop. While I'm waiting for him to finish his set of barbell curls, I dig around in his tape collection for his new Pink Floyd. I rewind it to the beginning and plonk down on the bed and stare up at the sackcloth ceiling. The first time Sean and me heard *The Wall*, we knew it was going to become an instant classic. There's nothing like it and there never will be ever again.

"What did you get up to last night?" I ask.

"Nothing much. And you?" Sean puffs.

"Went for pizzas and video at Michael's house."

"Who's Michael?"

"You remember the guy who did that backward somersault off the high diving board?

"Ja."

"Well, that's him." Sean stops for a second. "They've moved into the mine manager's house."

"Oh ja?" says Sean, eyeing out his biceps in the mirror.

"You should see this place, Sean. I'm not lying, there must be at least five bedrooms and they've all got their own bathrooms with wall-to-wall carpets and these gold taps."

"Interesting."

"And not just one lounge, but two."

"Why does someone need two lounges?"

"The one they use for entertaining posh guests. It's got these genuine leather couches and aircon and an electronic bar thing that pours your drink for you. I'm not lying, you can set it to how many tots you want and it pours the exact amount every time."

"Sounds good."

"I'm not finished. You must check the other lounge. You would cream yourself big time, Seanie."

"Why?"

"Because it's packed with electronic equipment and a heap of records and videos and TV games like you've never seen before. You know that Bang and Olufsen system you showed me in that magazine of yours?"

"Ja."

"That's exactly what they've got. With those same long thin speakers that you want."

"Must have cost a bomb," says Sean, puffing his cheeks out.

"You're telling me. I swear, Seanie, you must check this place. Oh ja, and then there's these double glass doors that zip open to the pool . . ."

Before I can finish my sentence Sean grabs the *Muscle & Fitness* I've been flipping through.

"Imagine having a chick with a body like that."

"Lemme see."

Sean holds up the page. It's a photo of a ripped lesbian in a bikini. "Don't tell me you would say no to a body like that."

"Who would say no? But I bet, Seanie, even if you trained your arse off twenty-four seven you wouldn't get your legs to look like her arms."

It's not even out my big mouth and I'm already regretting bringing up the war. Not that he has a complex about it or anything. But Sean acts like he doesn't notice. He turns the page.

"This is what I call a perfect body."

"I bet he pumps steroids," I say.

"No ways. The pros work out all the time. Imagine walking down the street with arms like that. You would pull heaps of chicks."

"Ja, fat furry ones who eat bananas. He's way too big."

"You nuts? There's no such thing as too big."

"Whatever. Listen, we should organise to do something together with Michael sometime. You two would get on."

"You reckon?"

"Ja, I reckon. He's also got heaps of ideas. Plus he's keen to do something with us."

"Like what?"

"Anything. It doesn't matter. He said he's keen to come fishing with us. Why don't we do that?"

"Ja, whatever. You can organise it." Sean pages through the magazine some more. "I bet you also wouldn't say no to a face like that," he says, and shows me this photo of a girl who looks like a guy after a sex change, with legs and arms bigger than ours put together.

"You're such a wanker," I laugh, and toss my slip-slop at him, but he ducks out the way.

"Come on, why don't you get off your lazy poepol and train with me for a change?"

"What, like now?"

"Ja, why not?"

"What about Eddie?"

"He didn't pitch."

"Typical. What about our camp meeting with Vernon?"

"What about it? We've got heaps of time. Come on, any other excuses?"

I think about it for a minute, then leap off the bed.

"Okay, let's do it! As long as you promise to come fishing with me and Michael."

"And I said, you organise it."

"Okay, I will." Before Sean knows what's hit him, I've ripped off my shirt. "Your turn, Seanie boy."

"What?"

"Come on, you said you want me to train with you."

"You're nuts, you know that?"

"I know. Vest off!"

"Okay, if that's the way you want it," laughs Sean, and strips down, including his rugby shorts. A second later we're both standing in front of the mirror in our jocks.

"Is that God's gift to mankind or what, hey Sean?"

"The before and after."

"Ja, you the before, me the after."

"Watch this," says Sean, and kicks into Mr Universe mode, puffing out his cheeks until his face turns red.

"Careful you don't blow a poepstring." That's how hard Sean's trying to pump his arms.

"Check those veins, Nick. Am I huge or what?" Sean's getting totally into it now, posing this way and that way, checking himself from the back, then the side. You can tell he's been studying Muscle & Fitness because he knows all the poses. "A couple more months and I'm gonna be massive. Feel that, Nick."

I give his arm a squeeze.

"Hard or what?"

"Hard to find."

Sean stops to rest.

"Out the way," I say.

Now it's my turn to do a Mr Universe demonstration, tensing my muscles until I'm also red in the face. Maybe it's the mirror or maybe I'm imagining it, but I'm looking bigger from the few times I've worked out with Sean and all the milk I've been downing.

"What you think?"

"You're huge," says Sean.

"You think so?" Suddenly I'm fully into this body-building thing.

"I wouldn't say so if I didn't mean it."

"You know what we need now?" I say.

"What?"

"Oil."

"You mean like Johnson's Baby Oil?"

"Ja, whatever. You have any?"

"I don't know. But I can go look."

Sean pulls on his shorts and bolts from the room. That's what I like about him; he's always game. While he's gone I look at myself, this way and that way. He's back in no time, carrying a half-empty bottle of sunflower oil.

"This is all I could find."

I take the bottle from him, flip open the lid and take a sniff.

"It smells like mixed herbs."

"It's the only oil we've got. Unless you want Castrol."

"What the hell," I say, and start pouring oil into my hand and rubbing it into my arms. I pour some more, not shy this time, and work it into my chest and abs. I hand the bottle to Sean and he does the same. We're both soon covered head to toe in salad dressing.

"Jissus, imagine if someone walked in now," giggles Sean like a girl, rubbing some more oil into his shoulders. "The stuff you talk me into."

"It takes two to tanga."

"You mean tango?"

"Who's the teacher now? Whatever. If we are going to do this we might as well do it right." I walk across to the window and yank the curtains closed.

"Maybe I should turn the light on?" says Sean.

"Okay, but just the bedside light. I'll organise some other music."

A minute later "We are the Champions" is blasting through the speakers and Sean and me are taking turns to pose in front of the mirror. I swear, with the bedside light dimmed and the music blaring and our bodies pumped and glistening with sunflower oil, Sean and I look just like Mr Universe. And between all the giggling and huffing and puffing, I'm thinking I haven't had this much fun in ages.

TEN

It takes so long to scrub the oil off and get dressed in our uniforms we end up arriving way late for our meeting with Mr Stevens. Eddie and Angelo are already sitting around the plastic table at the front of the hall listening to what Mr Stevens has to say.

"Sorry we're late." I head for the empty chair next to Eddie, who tries to trip me as I squeeze past.

"Sorry, Mr Stevens," says Sean and sits down next to Angelo.

"No problem, guys. I'm glad you decided to join us," says Mr Stevens, looking at his watch. "Okay, great, that looks like that's all of us. So how about we kick off with a prayer to start the proceedings?"

A drop of sweat rolls down my spine. We all bow our heads.

I still don't know what to make of this whole idea, but soon after his divorce Mr Stevens, who is from Rhodesia, got it into his head to start a youth leadership group. Before we knew what was happening we had become the chosen ones. And now the problem is Mr Stevens believes in us. And because his wife took everything and he's living alone in this small flat across from the slimes dam, maybe we don't want to disappoint him.

"We ask you Lord Jesus Christ to guide us and this beautiful country of ours through the darkness. We ask you to be a beacon of light and a . . . and a moral compass for your leaders of tomorrow. For, as you know, and as I have explained to the guys here, without your shining light we can't move forward."

Mr Stevens stops praying and a long silence follows. I open

my eyes. Eddie's looking at Sean and Sean is looking at me. Angelo still has his eyes closed. Mr Stevens is moving his lips, but nothing is coming out of them.

"You stink like garlic," Eddie whispers in my ear. I ignore him.

It all started with a casual chat and hot-cross buns after church, and us getting a bit carried away. Mr Stevens and this friend of his, Wayne Alpert, who was a corporal in the army, they wanted to know what teenagers are getting up to nowadays, what they want from life, that type of thing. I don't know why, but we started coming up with answers about stuff we had never thought about before. Like, ja, the youth of today are bored stiff and are looking for meaning and direction in their lives. And yes, maybe like Mr Alpert says, we need to pull our finger out our bum and and smell the coffee and find out what's really going down in our own country. Mr Stevens asked us if teenagers need more guidance and leadership and we all nodded our heads furiously, like it was something we've been thinking about our whole life. And then before we knew it Mr Stevens and Mr Alpert were organising the first meeting and calling us the future.

Out of the blue Mr Stevens says, "Amen", and opens his eyes and looks around him in a daze, as if he's forgotten where he is.

"So guys, where did we end off last week? Let me see here . . ." Mr Stevens flips through his black school exercise book.

"You said we were going to talk about the logistics for the team-build weekend," interrupts Sean before Mr Stevens has a chance to get on to some other boring subject, like analysing the words of the national anthem, which we did last time with Mr Alpert.

"Oh, that. Thanks for reminding me, Sean. You know guys, I've been giving this a lot of thought and I must shoot straight with you, I just don't know if now's the right time. In fact, the Lord is telling me that maybe we have to put it off until next term."

It's the same every time. Everything Mr Stevens does, he believes it's God speaking to him. He seriously does. Like, if he goes to buy the *Sunday Times*, it's because God has a message for him on the back page. I'm not exaggerating; Mr Stevens is so brainwashed by the Assembly of God he believes every move he makes is because God is telling him to. That's why we are still waiting for God to tell him what to do next with the youth group. And it doesn't look like God is in any hurry to get started.

"Ja, but you and Mr Alpert promised, Mr Stevens . . ."

Mr Stevens must see the disappointed look on our faces.

"Okay, how can I put this Sean . . . ?" Mr Stevens puts his hand together and stares up at the damp marks of the church hall ceiling. A swallow has built a nest in the corner, which I haven't noticed before. "The problem is the education department hasn't sent all the bucks through. And now with holiday and all and everything closed . . ."

"But you and Mr Alpert said last week we were A for Away . . ."

"Yes, maybe we did, but that was before I sat down afterwards and did the calculations."

"So you're saying we're not going on the team-build?"

"No, no, Sean, I'm not saying that. It's still A for Away. I'm just saying maybe we have to downscale our ambitions. Don't you guys rather want to do a team-build or survival course at the river? We can have a lekker braai afterwards? We don't have to go away to enjoy ourselves . . ."

"That's how I feel," says Angelo.

"But we already did that, Mr Stevens. I've already bought my sleeping bag for camp."

"You lie?"

"Nick's not lying, Mr Stevens. It's true what he says."

Now Mr Stevens looks seriously worried.

"And I've organised a tent and backpack," adds Sean.

"And we've been telling everybody about it," Eddie says.

"Geez, guys, I didn't realise you had your hearts so set on this trip."

"The guys are dead keen, Mr Stevens," says Sean. "Eddie and Angelo have never been away their whole lives."

"What, you guys have never left this town?" Eddie shakes his head, while Angelo just sits there. Mr Stevens looks up at the stain marks again. Next thing he'll be telling us he sees the face of Jesus in the massive one on the left. "Okay, okay. Just give me a minute." Nobody, not even Eddie, says a word while we wait for Mr Stevens to rework his calculations. "So with Angelo also now on board that makes five, maybe six total, at a cost of, let me see . . ." Angelo looks seriously not keen and I'm feeling quite sorry for the guy, because he's useless with the physical stuff. There's no ways he'll survive the army, even with cadet training. He's only here because his dad makes him come. "Okie dokie, not as bad as I thought." Mr Stevens takes the pen out of his mouth and sits back looking chuffed with himself. "Well, guys, there may be a solution to all this."

"What's that, Mr Stevens?"

"You heard the saying: *'n boer maak 'n plan*? Great. Because that's what we are gonna do, guys."

"Like we ask Father for the rest of the money?"

"We can't do that, Edward, it's not in the budget. Imagine if every Tom, Dick and Gerrie started asking Father for money for this and that. The church would be bankrupt in no time. No, there's another way. I don't know why I didn't think about it before. Let me ask you a question. What's coming up soon?"

"The Currie Cup final?"

"That as well. Something else?"

"The new *Dallas*?"

"The fête?"

"Exactly!"

"You mean we do a cake sale or something, Mr Stevens?"

"Now we're talking, Sean. We don't have much time but if we put our koppe together we can come up with a way to make some quick bucks. And we don't need that much, guys."

And for the rest of the meeting we have a blast coming up with crazy ideas to make money at the fête and the whole time Mr Stevens is scribbling like mad in his exercise book, nodding his head and chewing his pen non-stop and saying, "Ja, that's a good one", or, "I like that", or, "Maybe not, that will take too long to organise".

We eventually run out of ideas and jump straight to the team-build weekend instead. Mr Stevens is by now fully into the idea, drawing up lists of things we need to take with us and what rations we are going to eat, and who must do what and get what. And just as I'm thinking this youth group thing isn't so bad after all, Mr Stevens, who is so pumped up, decides to end the meeting by asking us to stand up and form a circle and sing "Die Stem" like we've never sung it before.

ELEVEN

My mom's standing at the kitchen table in her pyjamas, cutting the stems off her roses. She's one of those gardening types. Through the open door into the passage I can hear Simon and my dad. As usual both of them are glued vas to the TV, giving running commentary. My mom snips the stem off this white rose and holds it out to me.

"Smell." I take a sniff to keep her happy. "Don't you think it's the nicest perfume ever?"

"Ja, it's nice, Mom."

I head to the fridge, leaving my mom to her roses. I dig out the milk from behind the jug of Kool-Aid. Nobody is watching so I don't bother with a glass. There's a lonely piece of sausage lying on a plate so I also shove that into my mouth.

"Someone called Michael left a message for you," my mom says from the other side of the fridge door. "Two messages, in fact."

"What did he say?"

"Just that he would like you to call him when you get home." I take another swig of milk to wash down the sausage. "Who is Michael?"

I close the fridge door. "Just a new guy. What else did he say?"

"Nothing. What do you think of my arrangement? Nice, hey?"

"Very nice, Mom." It's like my mom is floating in another world. "When did he phone?"

"Sometime after lunch. You better phone him back. His number is next to the phone."

"I will get to it, Mom." I open the fridge again and stare into it. "Is there nothing to eat in this house?"

I don't know why, but this funny knot has crept into my guts.

The phone rings about ten times before Michael answers it.

"Hullo."

"Howzit, Michael. It's Nick Theron."

"Nick, who? Sorry, I think you've got the wrong number."

"It's me, Nick. I was at your house last night. I got a message from my mom to phone you."

"Sorry, are you sure you have the correct number? What did you say your name was?"

"Nick Theron. Don't you remember? We had pizzas and watched a video."

"I'm sorry, I really don't know any Nick Theron."

Now I'm seriously confused and wondering if I've got the wrong number. But it sounds just like Michael's voice.

"Is this the number for the Dempseys?"

"Dempsey? Buddy, this is the Stevenson household."

"Shit. Sorry, I must have the wrong number."

"Nick?"

"Yes?"

"It's Michael."

"What?"

Michael bursts out laughing over the phone while I work out what's going on.

"Sorry, buddy, I couldn't resist. I got you there, didn't I?"

"I swear I was starting to lose my marbles. Ja, you got me alright."

"So, how's it hanging?"

"Fine. And you?"

"Top drawer. You keen to do something?"

"Like when?"

"Like tonight, dude. I thought we could hang out together?"

"Just you and me?"

"Ja. Unless you have plans to hang out with your buddy Sean."

"We haven't organised anything yet."

"Cool bananas. Because I thought it would be fun if the two of us cruised the town like we talked about. What you think?

"You mean on our bikes?"

"You crazy? Get your butt over here and I'll show you."

I must be losing it because long after I put the phone down I'm still trying to remember when we talked about cruising town.

"Hey, hey, hey, nice threads, buddy."

Michael stands back from the front door and checks me up and down like I'm a chick.

"What, this? It's just an old Wrangler jacket."

"Wrangler? I didn't know they were still in business. Can I feel? Don't know when I last touched genuine Wrangler denim."

"Sure."

"Nice quality. And the jeans?"

"Also Wrangler. You can let go now." I swear, I feel like a cat.

"Matching threads *nogal*. You could be one of those Country and Western singers, like Joe ..."

"Cocker?"

"That's the guy. Wow, you really did go to town."

"I always dress like this. Anyway, look who's talking. You must have a new outfit for every day."

"You like? I was worried you wouldn't. Not Wrangler, I know, but I did my best."

"Ja, ja."

Michael is wearing those new stonewashed jeans that I've been wanting for ages, and a white Polo shirt and Adidas slops. There's no ways a guy would blow-dry his hair, but you would swear Michael does, it's so neat.

"Enough chit-chat. Unless you want to come inside and meet the parents, I say let's hit the road." Michael bangs the castle door behind him. "I'm really looking forward to my grand tour."

"Don't get your hopes too high. There's not much to see."

"I'm sure there's plenty. Especially with you as my tour guide. You must know all the hot spots."

"Talk about putting me under pressure. Thanks a lot, Michael."

"Don't mention it."

"Are we going to walk?"

"Walk? Are you crazy, dude?"

"There's no way we can both fit on my bike."

"Who says I haven't got one?"

"I thought you said you didn't have a bicycle."

"I don't."

"So. That's why I reckon we walk."

"I have a scrambler."

"Oh ja? Like what?"

"Honda XR200"

"Ja, right. You're bullshitting me, aren't you?"

"Would I bullshit you?"

"Yes."

"*Touché.*" Michael punches me on the shoulder. "No big deal, it's only a bike."

"'It's only a bike', he says. I still don't believe you."

"So, do you want to walk or go like Wrangler on a scrambler?"

"Difficult choice," I say, scratching my head.

"Thought so. Hang ten here."

Michael disappears down the side of the garage. I know he's bullshitting. And if it's a scrambler it's probably a 50cc like some of the standard nines and matrics have at school. I hang around the driveway waiting for him. It's one of those perfect nights: warm and still, with the moon dangling like a disco ball from a black velvet ceiling. Eventually there's a grinding noise from inside the garage and the double door lifts open automatically. And Michael isn't bullshitting; standing like a racehorse in the middle of the garage between the gold BMW and his mom's silver Ballade is a red XR. Michael's already on it, holding two helmets and his feet hardly touching the ground the bike is so tall. I jog up to the garage.

"Jissus, I really thought you were having me on."

"You approve? Try this on for this size." Michael tosses a helmet in my direction.

While I battle with the strap, Michael kickstarts the bike. It blasts into life on the second take. Michael revs the engine. The sound goes right to the bottom of my guts. There's no better sound in the world than the AK-47 rattle of a XR200. The adrenalin starts to pump.

"Hop on!" Michael shouts above the tuk-tuk-tuk of the idle.

"What do I hold onto?" I shout into his helmet.

"Me or fresh air. Your choice," he shouts back. I take hold of Michael's shirt, the adrenalin beginning to flow big time. "You ready?" I nod. "Okay, grip tight." Michael leans across and flicks the garage switch, then kicks the bike into gear and guns the engine.

As the door starts inching down on us he drops the clutch and I just about do a backward somersault. My arms are wrapped around Michael's waist before we even we hit the end of the driveway, holding on like there's no tomorrow.

It turns out to be the best night ever; we end up cruising all over the place. Michael rides like a pro because he did junior motocross in Joburg. Once he shows me how to lean into the corners with him, not against him, the bike tears into the circles and corners like a hot knife into butter.

"Okay, where to now?" Michael shouts after we've been riding around for a while.

"Keep going straight," I shout back.

Michael gears down and we cruise past a Skyline. Two girls about our age are sitting in the back, dolled up to go nowhere. As we motor past slowly one of the girls waves at us and I let go one hand and wave back. This must be the first time a chick has waved at me. It's true what Sean says – if you don't have a hot body or a car or a motorbike they aren't interested.

"Yeehaa!" Michael screams, and kicks into second and hits the throttle, and we leave the Skyline coughing in our dust.

We take a slow cruise up Voortrekker, past the fountain and into town. It always looks better at night; by day it's a dusty dump. It's March and the Christmas lights are still on, with half the coloured bulbs blown or broken. We pass the Galaxy.

"That's where we play Asteroids," I shout into Michael's ear.

"Who's we?"

"Sean, Eddie and me."

"What's that there?" shouts Michael pointing at the roadhouse and the rows of cars parked in front. "It looks festive."

"The Vegas. They do lekker burgers. If you want, I can stick you?"

"Already eaten. But let's take a look."

Michael slows the bike and pulls off onto the gravel. He keeps the engine idling. For a Thursday the place is quite busy. There's a family crammed into the Cressida next to us, all of them licking ice-creams. There must be at least five kids on the back seat, gawking at Michael's bike. Most of them look like the dad, with gingery hair and freckles.

"Christ. It's like stepping back in time," says Michael, looking around us.

"What you mean?"

"That's what I mean," he says, pointing to a guy walking back from the bogs. He looks like one of those retarded people my mom visits at the centre. "If that's not the missing link, I don't know what is. I swear, this town could be the set for *Deliverance II*."

"You sure you don't want me to stick you for a ice-cream?"

"No, I say let's keep moving."

We ride the town flat, me pointing out this and that the whole way – The Phoenix, where half the town goes every Saturday; my old junior school next to the slimes dam; the new Checkers where we sometimes race trolleys when we're bored; the Tropicana, which has been closed ever since the pool caved in on the one side. I take him past my old kindergarten, with its yellow jungle-gym and the sandpit of old car tires and the rusty red tractor that's still going to be there after the Russians blow the world up. Where Sean, Eddie and me used to play when we were still crawling around in shitty nappies.

We are passing the graveyard when Michael does a U-turn and decides it's time for a midnight stroll. I can't say I'm keen but it turns out to be quite interesting in a depressing sort of way because Michael seems really into all this morbid stuff. Like the biological process that goes on when you peg off, with these millions of bacteria chomping away at you from word go, and the different chemicals the people at Avbob use to make the body last longer. Stuff I've never thought about. After we've walked around for a while I realise it's true what my dad said about apartheid carrying on long after we're all dead, what with the blacks buried on the one side of the graveyard, and the whites on the side where the trees are.

"If you like, Michael, we can go past Sean's house on the way back?"

"Why don't we visit your buddy Eddie, instead? Didn't you say he lives somewhere around here?"

"Ja, but I don't know if it's a great idea."

"Why not?"

"It's just that . . ."

"Just what?"

"Just that it's really late."

"More like you're embarrassed about your own buddy."

"I'm not embarrassed. Why should I be embarrassed?"

"You tell me."

"Okay, if that's how you put it, let's go there."

So we turn into Dingaan and pull up in front of Eddie's house. The front stoep light is on. I lift open the gate and walk to the front door, almost breaking my neck on the broken cement. I work my way around the bits of metal and old car and motorbike parts on the stoep. Eddie's bike is lying turtle with its front wheel off. I look back. Michael is watching me. When I knock on the door the neighbour's dog goes ballistic in the backyard. Luckily it's kept chained to their washing line.

"Try again," Michael shouts.

I knock again, louder this time. I shrug my shoulders and

walk back to Michael at the gate.

"There's nobody at home."

"Okay, forget it," Michael says, and revs his bike. "Now I see why you're embarrassed."

When we get to my house, instead of turning up our driveway like I think he's going to, Michael carries on right past and turns into Jamboree Park instead. He cuts the engine next to the cricket field.

"And now?" I ask.

"The night is still young. How about we end it with a nightcap?"

"Oh ja. And where do we organise a nightcap?"

"Let's say I've already organised it. Are you up for it?"

"I suppose so."

"Good to hear. For a moment I was worried you were going to fade on me."

"Me fade? Never."

"That's my man. Hop off, I need to get something out."

I climb off and Michael lifts up the seat and brings out a plastic bag with something wrapped inside.

"*Voila*," he says and takes off his helmet. "You lead the way."

We start heading across the field. There's not a soul around. The club bar must have closed hours ago because all the lights are off. The moon has also disappeared. Now it's just a mass of stars, the Milky Way smeared from one end of the sky to the other. Michael bumps up against me and giggles.

"Sorry, bud. I can hardly see where I'm going. This must be how your buddy with the gammy leg walks."

"Funny. It's not that bad. How about we park off here?"

There's nothing grand about the grandstand; at the most it

takes fifty spectators. Like my dad says, there's only one sport in this town and it's just not cricket.

We climb to the top and flop down on the rough planks. Careful not to get a splinter through my spine I lie back and look for Orion's Belt, while Michael fiddles with the knot of the plastic bag. Eventually he gives up and rips the plastic open. I hear the snap of the seal being broken. Michael unscrews the top.

"Okay. Take a sip of this."

I sit up. "What is it?"

"A little something to celebrate the holidays." He passes me the bottle. I take a whiff and cough.

"Is it brandy or something?"

"Don't ask so many questions. Open your mouth."

Michael empties half the bottle into my mouth. I push his hand away and swallow, my eyeballs popping out of my head.

"Jissus, are you trying to kill me or something?"

"Kicks like a mule, doesn't it?"

"What is it?"

"Jim Beam. Bourbon."

"What's bourbone?"

"It's pronounced bourbon. It's a type of whisky. Comes from America. And don't even ask what it costs."

Michael lifts the bottle to his mouth and swallows loudly. This is the first time I've had neat whisky and I can feel it working through my veins. Michael passes the bottle back to me. I take another swig, but a small one this time. I hold onto the bottle, then pass it back to him and lie back on the rough planks. Michael takes another gulp.

"Where did you buy it from?"

"Didn't. I borrowed it from my dad's booze cabinet. Come,

move up."

I shift to the edge of the bench. Michael lies down so our heads are almost touching. We both stare up at the sky.

"I enjoyed tonight, Nick."

"Me too. It was fun."

"I'm really glad I met you. I don't know . . . It's like we really connect."

"Ja, no, definitely . . ."

"And what's strange is that I feel like I've known you for ages, yet it's only been a few days. I dunno if you maybe feel the same way?"

I'm not sure what I feel, but when Michael says it's like he's known me for ages it feels a bit weird. But good at the same time. "Ja, you're right."

"Because I thought maybe it's only me . . ."

"No, I also feel like that . . ."

"That's great, Nick. I would probably be bored out of my skull by now if we hadn't met. And you?"

"I haven't thought of it much, but ja. Can I have another sip?"

Michael passes me the bottle. "Got it?"

"Ja. You can let go."

Michael lets go of the bottle and my hand. I take a small glug and pass it back to him.

"How well do you know your constellations?"

"Not that well. Orion's Belt is about it."

"Can you see Orion's now?"

"Ja. It's straight up there."

"Okay, now look to the left of Orion's, across from the bottom of the dagger. Do you see that cluster of small bright stars that form a skew square?"

"I think so."

"That's called the Jewellery Box."

"You're right. It really does look like a jewellery box."

Michael sits up and hands me the Jim Beam. This time I take a big swig. It's getting to me already. I lie back again. Our shoulders are touching and it doesn't feel weird anymore.

The bottle goes to and fro. Michael shows me how to find the Southern Cross, which he says sailors used to work out north from south. We're soon giggling like schoolgirls and I'm feeling more amazing by the minute. Michael tells me he feels the same way. I'm drifting in and out of my own world until his voice is miles away. In no time I'm piloting my own private *Startrek* spaceship high above Jamboree Park. I hit the thruster button and before I know it I'm blasting through the galaxy, watching the stars rush by. Then I'm laughing like a hyena, calling Michael Mikey, and telling him he's crazy and I also feel like I've known him forever. His body is pushed up against me and he's also giggling like a hyena. And just as I'm convinced I can hold on to this feeling forever, my spaceship begins spinning and I start falling back to earth. Next thing I know I'm hanging over the side of the grandstand, puking my guts out.

TWELVE

Dinner has already started when I get back to the Jacaranda. I take an empty table near the window. It faces onto the carpark. The place is dead, with the usual background music. Richard Clayderman. It's always Clayderman or Gheorghe Zamfir and his panflute in these small towns. I bet they never see the royalties.

The friendly Afrikaans woman brings me the menu. She's got a nice arse, I'll say that for her. Not one of those flat numbers that spread out like a pizza. There's a guy with a sweaty face in a blue short-sleeve shirt and dark grey pants eating alone at the table opposite me. Can only be a rep; they all dress the same. I should know. There are also two couples, one of them with a whiney kid. That's all they must get here, reps and couples desperate for a romantic night out. Not that you can call the Jacaranda romantic; the lights are turned up way too bright. They should invest in a couple of dimmers. Even the ones you get from China aren't bad, and way cheaper.

The waiter is the same madala who carried my suitcase. He brings me the menu and flashes his big white smile. No ways those teeth are real; they're too perfect. He asks if I want to see the wine list. Or maybe a nice whisky to start?

"I don't drink the stuff, madala. Have you got Windhoek?" He shakes his head. Castle and Black Label. SAB horse piss. I run through the wine list.

"Okay, give me a bottle of the Chateau Libertas. A seven-fifty, not a dinkie, hey."

What the hell, it's only forty bucks.

The old guy comes back with my wine, shows me the label, opens it in front of me, pours some in the glass for me to taste, the whole tootie. I'm impressed. The wine tastes like Chateau should, so I give him the go ahead. And before I can stop him he's filled it right to the bloody brim.

Who would have thought? Thirty years. Thirty years for me to get it together to come back. Am I the only one? Or are there others I don't know about who've also booked into a room with a crack running across the roof?

The only person from here I'm still in touch with is my own flesh and blood. Simon. He's living in Australia, with his wife and three kids. Joined the chicken run. He left just before the elections. Thought all hell was going to break loose, that the blacks were going to murder us in our beds. He didn't say that was the reason, but I know it was. Why else would he leave? Maybe it turns out he's right. That one day we whites will have our throats slit by the darkies. Maybe Simon and the rest of them just got the date wrong.

My Madagascar rump arrives. It's drowning in mushroom and peppercorn sauce and is a carpet compared to what you get in the city. I don't know why I ordered it. I'm not even hungry – and the lump in my guts still hasn't shifted. The rep across the way doesn't have the same problem. He's tucking in like there's no tomorrow.

The last time I saw Simon was when he came out alone for a holiday four years ago. He even made a special trip to visit me at my old place in Pinelands. To check up on how I was doing after my divorce from Andrea. The way I carried on when he was here you would swear I was living in paradise. Knocking back the beers around my new Weber, telling him how perfect everything is. The weather, the women, the government, the economy, what more can a man want? Simon swallows my bullshit hook, line and sinker because he wants to believe it. He's not like those other South Africans living overseas. He wants to believe everything is hunky-dory. It's because he feels guilty he made the right decision by taking his family away from here. He feels bad he and Fiona are happy together and living in a safe neighbourhood in Brisbane. He plays along, and I help him believe I'm okay. That Andrea will see the light and, you read my lips Simey boy, any day now she'll be knocking on the door for the sake of the kids, begging to get together again. And no, contrary to what Andrea told you, what happened in the past has zero to do with what's happening in the present.

I ask the madala for a doggie-bag because there's no ways I'm going to get through this rump. Maybe I'll find some poor guy on the street who wants it. Shit, I almost forgot!

"Sorry, madala, have you got any more of those small packets of salt? . . . Ja, one's fine."

While he goes off to fetch my tube of bergie Colgate, I down the last of the Chateau and decide to call it a night just as Richard Clayderman gets going for the third time.

THIRTEEN

"You must check the boep on this one. I swear, he would give a hippo a run for its money," says Sean, squinting down the binocs.

"Lemme see," says Eddie, yanking on the strap.

"Hang on . . . They're getting ready to take a tea break."

"Come on, let me have a turn."

This must be the only decent thing about Eddie's house: it lies right across from where the cops trap. And I know it sounds dumb, but watching cops is way more fun than watching rugby or cricket on TV. At least that's what I think. It's even better now that we have a pair of binocs, which we found in Eddie's dad's cupboard among the Tex Bar wrappers and empty Lexington cartons and an open box of condoms. Although he's been dead for ages Eddie's mom still hasn't cleared out his dad's cupboard.

I twist the angle of the beer crate so I can put my feet up on Eddie's bed. I take another hard suck of the Dunhill we've been bouncing because it's the last one in the pack. To be honest I don't really care what's happening on the other side of the road, mainly because my head still feels like porridge.

"And now, ladies and gentlemen, the players will take a break," says Sean, still hogging the binocs and pretending he's Charles Fortune. Eddie takes the cigarette from me and sucks on it. "Cop with boep gets ready to stuff his face with bread and, yes, he now begins cement-mixing it with his coffee."

"How do you know it's coffee?" says Eddie.

"Whatever. Tea, coffee, what's the diffs?"

"Watch this one!" says Eddie, excited, as a Cortina flies into view at the top of Gemsbok.

I watch with Eddie and Sean as it barrels at a rate towards the cops and hits the wire. One of the cops leans forward in his folding chair and watches it fly past. He sits back and carries on chatting to his buddy.

"Did you get a hold of that?" says Sean. "He must have been doing at least a hundred. For fuck's sake, Eddie, don't gob all over it, I still want a last puff."

Sean hands Eddie the binocs and Eddie hands Sean what's left of the Dunhill and the copy of *Grensvegter* he's been reading.

"Where were you last night, Nick? I thought we were going to hang out."

I've been waiting for Sean to bring up the subject.

"I cruised the town with Michael on his motorbike."

"Who's Michael?"

"Nick's new best friend from Joburg," says Sean.

"Michael, the swimming oke we met at church? I didn't know you were chommies with him."

"I hardly know the guy, Sean, but ja, that Michael."

"What's he ride?" asks Eddie, like I expect him to.

"XR200."

"You bladdy serious?"

"Ja. It's amazing. You must check this thing, Eddie."

"Did he give you a go?"

"Not yet. But next time he will."

"Or maybe he will just buy you your own," says Sean.

I ignore Sean and start telling Eddie about the amazing time Michael and me had, about how Michael handles his XR, about us cruising up and down town. How we ended up at the cricket field and drank Jim Beam bourbon under the stars and how I puked down the side of the cricket stand.

"What's boarbone?" asks Eddie.

"It's a type of American whisky. And you pronounce it bourbon, not boarbone, you bonehead. And don't even ask what it costs. And here I'm puking all these bucks out–"

"I think we get the point," interrupts Sean.

"What you mean?"

"I mean, you haven't stopped gaaning on about Michael this, Michael that. You're sounding like a stuck record."

"A stuck record," laughs Eddie. "I like that."

"Bullshit. You asked me what I did last night, now I'm telling you."

"Thanks, but now you've told us."

"Next time I won't bother telling you. Anyway, I don't know what your problem is. Michael's keen to do something with us."

Sean turns back to the window. "Ag, just forget it. Pass me the binocs, Eddie."

I try concentrate on the blue skedonk puffing smoke and crawling along at snail's pace. An old black guy is behind the wheel. Cop with boep leaps into the road and flags the car down. You would swear he's parking a 747 the way he waves his arms about.

"Nail the black bastard!" shouts Eddie. He's still hogging the binocs.

It burns what Sean said. About me gaaning on about Michael.

The old guy looks about eighty. Even without the binocs I can see the cops are giving him the works, walking around the car and pointing at this and that – the indicators, the brake lights, kicking the tyres, the whole time shouting at him. The guy just stands there and takes it. His wife or whoever's in the passenger seat stays put. Eventually the cop with the boep tears a page from his book and sends the guy on his way.

"What a doos."

"Ag, Nick, he deserved it. I bet he bought his license at some shebeen. These houtkoppe weren't meant to be on the road in the first place."

"Oh, shut the hell up, Eddie," says Sean.

"What did I do now?" says Eddie, acting offended.

"You're talking out your arse," I say. "That's what you did."

"You are both talking out your arses. Anyway, who cares a stuff?" says Sean. "Let's talk about something more interesting."

"Like what?"

"Like, has Nicolas Theron decided yet if he's going to have a party?"

"I told you, I'm not into the hassle of organising it."

"What's there to organise? All you need is good music."

"And some jags chicks," chips in Eddie.

"It's easy for you to say. When last did one of you two have a party?" The answer is never. The last party we went to was my own, and that was when we were still in primary school. "Besides, let's say I did have a party, where are we going to find these so-called jags chicks, Eddie? We hardly know any chicks, never mind jags ones."

"What about Adele?" says Sean. "I'll ask her to come."

"Okay, apart from Adele, who else?"

"Vanessa's friend, Tanya Reynolds."

"That will be the day, Eddie. Why don't you just go to the tikkie box and phone up Miss World herself? You would have to pay Tanya to come to one of our parties."

Eddie has another go. "Okay, then, how about Rodney's sister?"

"She doesn't count."

"Why?"

"Because she's Rodney's sister, idiot. It's like asking your own sister on a date."

"Nick's right. It's like paying your sister to give you a love bite. I bet if you had a sister, Eddie, that's something you would do."

We all crack up at this. The mood in the room is suddenly lighter, as if somebody's opened the window and let in some fresh air.

"What you mean love bite, Sean? If Eddie had a sister, he would pay her to give him a blowjob."

"Very funny," says Eddie.

"There's only one person who would give Eddie a free blowjob, Nick."

"Who?"

"Eddie."

"Oh, shit, that's funny," I say, clutching onto my stomach. "You're going red in the face, Eddie."

"No, I'm not."

Sean wipes the tears from his face. "I bet Eddie doesn't even know what a blowjob is."

"Do you think I'm an idiot or something?" Sean and me look at each other, then crack up all over again.

"I wonder why it's called a blowjob," says Sean, after we've calmed down.

"Ja, why don't they call it a suckjob? But the job part's true. I swear, if I was a girl I wouldn't do it unless you paid me a huge whack. It must be like shoving your fist down when you want to puke. No ways."

I decide to give Sean and Eddie a demonstration, shoving my hand in and out of my mouth, then pretending to puke, which has both of them in stitches.

"Seriously, Nick, you only turn sixteen once, hey. You must have a party."

"I scheme so too," says Eddie.

And before I know it I'm buying into the whole idea and lapping up Sean's plans – Sean could sell sand to a camel dealer in the Sahara. He has the whole thing worked out A to Z. We will have it in our garage at home and he's going to sort out all the music and the lights, and we're going to ask Adele to invite a bunch of friends from her school; it doesn't matter if we don't know any of them because by the end of the night we will. And Eddie's going to be the bouncer and the barman, and I'm going to organise with my mom to make trays of sausage rolls and other snacks, and we'll ask Luke to buy us beers, but no hard tack because we don't want things to get totally out of hand.

"So how about it?" says Sean, after he's explained his grand vision to us.

I shrug my shoulders. "Okay, what the hell." I say it like it was never a big deal in the first place.

"That's our okie!" shouts Sean. And we give each other a round of high-fives. And Eddie punches the wall with his bare knuckles.

"You got anything for us to eat, Eddie?" says Sean, after a while. "I'm starving after all this thinking."

"Just bread."

"With what?"

"Polony."

"I dunno how you can eat that stuff. There's pig's balls in it."

"Bullshit."

"That as well. Nick, tell him why it's so pink."

"To disguise all the balls and derms that go into it."

"I swear, not even Angelo's dog will go near that stuff. Don't you have peanut-butter or something, Eddie?"

"I dunno. Maybe there's some jam."

So we troop after Eddie into the kitchen and sit round the table and make doorstop sarmies with white margarine and what's left at the bottom of the apricot jam tin. You would think a grenade's gone off by the time we're finished.

"Luke, you want a polony sarmie?" shouts Eddie through the hatch between the kitchen and the lounge.

"No thanks, boet," comes Luke's Rod Stewart voice through the hatch. "But you can gooi me another Blackie if you want."

"Are we hitting the pool later?"

"What a kwessie," says Sean.

"You asking Adele?"

"Think I should?"

"Ja, I do."

"Okay, maybe I will."

Eddie comes back with Luke's beer.

"You okes want to hear a good story?"

Before we can say yes or no Eddie's leading the way into the lounge, where Luke is lying on the couch with his bare feet up on the coffee table.

Luke Scheepers is a Recce or a parabat – I'm forever mixing up the two – and I would be lying if I said I wasn't a bit bang of him. I don't mean scared in the normal *Chainsaw Massacre* way, or that he'll stuff you up if you look at him wrong sort of way. He's actually a decent guy, calm and friendly, and he's always got time for us. But once he tells you what he's done and Eddie's shown you some stuff to prove it, you are not so sure anymore. It's like now and then you get a cold shiver down your back when Luke Scheepers is around. It's like you can't put two and two together, this calm guy and the stuff he tells us.

This must be about the tenth time Luke has been to the border. He's always going or coming back. He must have more contacts than anybody. That's what they call it in the SADF, "contacts". This time he's been back for about a week and I swear he looks like Rambo. His hair is shaved on the sides in a GI Joe-style and the skin on his neck is almost black from the sun. And I'm not exaggerating like I normally do, but he has these ripped muscles everywhere, especially his arms, which look like engine pistons. Even his neck is one bulging muscle, with a thick vein running down the side. Whenever Luke gets back from the border he looks fit as all hell. One look at him and you also want to sign up with the Recces.

I can tell Eddie's chuffed as all hell with him because it's usually non-stop Luke this and Luke that when his brother's home. But I suppose I would also act like him if he was my brother. He must think Eddie's a total pain in the arse, when all he wants to do is rest, drink beer and watch TV.

While Eddie leads the way and hands Luke his beer, Sean and me hover near the door with our marg and apricot jam sarmies.

"What you watching?" Eddie asks him, all casual-like.

"Ag, just some Western," says Luke, and cracks open the Black Label with his BIC lighter. He takes a swig, burps, but softly, letting the air out slowly. He's not wearing a shirt and his stomach muscles are really ripped. I try not to stare, but it's not easy.

"Can I have a sip?" says Eddie, just to impress us. Luke hands Eddie the bottle, who takes a gulp. And then another one.

"Luke, why don't you tell Nick and Sean about that last time in Angola," says Eddie, handing the bottle back.

"What last time?" says Luke, and drags his Texan Plains across the coffee table with his foot.

"You know, that night you told me about."

"Oh that. Just the usual shit," says Luke in that calm voice of his. You can see he isn't in the mood to talk and I think we should maybe leave him in peace and get the hell out of here. Like maybe wait for another day to hear his story. But Eddie wants Luke to tell us now so he can brag afterwards.

"Tell them about the ambush, Luke, like what happened. Sean and Nick want to hear."

And he turns to us for moral support and we nod our heads.

"Ja, we're keen, Luke," says Sean for both of us.

Luke keeps staring at the TV. I reckon he's thinking the only way to get rid of us is to tell his story. If he wanted to he could squash us like three fat mosquitos. But luckily he's not that type of guy. He really takes good care of Eddie, especially since their dad died two years ago. That's why nobody ever lays a hand on Eddie at school. It would be like putting a .38 Special to your head and pulling the trigger.

"I dunno why you guys want to hear this shit, but okay," says Luke.

He turns the volume down, but carries on staring at the TV. Only now do Sean and me move more into the room and find a place on the carpet. And then Luke starts telling us about this night he and four of his company had to sleep in the bush somewhere in Angola. How they weren't even sure where they were exactly because they had lost their bearings earlier in the day after tracking a group of terrorists. How they lay there nipping themselves in their sleeping bags, listening to the lions and hyenas circle around the camp, but couldn't light a fire because the SWAPO terrs might see it.

Luke is telling us the story in this calm voice of his, as if he is telling us about a Sunday tea party. Meanwhile Sean and me, and I bet even Eddie, who has heard the story before, are lapping it up.

But that's not half of it. Sometime during the night one of the guys hears this sound like footsteps and twigs breaking and soft voices. He tugs at Luke's sleeping bag, but Luke's already wide awake. And so are all the other guys in his company. They whisper to each other. They're sure it's the group of Swapo terrorists they've been following during the day. Sean's mouth is hanging so wide open I can see his tonsils and bits of bread stuck to his teeth.

And before they know it the footsteps are coming straight in the direction of their camp. And Luke reckons there must be at least ten of them. He tells us, still in this calm voice, how they've got no choice but to engage – that's the word he uses, "engage" – because they are sitting ducks. While Luke explains, Eddie keeps looking at us, then back at Luke, then back at us.

Luke lights another Texan from the first one. The ashtray on the couch is overflowing with stompies. It's one of those perlemoen ashtrays you get when you go on holiday to places like Margate or Umhlanga.

And now the worst bit comes. Luke tells us how all hell breaks loose as the enemy walks straight into their camp without even realising it. And because it's so dark, Luke and the guys in his company wait until the very last second before letting them have it. And the terrs don't know what the fuck has hit them. Luke says half of them are dead before the rest of their black brothers have a clue what's going on. There's lots of screaming going on, not just from dying Swapo, but from our side as well.

Luke, who is now staring at the ducks flying above the TV, says it's the adrenalin, you can't help yourself, it just takes over.

It's so dark all they can see are black shadows. So they just keep shooting and shooting, until there aren't any shadows left to shoot.

"That's it," says Luke, and then stops talking and turns the volume up again.

"But what happened next, Luke?" asks Eddie. I don't need to hear any more.

"That's it, boetie. Finito. Nothing more to tell except terrs lying everywhere, some moaning and groaning. The usual."

Sean now asks a question. "What did you do with the injured ones, Luke, the one's that didn't die, what did you do with them?"

Luke turns and looks at Sean as if he doesn't understand the question. Eddie also looks at Sean as if he's stupid or something. I don't know where to look. Eventually Luke turns back to the TV and says in that calm voice of his, "'n Boer maak 'n plan. Not so boetie?" And he roughs up Eddie's hair. And Eddie laughs and looks real chuffed with himself.

FOURTEEN

"Don't forget you owe me," I tell Eddie, after we collect our ice-creams and head back to the pool. As usual, he doesn't have a cent to his name.

"Ja, ja," says Eddie, chuffed he's scored a free cone, although it's only a boring Classic. There's no ways I'm going see my money again, but I know that already. By the time we get back to our towels my Choc-99 is running down my fingers. Gavin Joubert and Rodney Meyer are busy unpacking their stuff. Just because they're going to be in Eddie's class next term they suddenly think we're all best buddies.

"What happened to Sean?" asks Eddie.

"His toppie said he had to mow the lawn."

"Isn't that what garden boys are for?"

"The oke's mother or auntie or whatever pegged. He's gone back to Malawi."

You would swear Eddie's never eaten an ice-cream before, he's shoving it in so fast.

"Close your legs, Eddie, I can see your bladdy balsak," Rodney says.

Eddie's cozzie is a pair of old rugby shorts with a split down the middle.

"So what?"

"So what? You're making me naar."

Eddie closes his legs. I break off the bottom of my cone, hold it up to the light and inspect the inside. Eddie starts giggling like a schoolgirl.

"What's so funny?" I say.

"Nick, tell Gav about the time you found that cockroach. I'll never forget that."

"Why do you think I break off the end? You think it's for my health?" Actually, it is for my health, but it doesn't matter; it goes way over Eddie's head.

"I promise you, Gav, it wasn't a tiny cockroach or anything. You should have seen this thing." Eddie opens his arms wide. "It was one of those fat Parktown prawns you get in Pretoria."

"Thanks for reminding me, Eddie. For your information it wasn't a fat Parktown prawn. It wasn't bigger than this." And I show Eddie my middle finger. Gavin and Rodney have also started giggling like schoolgirls. "I swear, that's the most disgusting thing that's ever happened to me."

"The roach must have thought he was being ambushed by one those trapdoor spiders," says Rodney.

"Meanwhile old Theron here is happily munching away and coming closer and closer."

I also can't help smiling because it's funny now I come to think of it.

"But it wasn't as funny as you're making out."

Eddie and Rodney are already licking their fingers and I'm not even halfway through. Eddie digs a bogey from out of his nose and wipes it on the grass.

"Shit, man, that's disgusting. Can't you see I'm still eating?"

"Your fault if you want to eat so slow."

"At least I taste my food."

"Is that now hot or what?"

"What?"

"Tanya Reynolds."

"Where?"

"Right there, man. Lying next to the superslide."
"Okay, okay, I spot her. Who is that she's with?"
"Malcolm Swart."
"That doos?"
"She's going steady with him."
"Who says?"
"Everybody."
"But he's like twenty."
"So? These hot chicks are into old guys. Malcolm's got a car and his own flat at Mount View."
"Dump View, more like it. Is his the red XR-6?"
"Ja. It's a beast. Imagine those legs wrapped around you."
"Don't even say it, Eddie."
"Enough to give you bladdy bal cramp. Jissus, imagine being that Coke bottle."
"Eddie, are you jags or what? But why Malcolm Swart? He's such a twat."

"Hi, guys," says this voice behind us.

I twist round on my towel and see his shadow before I see him. Michael. Blocking out the sun in a white cut-off T-shirt and Polaroids, holding his helmet. I hop onto my feet.

"Hey, howzit going, Michael?"

"Good, good. If I had known you were coming to the pool I could have given you a lift."

"We sort of decided at the last minute."

Michael looks past me to Eddie and Gavin and Rodney, who are sitting there like meerkats, waiting for the next move.

"Mind if I join you guys?" Michael says, and throws his stuff down on the grass. Rodney moves up to make space for him.

"Okes, this is Michael."

Rodney and Gavin reach across and shake his hand.

"I'm Eddie. We met at church."

"Yes, how are you doing, Eddie? Short for Edward?"

"No, it's short for Eddie," chirps Gavin from the peanut gallery.

Michael shakes Eddie's hand, then spreads his towel on the grass and drops his denim shorts. He's wearing that black Speedo again. He doesn't even have a farmer tan.

"Where's Beacon Island?"

"What?"

"There, on your towel."

"Oh, that. It's a hotel in Plett."

"Where's Plett?"

"Don't you know anything, Eddie?" It's bladdy embarrassing the way he goes on sometimes.

"What's the water like?" says Michael, changing subject.

"Like bathwater," says Rodney.

"Ja, from all the lighties pissing in it," says Gavin. "So where did you learn to dive like that?"

Instead of ignoring Gavin, Michael starts telling us about his school swimming team and their diving instructor who would have made it into the Olympic team if it wasn't for the boycotts. He's soon got Eddie and Gavin and Rodney lapping up every word because they start asking him questions about the places he's lived, what his dad does, about his XR200, that type of thing. Michael's already told me half of it, but it's interesting hearing it again. With all the things he's done you would never say he's seventeen.

"So that's my story," says Michael eventually. He stands up. "I need something to drink. You guys want something?"

Eddie looks up at him. "You mean you're sticking?"

"If that means paying, yes, I'm sticking."

Eddie looks at the rest of us, like he can't believe what he's hearing. "You serious, china?"

"Why wouldn't I be serious, Japan?"

"In that case I won't say no, I'll have a Fanta," he says.

"What about you two?"

"Grape Fanta," says Rodney.

"Me too," says Gavin. "Hell, thanks, Michael."

"No problem. Do you want something, Nick?"

"I won't say no to a Creme Soda. Can I give you some money?"

Michael waves my hand away. "Another time."

"Is he loaded or what?" says Gavin, after Michael has gone off to fetch.

"Maybe he's just generous. You should take some lessons," says Rodney.

"Michael is big time generous," I say. "I have to keep saying no."

"If I was you I wouldn't say no."

"But you're not me, Eddie."

"So why's he hanging out with you all the time?"

"What you mean all the time, Eddie? It's only been a few times. I'm just making an effort to be friendly. Not like you."

"Maybe he wants Theron's bod. Ja, that's must be it. The oke's a moffie. Full stop."

"You talk such shit, Gavin. I don't know why I bother trying to explain."

"What you reckon, Roddie?"

"Must be. Only moffies wear Speedos."

"Lifesavers wear Speedos?"

"In that case, lifesavers are moffies."

Rodney and Gavin are still congratulating themselves when Michael arrives back with the cold drinks and hands them out.

"No problem," he says after we've said thanks for the tenth time. "It's only money."

"You hear that, Nick?" says Eddie.

"What?"

"It's only money."

"Why, did Nick lend you money?" says Michael.

"Ja."

"How much?"

"Thirty cents."

"For what?"

"An ice-cream."

"And he wants it back?"

"Ja. Can you believe it?"

"It's the principle, Eddie. And it's not the first time."

"Come now, Nick," says Michael. "I'm sure you can afford to give your bud here thirty cents."

"Ja, Nick, you mustn't be so suinig."

"Thanks, Gavin. If I want your opinion I'll ask for it."

"Hey, check-check, look who the dog's dragged in," says Rodney, and whistles.

Like meercats we spin round and spot Sean walking across the grass towards us, flicking his kuif. Maybe it's the light, but his limp looks worse than usual. I wave, but he's already spotted us under the tree. His shirt is off and he looks pumped, like he's been working out or doing push-ups before he came to the pool.

"Ze elephant man cometh, ja?" says Michael, in this German accent. Rodney and Gavin pack up at this. "Who's that?"

"Sean".

Michael digs his toe into my side. "Oops!"

It takes Sean forever to cross the open stretch of grass between the ticket office and where we are lying.

"Howzit, okes," Sean says, and chucks his school haversack to the ground. He looks around at us, then at Gavin and Rodney.

"What's so funny?"

Gavin elbows Rodney in the ribs. "Come on, quit it, stop making me laugh." But Gavin can't keep a straight face and they both pack up giggling again.

"What's the big joke?"

"Don't look at me," says Rodney, trying to keep a straight face.

I shrug my shoulders and turn to Michael, who is watching all this go down.

"I'm Michael," he says, and stretches out his hand, not bothering to get up. "Your friends are just playing silly buggers with you. Hey, you two, behave yourselves."

"I'm Sean. Anyway, who cares a stuff?"

Sean is still looking seriously confused long after he's shaken hands with Michael. He spreads his towel next to me.

"Seanie, where's the hot chick you supposed to be bringing?" says Eddie.

Sean gives me this pissed-off look.

"I just said you might bring Adele with. That's all."

"She's got netball practice."

"In the holidays?"

"They're going on camp, if you must know, Eddie."

"Who's Adele," asks Michael.

"Sean's stukkie," says Eddie.

"Sean wishes Adele Du Plessis was his stukkie," chirps Gavin. "They've only been on one date."

"Why, is she a babe?" asks Michael, while he smears himself with baby oil.

"I wouldn't say no."

"You wouldn't say no to your mother."

"You wouldn't say no to your grannie."

"You wouldn't say no to your old man."

"Fuck you."

"Fuck you, too, Gavin."

"Hey, Sean, have you pomped her yet?"

"I can't believe this shit. Did anyone ever tell you that you're a sicko, Gavin?"

"Ja, lank times. Apparently Steve van der Spuy and half the matric guys at St Helena have pulled into her."

"You talk such crap Gavin." I'm way regretting even mentioning the word Adele.

"I love it! You lot are hilarious, you know that?" Michael says, which isn't such a good thing because now we'll never hear the end of it. That's how Gavin Joubert and Rodney Dreyer are. Also Eddie if you don't put him in his place. But eventually Michael turns his back to them.

"Don't look so serious, buddy, they're just ragging you."

"Do you see the worry on my face?"

"So Nick tells me you've got your junior colours in fishing."

Sean hands me another pissed-off look, but I ignore it. "Don't be shy, Sean. Tell Michael how you came first in provincials."

"It's no big deal. And it was northern districts, not provincials."

"Same thing. Sean's just being modest, Michael. It is a big deal. He was competing against guys twice his age and he beat them hands down."

"I'm impressed. But seriously, what do you have to do to win a fishing competition?"

"You have to catch a moerse big fish," says Gavin, who's been listening in and who knows squat about fishing.

"There's more to it than that, Gavin," says Sean back.

"Of course there is. It must be similar to a diving competition, where you are judged on different aspects. Am I right?"

"Ja, that type of thing."

"I don't know if Nick said anything to you, but I would love to go fishing with you guys sometime. He's been telling me all about your fishing trips."

"Half the time you sit there doing nothing, if that's what you mean?"

"That's what I also told Michael."

"Yes, but just hanging out at the river with your buddies and having a fire going while you fish, it all sounds like a blast. When are you planning to go next?"

"Depends . . ."

"On what?"

"Like if I'm in the mood, or if it decides to rain."

"Why don't we go Saturday, Sean?" I say.

"This Saturday?"

"Ja, like we usually do."

"I'm there like a bear," says Michael.

"Shit, I just remembered!"

"What?"

"I'm not going to be here on the weekend."

"Why, where you going to be?"

"Joburg. We have to visit my uncle."

"He's got cancer," Eddie says on my behalf.

"Okay, how about Monday? Will you be back by then?"

"Ja. We're only going for the one night."

"So what you think, Sean. Monday good for you?"

"Whatever."

"Brilliant! I love it when a plan comes together."

"Isn't that what the guy in the A-Team says?"

"Who, BA?"

"No man, the leader. The white oke with the cigar. Whatsisname?"

Rodney jumps up. "You asking me? I'm going for a goof."

"You can use one of Sean's rods, Michael. He's got heaps. If that's okay with you, Sean?"

"I'd really appreciate that, Sean. I'm chuffed, us going fishing next Monday. What about you two? You coming with?"

But Gavin and Rodney are too busy giving each other Chinese bangles to be interested.

FIFTEEN

"Hey there, if you've just tuned in, you are listening to the Coca Cola countdown. I'm David Gresham, with you till ten am. And we're counting down, we're counting down all the way to this week's new Number One. Right, next up, at thirty-six, Rastaman Eddie Grant with, "I Just Wanna Dance" . . . Enjoy."

I poke my arm through the duvet and fumble around for the snooze button. For the next half-hour or whatever it is I'm floating in that half-awake, half-asleep, half-dead state, where time is twisted and weird. "At number big Three-O we have Alphaville, falling twelve storeys from eighteen last week . . ." This time I hit the Off button. Someone must have come in the night and glued my eyes shut with Bostik; I can hardly open them. I lift the duvet: five-past-seven. I pull the duvet back over my head, wishing I was dead.

Across the way Simon is sawing down a tree. I hang over the side of the bed, dig out a takkie and toss it across the room. It's way off target. I find the other one. This time I take better aim and the takkie connects with Simon's head. He lets out an animal groan, turns over and goes back to sleep.

I hear my dad's footsteps down the passage. The door swings open. I play dead.

"Wake up you two. Time to get up."

Silence. My dad walks into the room and rips open the curtains.

"Come on, Simon, up you get. I want you guys packed and ready in fifteen."

"I don't want to wake up," groans Simon. "I'm not feeling so good."

"What's wrong?"

"My tummy's sore. I think I've got food poisoning."

Simon comes up with amazing excuses; and he must think my dad suffers from amnesia.

"Sorry to hear, but you know what?"

"What?" moans Simon. A hopeful moan.

"Too bad."

Simon lets out another dying groan.

"Are you awake, Nicolas? Or are you also suffering from food poisoning? I'm getting worried it may be contagious." Funny. I keep staring at this mosquito smear on the wall. It's been there for yonks. "Hey, boy, you awake?"

I let out this grunt to make him happy, which he must translate as, "Ja, dad, I'm wide awake and ready to go. I can't wait."

"Good. We will see you both at breakfast in ten."

My dad doesn't bother closing the door behind him. I wait for his footsteps to disappear down the passage before flipping over and staring up at the ceiling.

Talk about crap luck. My uncle's only thirty-two and he's dying from cancer. He's had it for quite a long time now, about six months, but even so it's a big shock when you hear the doctor tell your parents he's got less than a month to live. I don't know how they know these things, they just do.

It's all a bit weird because my uncle was such a fit guy and into his sports. Especially tennis – he was mad about tennis. Ever since school he's been in the first team. Same in the army. That's how good he was. If you saw the photos we have of him before he klaared out you would say he was the healthiest guy around. If anyone was going to live forever it was my uncle. It's so flipping true what Sean says: life's a bitch and then you die.

Nobody has much to say as we drive the road to Joburg because we are all quite morbid about the whole thing. Only Simon, who's too young and dumb to know what's going on, is his usual self. For a change I'm actually quite happy to have him around.

"Why's Oomie been sick for so long?" he says as we leave the mine dumps and mielie fields behind and hit the N1.

That's what he calls him, Oomie, because he can't pronounce Jacques, my uncle's actual name. I pretend not to listen, and keep staring out of the window, trying not to count telephone poles. It's an addiction, this counting telephone poles; it drives me crazy sometimes. My mom's the only one to take notice of Simon's dumb question.

"Jacques has a serious illness, Simon. One that takes a long time to get better from."

I know my mom's lying. We all know my uncle is going to die. The doctors said so.

"But he's been sick for ages, I want to know when he's going to get better?"

"I don't know, sweetie, but we must all pray and hope he gets well."

I don't know why my mom doesn't just tell Simon the truth. But I can't be bothered to get involved. My dad's also not bothered because he keeps staring straight ahead at the road, his jaw muscles popping up and down like a pulse. He's hardly said a word since we left home early this morning. My uncle is his younger brother so he must be feeling it the most. I'm not sure how I would feel if Simon got cancer, but it won't be as bad as my dad is feeling right now. Then again, if somebody like Sean got it ... I would put a gun to my head and pull the trigger.

"Mom, can I sit in front with you?" Simon asks in that baby voice of his, the voice he uses whenever he wants something. My mom looks across at my dad before answering.

"Okay, Simey, as long as you promise not to disturb dad while he's driving."

Simon throws me a chuffed look, then climbs over the seat and squeezes in next to my mom. Like I said, I can't be bothered. I've got enough to deal with. Between counting telephone poles and wondering who I'm going to invite to my party and whether the whole thing's actually a crap idea, I can't help thinking about my uncle lying on his hospital bed. I wonder what he's thinking this very minute. Everybody knows there's no cure for what he's got so he must know he's going to die, even if the doctors haven't told him.

The one-seventy-five-kay sign for Joburg comes up and my mom hands the Lemon Creams around. It's always Lemon Creams. I wonder what it's like to know you are going to die. My uncle must lie awake at night thinking about it, imagining what nothingness feels like. I hope he believes in life after death, even if I don't, because if you believe there's something better waiting you are maybe less poep-scared about dying.

Sixty-four, sixty-five, sixty-six . . . when Simon blurts out of the blue, "Is Oomie going to die?"

Even I'm caught off-guard because I lose count and turn from the window and look first at my mom and then my dad. My mom doesn't know what to say so I decide to say it for her.

"Are you dumb, or what, Simon? Of course he's going to die. Why do you think we are driving all the way to Joburg? It's not for a Sunday picnic if that's what you think."

And now everyone in the car gets upset – my dad, my mom, me, Simon. My mom starts crying and tries to hide it, but she can't, and then Simon starts bawling his eyes out. The muscles in my dad's jaw begin pulsing even faster.

"I don't want Oomie to die, Mom."

And now I feel awful that I opened my mouth, but it's too late to do anything about it.

"Sorry, Mom," is all I can say, before turning back to the window and counting from scratch again.

My dad heads straight for the hospital as soon as we hit Joburg. He's still hardly said a word, which isn't like him; he usually talks non-stop when we go somewhere in the car, pointing out this and that the whole way. He could have been a game ranger with all the stuff he knows about trees and mountains and animals. Instead he ended up spending half his life two kays underground.

When we get to the hospital, which is actually called a hospice, my dad pulls into the parking lot and tells Simon and me to wait in the car.

"I want to come with," whines Simon. "I need to pee."

"I also need to pee, Dad," I say, and I'm not lying. My bladder is about to explode; we haven't stopped once the whole way. If it wasn't for the pee I would be happy to stay put and listen to the radio. I have a knot in my guts and I haven't even stepped a foot out of the car.

You can see they've tried to make the place nice for the visitors and patients, with a pretty garden with roses and a friendly guy at the gate, but it's still a place where people go to die. It's not like visiting a hospital.

Because my dad doesn't want Simon peeing in his pants or in the flowerbed next to the car he has no choice but to take us with. So we all climb out and traipse inside, my dad walking way out in front, the rest of us behind, my mom holding Simon's hand. As soon as we're through the revolving doors Simon and me bolt straight for the toilets, which are next to the reception office. I don't know who needs a pee more, Simon or me, but luckily there's a proper toilet and a urinal thing.

"You use that," I tell him.

I go into the toilet and lock the door behind me. I can hardly get my zip open it's so urgent, and I nearly pee all over the seat. I can hear Simon on the other side, pulling up his pants. He still pulls his pants right down whenever he takes a slash, like it's a number two.

"Have you washed your hands?" I say over the top of the wall. Simon never washes his hands, even after a number two. That's how unhygienic he is. But before I have a chance to make sure he has, I hear him pull open the door and disappear out of there.

My mom and dad are speaking to this woman doctor with grey hair in a bun and these old-fashioned glasses with thick black frames that you see in old black-and-white movies. She seems the real serious type, but I suppose you can't exactly start cracking jokes in a place like this. I have to come really close to hear what she's saying because she's almost whispering, as if she doesn't want anybody else to hear.

"Jacques is feeling very little pain," the doctor is telling my parents. "He stopped eating a few days ago. We've been feeding him intravenously." My dad nods his head, but doesn't say anything, so she carries on. "He's been slipping in and out of consciousness for the past few days, though I have to tell you, he's hardly been awake today." My mom and dad nod some more. Simon must sense something serious is going on because he's keeping his mouth closed for a change. "Once it spreads to the brain it's just a matter of time."

I'm hearing the doctor's words, but I'm not hearing them. It's hard to explain.

"Can we see him?" my dad asks in a croaky voice.

"Yes, of course." And the lady doctor looks at me and Simon, then back to my dad.

"They should be fine," he says, and turns to us. "You guys want to visit your uncle? You don't have to if you don't want to."

Simon looks up at me and we both nod at the same time.

We've come all this way.

We follow the doctor down the passage. My mom reaches for my hand, but I pull it away gently so she doesn't notice. Instead she grips onto Simon and my dad's hand, and I follow behind them. We pass a room with the door half-open. I try not look, but it's too late. A young girl is lying on the bed, with these hollow cheeks and tubes coming out of her nose. She must be about my age, maybe even younger; it's hard to tell. A black nurse is standing over her, wiping her head with a facecloth. We pass another open door, but this time I keep my eyes straight ahead.

Right at the end of the passage the doctor with the old-fashioned glasses comes to a halt in front of Room 18.

"Would you mind waiting here a moment?"

She disappears into the room and closes the door behind her, while we stand around like lost farts. The door opens a few seconds later.

"I will leave you alone now, but I am next door if you need me."

My dad leads the way. I can't see much at first because the curtains are drawn and the lights are off. But my eyes soon get used to the dark and I can make out my uncle's bed in the far corner. There's a very soft yellow light glowing above it. The room has a strange sweet smell I've never smelled before. It's not the usual hospital smell.

The walk from the door to the bed feels like miles. Simon and me stick to my mom's back.

"Oh my God!" my mom whispers, sucking in her breath.

I step out from behind her. I can hardly recognise my uncle. It's him but it's not him, the skeleton lying on the bed, covered in paper-thin skin. There's nothing much else. All the muscles have disappeared from his face and he has no hair, and it's as if his head has caved in, like a soccer ball with a puncture. His eyes are closed and his breathing heavy and slow, struggling to get air. My mom now starts crying, very softly, trying not to. Simon stares up at her with big round eyes. My dad says nothing. There's nothing to say. I just stand there, this prickly numbness seeping through my body.

SIXTEEN

Maybe it's this thing with my uncle but I'm in a weird mood after we get back from Joburg. It's like I don't have the energy to do anything. I can't even be bothered to answer Sean or Michael's messages on the machine. I'm in such a weird mood I end up hanging out all afternoon with my mom, checking out old photo albums

"I don't know why you even bother with that book, Mom. There's no ways you'll finish it," I tell her as I work the gears of my dad's La-Z-Boy, back and forth, back and forth. The book she's reading is thicker than a loaf of government special; she's been at it for months. It's written by some Russian; from what

I can make out from the back cover it's one of those depressing sagas that my mom loves.

But my mom's not concentrating; every two minutes she looks out the window and stares at nothing. I pretend not to notice, but when the photo albums come out the drawer you just know.

Thanks to my mom we have stacks of albums. She reckons photos help you remember who you are. Like, if you know where you come from you know yourself better, that type of thing. She will go totally overboard sometimes, telling my dad to take photos of everything he sees. Even if my mom bakes a fancy cake she'll make us all stand behind it while my dad snaps away with his Pentax. She must have been Japanese in a past life.

My grandfather was also Japanese in his past life because there are heaps of photos of my gran. Looking at these black and white ones it's hard to imagine my gran was once my age. She died about three years ago, also from cancer. It must run in the family, which means I might get it one day.

I don't want to sound sicko and all, but my gran was beautiful like my mom. My favourite is this ancient black-and-white photo of them on holiday in Paris, sitting on the back of a park bench, with the Eiffel Tower behind – Eddie actually believed me when I told him the Eiffel Tower is in Pretoria. Talk about doff. My gran has her arms around my grandfather; you've never seen two people looking so happy together. You would swear they were on honeymoon or something. But they weren't because they were already ancient when the photo was taken – at least forty. It's just that they were so into each other that they could look like this after all those years together. It's my favourite photo of them, even though it makes me bit depressed every time I look at it.

Looking at old photos must be a craving my mom and I both suffer from. Like the craving my dad gets for slap chips from Vegas. Or the one Simon has for grape-flavoured Kool Aid.

One thing I like about my mom is she knows when I'm not in the mood for small talk. We can sit together for ages and not say anything. She's definitely not pushy like Eddie's mom, who can be a total bulldog.

After a few pages the photos are just of my gran. And she's looking nothing like that time in Paris. That's how quick things change. That's how quick you get old. After a few pages she looks like any other grannie you see in the street. Especially if they get their hair done at Rochelle's. When old people walk out of La Rochelle they look like they've popped out a sausage machine. I'm not even a trained hairdresser and I could do a better job.

Only when you look closer at these photos of my gran – there's a couple of her watching Simon blow out the candles on his third birthday, another one of her holding him when he was still in nappies, and one of her in a big hat watching my uncle play tennis at the Joburg club – only then can you see it's the same person. Even if she were a hundred years old the eyes would be the same as those in the photo of her with my grandfather at the Eiffel Tower.

Come to think of it now, I really miss my gran. Not to mention my gramps and my sister who I can hardly remember. And before I know it I'm missing my Uncle Jacques. And he's not even dead yet.

And then there are the photos of me and Simon and our friends when we were only this high. The best one is of me and Sean and Eddie in the bath together. If you peel away the *Three*

Musketeers sticker you will see Eddie's hard-on. And he wasn't even four when the photo was taken at our old house with the huge green bathroom. There's another photo of us in the under-eight soccer team, with each of us taking a turn to hold the trophy, and Gavin Joubert picking his nose in the background. Because of his leg Sean always had to be goalie. Then a photo of Sean and me in the school play. Another one of us blowing the candles out at my sixth birthday. The photos carry on forever, just about all of them with Sean, Eddie and me.

I look up to catch my mom staring out the window again. I know I should ask what she's thinking about and all that, but I don't bother.

It's almost four o' clock by the time I throw the clutch, gear the La-Z-Boy down, and jerk forward to *P1*. My dad would blow a poepstring if he saw the way I rode his chair when he's not around.

"I'm going out, Mom."

My mom says it's fine, I must have a good time. I don't know why, but I actually feel bad leaving her alone with her depressing book and all these photos to remind her of things she maybe doesn't want to be reminded of.

SEVENTEEN

The gold BM is parked in the driveway. Meaning: Michael's mom and dad are at home for a change. As I'm walking up to the front door I spot them sitting under this gazebo thing at the far end of the garden, reading the newspaper. Michael's mom is wearing a bikini top and sunglasses – for an older woman she's quite hot. Michael's dad also has his shirt off, but is wearing long khaki pants. He spots me and waves. I wave back. I'm still deciding if I must go over and introduce myself when the maid answers the door. She's dressed in a posh red and white maid's outfit that looks like it's just come out of the wash.

"Is Michael here?"

"Yes, I'll show him to you."

She says it in this perfect English and doesn't say master or madam like all the other maids. Her name is Doris or Dorothy and has been with the Dempseys since day dot. Even though I've been here a couple of times already, Doris (or whatever her name is), must show me the way to Michael's room. We pass a sculpture of a kaal woman with no arms, which I haven't noticed before. As I said before, my mom would go mad for the Dempseys' art. The maid knocks on Michael's door. "A young man for you, Mikey."

"Who is it?" comes Michael's voice from the other side.

The maid looks at me.

"It's me, Nick."

If this was Sean or Eddie's house, or anybody else's for that matter, I would just barge in. I stare at the door like an idiot, waiting. The door opens. Michael looks as if he's just woken up, with his hair all over the place.

"Thanks, Doreen."

The maid turns and disappears down the passage. I'm already regretting I didn't phone first.

"Hey, buddy, how is it hanging?"

"Alright, thanks. Have you been dossing? I can come back later if you want."

"No worries. Come in."

I follow Michael into his bedroom. It's more like a flat than a bedroom, with its own bathroom and all. Michael shuts the door behind us and chucks the pile of clothes off the chair. His bed is a mess, books scattered all over the place.

"What you reading?"

"Just some stuff for an essay. Nothing you would be interested in."

"Why do you say that?"

"I don't know, but you don't strike me as someone who reads."

"I'm actually quite into books, and my mom and dad are forever reading."

Michael leans over the side of the bed and slides a book across the carpet.

"Okay, tell me what you think of Hermann Hesse?"

"The name sounds familiar. What else did he write, besides this one?"

Michael slides another book across to me.

"*Thus Spoke* who?"

"You telling me you haven't heard of Nietzsche?"

"Wat se? It looks like something my mom would read."

Michael reaches up to the bookshelf.

"I forgot I had this. Catch."

"*Clockwork Orange*. Same as the movie you were telling me about?"

"The movie was based on the book. Let me know what you think."

"Thanks. You saying I can lend it?"

"No, I'm saying you can borrow it."

"Sorry, that's what I meant."

"Take this one also."

"*Lord of the Flies*. I've already read it."

"Read it again."

"I wouldn't mind. It's really good."

"Why is it really good?"

"Ag, I don't know, I just liked the story of these kids stuck on this island with no rules, watching them turn savage."

"So you believe if the world had no rules we would all become savages."

"For sure. It would be chaos."

"Sounds good to me."

"What, no rules or chaos?"

"Both."

"Shit, I dunno. Check what happened in *Lord of the Flies*."

"Survival of the fittest. It's nature's way. Only the weak want rules."

"You reckon?"

"Of course. Imagine, Nick, no rules means you could do whatever you wanted, nobody telling you do this, do that. It would be a total rush. Like, you could walk down the street and see a hot woman . . . What's the name of that girl Sean's into?"

"Adele."

"That's right, Adele. Now imagine you spot Adele walking

alone and you felt like some action. If there were no rules you could take her on the spot. And don't tell me you wouldn't?"

"Shit, I don't know, it doesn't sound right."

"Would you or wouldn't you? Yes or no?"

"Seriously, I don't know."

"Of course you would. But you dudes in this verkrampte place are so caught up in your tiny worlds you can't think out the box. Do yourself a favour and read *Clockwork Orange*."

"I'm going to."

"Good, because maybe you'll think a bit differently afterwards. So . . . How was Joburg?"

"Okay, I guess."

"Who was it you visited?"

"My uncle."

"That's right, he's got cancer or something? Must have been a blast."

"That's no lie."

"And besides visiting the sick?"

"Nothing much. Except I came to tell you I'm organising a party."

"A party?"

"Ja. I'm turning sixteen next Saturday."

"I didn't know you were fifteen."

"How old did you think I was?"

"I don't know," says Michael. "More like fourteen. So, where's the party?"

I start laying out our plans to Michael, about how we've decided to have the party in Sean's double garage and that he's sorting out the music and the lights, and Eddie's getting his brother to buy us a few cases of beer, and we're going to invite a whole bunch of people, including some hot girls.

"Why are you smiling?"

"Nothing. Carry on."

"That's it, I'm finished. So what do you think?"

"In a garage, Nick? You're having your party in a garage?"

"Ja, what's wrong with that?"

"Each to their own, I guess. At least now I know where the word garage-party comes from. Nothing personal, but no ways I would celebrate my sixteenth in a garage. Surely you can come up with something a little more ambitious than that?"

"Like what?"

I can feel my ears burning. Michael puts his book down and folds his pillow in half and leans back against it. Maybe Michael is right. Maybe it is a dumb idea.

"Jesus, why didn't I think of it before?" Michael blurts.

"What?"

"I'm such a selfish bastard, Nick."

"I don't know what you're on about."

"I mean, it's your big one-six coming up and here I am giving you a hard time."

"So, you're saying you're keen to come?"

"Please, of course I'm keen. Do you really think I wouldn't be there for you?"

"Well, I thought . . ."

Michael is now sitting upright, his blue eyes shining.

"Seriously, who do you think I am, Nick? I mean, how can I not be at your party? After all, we are buddies."

"I just thought maybe you weren't so keen on the idea . . ."

"We are buddies, hey?"

"Ja, of course."

"Good, because then I'm with you all the way. And I'm not only coming to your party, I've decided something else, too."

"What's that?"
"There's no ways you're having it in some greasy garage."
"Why, where are we going to have it?"
"Right here."

I'm still revved up when I get back to the house. It's going to be way better than I imagined because Michael has some great ideas from all the parties he's been to in Joburg. It's flipping true what he says about us living in the Dark Ages.

As I come up the driveway I spot Sean and Simon on the front lawn, messing around with my soccer ball. Sean is dribbling the ball around Simon, acting the idiot, Simon chasing him, laughing hysterically. Sean is seven years older than my brother and he's pretending he's having a good time. Sean sees me and collapses in a heap. Simon takes the ball and dribbles it away and boots it between Sean's slops, which they've been using for goalposts.

"Nice one, Simey!" Sean shouts. Simon sprints around the garden, believing he's Maradona or something. I don't know what Sean sees in Simon; it's irritating the way the two of them carry on sometimes.

"Where've you been, man?" says Sean, panting like a dog. "Didn't you get my messages or something?"

"What messages?"

"To phone when you got back?"

"Sorry, I forgot."

"It's okay."

"I said I'm sorry."

"And I said it's okay."

Simon sits himself down on the ball and watches us from a few feet away.

"Okay Simon, you can go now."

"Leave him alone," says Sean. "You can stay if you want, Simon. You were here first." Sean walks over to his haversack. "While you were away I organised some cool music we can use for our party." He lifts out a Checkers packet stuffed with tapes and brings it over. I'm trying to ignore Simon, who is still watching us, as if he's actually interested.

"There's been a change of plan, Sean."

"A change of plan? Like how?"

"Well, it's just that Michael and me decided to have the party at his house instead. That's where I've just come from. And that's why I forgot to phone you back."

"Slow down. You're speaking Greek."

Simon giggles and I give him a look and he shuts up.

"Let me get this right. Are you telling me we must forget everything we've done so far because you've now decided to have the party someplace else?"

"I'm not saying that." Or maybe I am saying that. I don't know what I'm saying. "All I'm telling you is that Michael came up with this lekker idea to have a pool party at his house instead. He said he'd help organise the whole thing. I promise you, Sean, if you saw this place you would also think it's a much better plan."

But Sean doesn't let me know what he thinks; instead he turns his back to me and stares at Simon, who by this time is bored with our conversation and is dribbling the ball again, acting his usual dumb self.

"You want to know what I think?" says Sean, his back still to me.

"Of course, I do. Why would I have bothered to tell you in the first place?"

"You can have your party wherever you want, Nick. And by the way, I also came here to say I'm sorry to hear about your uncle being so sick and all. But I can see you're not interested."

Before I can ask what he means by that, Sean is on his feet and chasing after Simon.

EIGHTEEN

It ends up being a seriously bad day. The moment I get back from the café with the milk and bread and walk into the house and the flyscreen bangs behind me and my mom doesn't shout the usual about us living in a stable, I know something's happened. I find them in the lounge, my mom and dad sitting on the couch, with Simon squeezed between them, talking in soft voices. The only time you talk in soft voices is in a library or if something's wrong. The photo albums from this afternoon are still lying all over the place.

"What's the matter?"

"You better come sit down, Nicolas."

"I'm fine. Is it Uncle Jacques?"

My mom nods.

"Oh." I take a deep breath. I've been expecting it, but not so soon. I flop down on my dad's chair. "When?"

"An hour ago. The hospice just phoned us," my mom says.

What was I doing the exact moment my uncle's heart stopped? Clocking up a bonus score on Madeira Café's pinball machine.

I look at my dad. His eyes are red. I've never seen him cry. And I don't know if I could handle it if he started now. Next to him my mom blows her nose into a tissue. I can handle my mom crying. It's her job to cry for the rest of us.

"When's the funeral?"

My dad clears his throat to squeeze the word out. "Saturday."

"Are we going to Oomie's funeral?" asks Simon, looking up at my mom while he weaves his fingers in and out of hers.

"Yes, sweetie, we'll all go."

"I don't know if I want to go."

I'm not that big into funerals. Not that I'm an expert or anything; the only funeral I've ever been to was that of Mrs Graham, our standard two teacher who was hit by a runaway mine truck on her way to the shop.

"It's your choice, Nick," says my dad. "You don't have to go if you don't want to."

But when he says it like this, I suddenly want to go. It doesn't seem right not to.

I didn't realise my uncle knew so many people because there's a crowd at the funeral, including some posh-looking types. And the funeral service, which is held in a stone church in Hillbrow, isn't as bad as I imagined. There's a really good black choir who knows how to hold a tune and the priest doesn't go on and on like Father Dominic does sometimes, and near the end some friends of my uncle walk up to the front and say some really nice things about him. And not in a way that blows him up into something he wasn't; the way they describe him is the way I knew him. My dad also gets up to say a few words, but he's so choked up he can hardly get past the first sentence. Every few seconds he has to stop and blow into his hanky; before you know it half the church is hauling out their hankies and doing the same. It's all pretty sad and emotional.

After the church service we follow the black Merc to the graveyard, which ends up being miles away. My dad has to jump three red robots to keep up because he doesn't know the directions to the graveyard, and we've got this convoy on our tail that thinks he does. We are so busy keeping up with the Merc it helps takes my mind off things.

While we stand around waiting for everyone to arrive and the guys from AVBOB to get organised, a couple of people walk up to my parents to chat. Except for a few distant relatives, I don't recognise any of them; my uncle never married and he was my dad's only brother, so I don't have much in the way of cousins. My mom hasn't let go of my dad's hand since we climbed out the car and she does most of the talking. Every now and then she points to Simon and me standing in the shade of this jacaranda tree, but luckily nobody comes over to speak to us. Right now I'm really not in the mood for small talk.

For once I don't mind looking after Simon. He could be a magician's assistant, dressed in his black jacket that's way too big for him and his black hair slicked back. I can't exactly talk, what with the brown suit I wore for my confirmation and my black school shoes and the white running socks I borrowed from my dad because I forgot my socks at home. It's a good thing we don't know anyone.

"Are they going to use the coffin again when they've finished burying Oomie?" asks Simon.

"Of course not, dummie. It's going to stay in the ground until the worms eat it."

"Not even the gold handles? Won't they use those again?"

I don't bother answering. It's a dumb question, but part of me thinks maybe Simon has a point. I reckon if my uncle had the choice he would have gone for a much cheaper coffin. Maybe one of those pine jobbies with the rope handles. That's the type of guy he was.

Eventually everybody is ready and the priest begins to read from his Bible. The world goes into slow motion as my dad and three big guys in black suits shift my uncle's coffin into position. My dad steps right to the edge of the grave as the coffin is lowered into the hole and swallowed up by the earth. The priest reads some more from his Bible. The birds in the jacaranda carry on above our heads as if it's just another day. My mom steps forward and holds onto my dad's arm. My dad throws a fistful of sand into the hole. Other people do the same. There's the loud thud of a stone hitting the coffin lid.

I bite my lip; it doesn't help because the tears keep coming. I turn and face the other way because there's no ways I want Simon to see me like this. I also want to be at the hole, throwing red Joburg sand into my uncle's grave. But I stay put, with Simey under the jacaranda tree, biting my lip until I taste the salty blood.

NINETEEN

It takes a couple of seconds to work out where I am. My heart is beating out of control and the sheets are soaking wet and everything is crazy and back to front and upside down. But once I work out I'm in Room 104 of the Jacaranda Hotel and it's eleven forty-eight pm and I'm forty-five years old, not fifteen, my heart slows down and I breathe in and out deeply and slowly pull myself together. As I've learnt to do a hundred times before.

I get up and push open the other window as far as it will go, then switch the TV on, first making sure the sound is off. I pour a glass of water from the basin in the bathroom and climb back into bed. Some people count sheep to help them sleep; I stare at the TV. It's the only thing that works for me.

There's nothing much to watch, but what can you expect when you only have two channels to choose from. The Jacaranda should do itself a favour and invest in DSTV. I flick back and forth between eTV – wall-to-wall adverts – and SABC 3, which has dug up some old documentary of cops and blacks running amok in the townships, and then later a hall packed with people bawling their eyes out. All this pussyfooting about, trying to be civilised about the past – they should have seized the moment and done it Africa-style when they had the chance.

It's the same every time: these crazy dreams and the wet sheets. I tried to explain it to Jen because she's the one who has to put up with it. I said try imagine a wine glass shattering into a thousand bits and you have to piece it all together again. Sometimes it takes days. Andrea and the divorce lawyer reckoned I should see a shrink. I told them I don't do shrinks. And then I met Jen, and she also reckoned I should talk to someone.

I carry on staring at the TV, at all these people letting it hang out. What about those who haven't owned up to the past? How many are there like me, sitting night after night in front of the TV with a Blackie in one hand and the remote in the other, our cute kids asleep on the couch next to us, our peroxided wives doing the dishes? Pretending to everyone, including our own wives. Not that our wives really want to know about it. Day after day, year after year we carry on like nothing's happened. Clock in at work eight am sharp, watch our rugby on the weekend, stand around the braai with our mates, our boeps touching the Weber. Pretending past is past.

TWENTY

"Am I doing this right, Seanie?"

Sean puts his rod down and walks over to Michael sitting on the broken wall of the old pumphouse.

"Looks okay. Tighten the line a bit, or no ways you'll feel it when a fish bites."

"Got you." Michael gives the coffee grinder a few cranks, reeling in the slack. Sean walks back to his rod. "Is this the life or what? Hey, Sean, what do I do when a fish bites?"

"Not when, if," Eddie says behind us, busting his lungs trying to get the fire going.

"All depends," says Sean. "If it's just a nibble you do nothing. But if it's a big take, then you must strike."

"What, like this?" Michael gives the rod Sean lent him a serious yank.

"You don't have to do it so hard. You only do that when you want to make sure the fish is vas on the hook."

"How do you know that?"

"You jump in with your goggles and snorkel. Nick, gooi me the petrol, this wood's papnat."

"I dunno," explains Sean. "It's just a feeling you get after you've been fishing a few times. He's not showing it but I can see Sean's starting to get irritated with Michael's non-stop questions. He has a point.

"Got ya. So this is what you've earned colours for?"

"It's no big deal."

"Okay, we're in business, china," says Eddie, screwing the cap back on the petrol can and wiping his hands on his shorts. "Works like a dream."

"Nice one, Eddie. I reckon we braai early."

Eddie and me study the sky, the heavy black clouds that have been hanging around all morning, getting darker by the minute.

"Kak weather. Dunno why we even bothered," says Eddie.

Michael is still stuck on his earlier topic. "Of course it's a big deal, Sean. They don't just give you colours for nothing. Even if it's for fishing. You have to deserve it."

"Guess what Nick and me have our colours in?"

"What?"

"B-A."

"Meaning?"

"Bugger All," laughs Eddie, stomping into the water.

"What the hell you doing, Eddie? You're scaring the flippin' fish away," says Sean.

"I'm just washing the petrol off my hands, man."

"Well, don't make such a racket about it."

Eddie climbs back up the bank, squats next to the fire and pulls out his ciggies. He leans into the flames and lights up.

"Donder! You smell that? My bladdy hair nearly caught on fire."

"Serves you right for not offering."

Eddie blows a smoke ring into the air. The smell of Gunston wafts across. Eddie flicks a pebble into the water.

"Cut that out, man."

But Eddie finds another one and does it again. This time the pebble lands close to Michael. Michael doesn't even turn around.

"Didn't you hear what your buddy said?"

"Whatever."

Eddie lies back on the grass and blows another smoke ring into the dark sky. I don't know why he bothers coming fishing with us. He's not built for it. I'm a dedicated pro compared to him. I move across to where Sean's sitting. Michael's leaning back against the willow, his cap pulled low.

"I reckon it's going to piss down, Seanie."

"You think so?"

"For sure."

Another of Eddie's smoke rings drifts slowly over us like a UFO.

"Seanie, can I have one of your Dunhills?"

Sean hands me the pack. I don't offer Michael because he doesn't smoke. He reckons it's bad for your health.

"Hey, Nick, why don't you tell us about the funeral?"

"What's there to tell, Michael?"

"I wonder what it's like to vrek," says Eddie, sliding down the grass and joining us.

"That's profound, my man," says Michael.

"Eddie's just weird," says Sean.

"Look who's talking? Anyway, what's weird about it? We're all going to peg one day."

Michael twists his cap to the back of his head. "It's a good question. Like, imagine never ever existing again. From the moment your heart stops until infinity you become black nothingness."

"That's why I don't think about it," says Sean.

"No, I don't worry about that. I just think about being gooied into a hole in the ground and maybe I'm not fully dead yet . . ."

"How can you not be fully dead, Eddie? You're dead or you're not dead."

"Listen to what I'm saying, Sean. Like my body is dead but my brain is still ticking over. Fok, imagine that, hey?"

"Don't laugh, Sean. It happens. I read this article about it in *Scientific American*," says Michael.

"Ja, I also read it."

"Like hell you did, Eddie. Unless it was in your mom's *Huisgenoot*."

"Ja, how did you know?"

"Seriously Sean, you can't deny reality."

"I'm not denying anything."

"So you're telling me you never think about dying?"

"I didn't say that. I just don't see the point of it. If it's going to happen anyway, why bother thinking about it?"

"Why don't we talk about something else?"

"Nick's right."

"No, he isn't," says Michael. He's a dog at a bone.

Sean doesn't bother replying, just shakes his head like he does when he disagrees with something. "Michael should meet Eddie's boet. They'd get on like a house on fire."

"And why's that, Sean?"

"Because Luke's an expert on dying," I say on behalf of Sean. "He's killed heaps of people. Not so, Eddie?"

Eddie nods, chuffed as anything.

"How do you know he's killed heaps of people?"

"Because he's a Recce. And, besides, he told us so."

"Eddie, tell Michael about the shoebox."

"Ag, it's no big deal."

"Jesus, dudes, talk about dragging out the suspense. What's the deal with the shoebox?"

"Like Eddie says, it's no big deal, but Luke has this shoebox at the back of his cupboard filled with . . . Can I tell him, Eddie?"

"Come on, Nick, spit it out . . . Size fourteen Bata shoes? Silkworms, what?"

"Ears."

"What you mean, ears?

"Swapo ears. From Angola."

"That's pretty cool. But you're sure they're ears?"

"Of course I'm sure," says Eddie, chuffed as all hell that Michael thinks it's cool.

"And you've all seen them?"

"Ja," I say, "they're tied together into this long necklace. They look like pieces of kudu biltong."

"How many are there?"

"Heaps. At least twenty, hey Eddie?"

"At least."

"I'm impressed, dudes. And here I thought you were boy scouts. So when do I get to see them?"

"Ag, anytime."

"Ja, like hell, Eddie," I say. "Luke would kill us all if he caught us scratching in his cupboard . . . Hey, told you it's going to rain, a fat drop just landed on my head. Are we going to chuck, Sean?"

"Don't be a wuss, Nick, we just got here."

"You don't know these Free State storms, Michael. They come from nowhere."

"Can't be worse than what you get in the Highveld. Anyway, if it does start pissing, you dudes can hang out at my place. What you say, Sean?"

"Same diffs."

Sean rebaits and then moves further up the river. I decide to follow him.

"Had any bites?"

"Nothing much."

Michael and Eddie are acting all buddy-buddy. Eddie's probably telling him a Luke story.

"You guys still going to Rocky tonight?"

"Ja."

"Mind if I come with?"

"What about your friend?"

"What about him?"

"Is he also coming?"

"I haven't asked. Anyway, he's not into the same movies as us. I thought it would be lekker if we did something together for a change. Just you, Eddie and me."

"Ja, it would be. For a change."

"So, let's do it."

I can see Sean's chuffed, which makes me chuffed.

"Whoa!" shouts Michael from across the way, jumping to his feet. "I got a serious take!"

"Like hell he did. We better go check."

I jog back to Michael and Eddie.

"You sure it was a big take, Michael?"

"Is Mother Theresa a virgin? Of course I'm sure. There! It did it again." This time I see it. A big take, followed by a few small nibbles. Even Eddie is sitting up and taking note. My heart starts beating.

"Sean, come quick!"

Sean lays his rod down and sprints across.

"What do I do now, Seanie? Must I strike?"

"Not yet. Wait for another big bite like that first one." The words are hardly out of Sean's mouth when the end of Michael's rod bends double and his reel screams. "Now!"

Sean's wasting his breath because the fish is vas and all Michael has to do is hang on and start reeling like mad. It's a total rush.

"This is amazing," shouts Michael, as he strikes and reels in, strikes and reels in some more. "Am I doing good or am I doing good, Seanie? Come on, you fucker, come to papa."

"Don't let your line go slack. You mustn't let your line go slack," says Sean, hopping about like he needs to pee.

"Got you, Seanie. Don't let my line go slack."

We're all now staring out at the muddy water, waiting for the fish to surface. A flash of lightning cracks open the sky. Billy-billy one, billy-billy two . . . billy-billy six, and then the thunder.

Which means the rain isn't even two kays away.

"Nick, grab the net," shouts Sean.

I climb the bank and rush over to our bags and grab Sean's net. It's still got the plastic wrapper around the handle.

"Eddie! The wors is burning."

I quickly turn the braai grid and sprint back to Sean.

"Can you see it yet?"

"Ja, it just came up. Keep reeling, Michael. There it is!"

Now I also spot it, its white belly twisting and turning against the line.

"Come on, baby, come to me," whispers Michael to the fish, like he's chaffing a chick. "What you reckon it is, Seanie?"

"A barbel, I scheme."

Sean's right. The head breaks through the surface of the water and it's definitely a barbel, what with the whiskers and all. And it's huge. Longer than my arm.

"Keep reeling, you mustn't let it get into the reeds."

Sean wades into the water. He reaches out with his net, trying to get close. Behind us Michael reels, strikes, reels, strikes. Every time he strikes the barbel's head jerks out of the water.

"You don't have to do that," says Sean.

"What?"

"Striking. He's had it." Sean wades in deeper.

"Hey, what are you doing?"

"Netting him for you."

"No ways, it's my fish. I'm bringing it in."

Sean looks over his shoulder and gives me this surprised look. "Your choice."

"Fucking right, my choice," says Michael. He's now standing in the water with us, hauling the barbel closer and closer to the side. He's got this crazy look in his eyes. Michael, that is.

He's seriously excited. The barbel's too big to lift out of the water. Michael tries to grab the line with his hand but misses and almost loses his balance. Eddie packs up laughing.

"You cheeky little bastard. Give me a hand, Nick!"

"Sure you don't want to use Sean's net?"

"No. Make yourself useful and grab the line."

I manage to get hold of the line and start hauling the barbel towards the shallow water. Luckily, it's given up the fight. I drag it along the mud.

"Keep going. You're doing well, bud."

To make a hundred per cent sure I drag it up onto the grass. The barbel lies there, hardly moving, except for its gills opening and closing, struggling for air. It must have swallowed the hook because there's no sign of it. Michael tosses Sean's rod onto the grass and scrambles over to where I'm standing. For a few seconds Michael and me just stand there staring at the barbel. It stares back at us through its pale eyes. Michael is still panting from the effort. Eddie slides down the bank, juggling a piece of sausage.

"Fokken nice one, Michael."

"Thanks, buddy. What you reckon, Seanie?"

"Ja, nice one," says Sean, who is still knee-deep in the water, pretending to be busy with his net. Another flash lights up the sky.

Michael digs his foot into the barbel's side. This funny grunting sound comes out of its mouth when he does it. Eddie giggles. Michael does it again, this time harder. The barbel does it again. "Hey, I think the fish is trying to tell us something. Listen." Michael does it again, but nothing happens this time, so he gives it a serious stomp. "You hear that, Seanie? Come on, you've got your colours in fishing. What's he saying?"

"That maybe you should let him go," says Sean softly, his back to us.

"What did you say?"

"I said maybe you should let him go."

"You boys hear that? Sean thinks we should let my fish go. What do you think, Nick?"

"Maybe Sean's right. It's just a barbel, Michael. You can't eat it."

"Now it's just a barbel."

"I didn't mean it like that."

"And you, Eddie? What should we do with it?"

Eddie looks at me, sausage fat smeared around his mouth. I say nothing.

"Ag, I don't care. It's your fish."

"Thanks, Eddie. That's what I thought. You have a go."

"With what?"

"Get the fish to talk."

"Seriously?"

"Seriously."

Eddie makes a whole show of it. He takes two steps back, checks the wind direction, points at the rugby poles and then steps in and gives the barbel a serious boot. The barbel lands about three feet away.

"Fuck! I didn't mean that hard, psycho boy," laughs Michael.

I look at Sean, but he's looking the other way, staring at the river, at the raindrops beginning to slap the water.

"Why don't you have a go, Nick?"

"No thanks."

"Suit yourself. So what now, Eddie?"

"I dunno, what?"

"I say let's put these guys out of their misery. Give me your knife." Eddie hands Michael his knife. It's also smeared with sausage fat.

"Who wants to do the honours? Nick?"

"No ways."

"Thought so."

Sean is now also watching what Michael is going to do next. Michael kneels down next to the barbel and cuts the line just before its mouth. Its gills are still opening and closing, but much slower now. Holding the knife with both hands Michael lifts it above his head. He's looking straight at Sean. Sean stares back, blank like.

"You ready, Eddie?"

Eddie looks at me, shrugs. "Ja, go for it."

I'm still thinking Michael's having us on when, next thing, he drives the knife straight through the barbel's head.

TWENTY - ONE

"Maybe I should make a run for it."

"More like a swim. You mad or what, Sean? Hang around here until it stops."

"Suppose you're right."

We carry on staring out the window, at the rain whipping against the glass like a pack of starving wild dogs trying to get inside. It hasn't come down like this in ages, but it's way better than living in a dust bowl, chewing sand day after day. I'm not exaggerating; it's been so bad lately you could hardly see the sun the sky was so brown with mielie-field dust.

"We're flippin' lucky we got out of there in time."

"Ja. We could have been in the dwang."

"I bet they never get storms like this overseas."

"Or dust."

"True."

"Right, boys, here we go," says Michael coming into the room, towing Eddie behind him with a tray. "Toss it down there, Edward."

"Looks like a feast, Michael."

"Just some sarmies. That's if you guys want."

"What a ques. I'm starving," I say.

"You don't want to borrow a pullover, Sean? You look like a drowned rat."

"No, I'm alright, Michael."

"Your choice, buddy. Okay, let's see what we've here . . . Cheese, mustard and ham. Sorry, that's it."

"Eddie's sad there's no polony," I say, helping myself to a sarmie. Maybe I'm just hungry but they're the best things I've tasted in a long time. "Can I grab a mug of Milo, Michael?"

"Help yourself, boys."

I hand Sean the mug with a cow on it. Another blast of thunder rattles the windows.

"Christ, get a hold of that one! I swear, this is most definitely the arse end of the world."

"You guys are also living here now," I say.

"Not for long if I have anything to do with it. I still can't believe the old boy took on this consulting job."

"Ag, it's not so bad."

"It's worse than bad. You lot just haven't experienced anything else to know better. If it's not the dust, it's the rain."

Eddie wipes his mouth on his sleeve and burps. "Now that was lekker."

"Ja, thanks Michael," I say. "Way better than the usual apricot jam and Stork marg. Hey, Sean?"

"That's for sure. They were good, thanks, Michael."

"No, thanks to you, buddy, for taking me fishing. It was a total jol. And how was that fish I caught? I still can't believe it. My first time ever and I catch something. What do you think it weighed?"

"About four kilos."

"I reckon about ten."

"You would, Eddie."

Sean walks back to the window. "Looks like it's cutting back. Maybe I should take the gap."

"What's the rush, buddy? Chill out here for a while."

"Michael's right, Sean. Chill out here for a while."

"All those books up there. How many of them have you read?" asks Eddie.

"Most of them."

"Michael's not joking, Eddie." Eddie pulls out a fat hardcover. "Chips, guys, Eddie's about to blow a fuse. I bet you can't even pronounce the title of that one."

"You're so bladdy funny, Nick. It's *Thus Spoke Zara* . . . What the hell . . . Who is this Zara Two Stroke? A Greek or something."

"Told you you wouldn't be able to pronounce it."

"Zara Two Stroke. That's funny, Edward. But instead of

143

talking crap, boys, why don't we do something?"

"How about a video? You must see Michael's collection, Sean"

"VCR's packed up," interrupts Michael.

"Since when?"

"Since two days ago."

"Okay, how about Monopoly or something like that?"

"Boring."

"What then, Michael?"

"Hey, okes, I know," says Eddie. "Let's phone someone."

"And say what?"

"Man, like we did with Craig Jennings."

"I like," says Michael. "What did you do with Craig Jennings?"

"Sean, do your Mr Alpert act for Michael."

"And now who, may I ask, is Mr Alpert?"

"Our cadet instructor. Sean, show Michael."

"I'm not in the mood."

"Come on, don't be so skaam."

Eddie grabs the gap and goes off with his own korporaal act. It's such a disaster we all end up in stitches. Even Michael.

"Jissus, Eddie, you sound like something the cat puked up. Come, you show us, Sean. You do it best."

"Like just so, menere?" says Sean.

"See what I mean, Michael?"

"So who are we going to phone?" says Eddie.

"How about Angelo's boet?" Like I said before, Angelo is our own Piggy from *Lord of the Flies*.

"Angelo?"

"This fat Greek guy at school."

"Okay, if not, why not?" says Michael. "Let's phone Angelo's boet. I want to hear this. Are you ready to go, buddy?"

"And say what?"

"Just do your corporal act, the same as you did with Craig."

Michael jumps up. "While you get your act together, I'll fetch the cordless."

"So you going to do it, Sean?"

"If you're so keen, why don't you do it?"

"You know I'm useless at accents. Come on, Michael will be seriously impressed."

"Is that what it's about?"

"Ag, you know what I mean. It will be a total lag. Please . . . Pretty please?"

Sean turns back to the window. "Stop gaaning on, Nick. I'll do it."

"So what's the number?"

Eddie flips through the phone book. "Does it start with a C or a K?"

"C, idiot. Constantine."

"Okay, I found it. There are two of them."

"The one's his uncle who owns that café next to the pawn shop. Angelo is the one on De La Rey."

Michael hands the cordless phone to Sean. "All yours buddy. Move up, you two."

Eddie and me make space for Michael on the bed.

"You ready, Seanie?"

"Whatever. Read me the number."

Eddie reads out Angelo's number. Michael grips my thigh. "This, I'm going to enjoy."

"I just pray Dimitri doesn't guess it's us."

"Is it ringing, Seanie?" Sean nods, pacing up and down by the window. "Don't forget to . . ."

"Gooie môre? Kan ek met Dimitri praat? Dankie . . . Hullo, is dit Dimitri Constantinople wat praat? Wat se? . . . Jammer. Hoe spel jy dit? Nou, waar's my blerry potlood? Het hom. Engels of Afrikaans? . . . Englishman? How are you today Meneer Constantine? . . . You are very well? That is good to hear. And how is the weather today in your part of this beautiful country of ours? . . . Yes, we are also enjoying the most beautiful weather here in the Syringa city of Pretoria.

I give Sean the thumbs up. He's so brilliant.

"Listen, Mr Constantine, you are speaking to Commandant Le . . . sorry this line is not good. Like I am saying, you are speaking to Corporal Theunis Le Roux from the South African Defence Force, from the Department of Call-ups. I just want to ask you a few questions . . . Don't sound so worried, Mr Constance, this is just a formality. As long as you are honest with me I will be honest with you. Do you understand? Verstaan jy? . . . That's very good. You sound like a very decent chap . . . as the Englishman would say. Now, let us begin, Mr Dimitri. What is your age? Fifteen. And what is your colour? Blanke. This blerry potlood of mine . . ."

I elbow Eddie in the ribs to stop his giggling. Michael's staring at Sean like he's enjoying the show, but trying hard not to.

"And your sex is male? Manlik. Excellent. Can you just wait a second while we check for you on our system, Mr Dimitri?"

Sean covers his hand over the phone. He's biting his lip, fighting the giggles.

"How am I doing?"

"Bladdy brilliant, Seanie. I know, I've been trying . . . Eddie, shoosh, man. You're gonna give the whole act away."

"I can't help it," giggles Eddie, the tears running down his face.

Somehow Sean manages to pull himself together again.

"Thank you for waiting, Mr Dimitri, the system is again working. Ek sien here that according to our records you have not reported for your call-up. Is that true, Mr Constantine? Is dit waar? . . . You did not receive your call-up papers? Not according to our records, sir. In fact, if I look here into your brown folder, which I have here right on the desk before me, next to my . . . next to my mug of . . . my mug of Ricoffy, you were sent call-up papers. Not once, not twice, but three times, Mr Dimitri. No buts, buts, Meneer, you do realise that this is a serious offence not to report for duty? Dimitri, are you still there? . . . Good. That is why I am phoning you today, to find out why you have not reported for duty." Sean grabs the phone book from Eddie. "Let me see again where you must have reported to." He holds the phone to the telephone directory and makes a racket flipping through the pages. "Ek het hom. Here it is . . . Parabats, third Battalion, Kuruman training base. What do you say to that, Meneer Dimitri? It is a great honour to serve in the special forces . . . Meneer, are those tears of joy I hear you crying? Are you still there? Hullo? Wie praat nou . . . ? Ja, nee, jammer Meneer . . . This is Captain Le Roux from . . . No, this is not a joke, Meneer . . . I am Corporal Le Roux from the South African Defence . . . It is not a joke, Meneer. But I have to go now . . ."

Sean rushes across the room. "Shit! How do you switch this thing off?"

Michael grabs the phone from him and hits the Off button.

"Who was that at the end, Seanie?" I say through the tears.

"Dimitri's toppie. He must have been listening the whole time."

Sean flops himself down next to Eddie, who gives him a fat high five.

"That was so bladdy brilliant, Sean," I say. "You agree, Michael? Was that good or what?"

"Nice one, buddy. I'm quite impressed."

"Quite impressed? You were fantastic, Seanie. You should be a flippin' actor."

"You reckon so?"

"Hundred-and-ten per cent."

Michael stands up and stretches.

"Okay, don't go blow the guy's ego now. It was good, but it wasn't brilliant."

Sean checks his watch and jumps up again. "I'm gonna make a run for it. Thanks for the sarmies and Milo."

"No problem," says Michael.

"I must also chuck," says Eddie, jumping up, leaving me on the bed with Michael.

"Me too."

"Stay awhile, Nick."

"No, I better go. Before it starts coming down again."

"Come on, what's the big rush? And we still need to organise a couple of things for your party."

"I thought we've organised everything."

"There are still a few loose ends we haven't talked about."

"Oh. I didn't realise. Shouldn't we all do it together then?"

"No need."

Eddie and Sean are standing at the door, their backpacks on, waiting.

"Go so long, I'll catch up with you."

TWENTY - TWO

Michael cuts the pack for the hundredth time. It's like there's something bugging him but he won't come out with it. Like you would swear he's jealous or something like that.

"What are the matches for?"

"Poker."

"You mean like gambling poker?"

"Yes, I mean like gambling poker."

"I don't have any money with me."

"I'll lend you some."

"What if I lose?"

"And I thought Elephant Man was negative! What if you win? Have you thought of that?"

"I've never won a thing in my life. Not even a church raffle. You shouldn't call him that."

"Whatever."

"Why don't we just play for matches so we don't owe each other afterwards?"

"What's the fun in that? Don't look at your cards yet." Michael empties the matches onto the floor and splits them matches into two heaps. "Okay, we will start with a rand a match. Even your friend Eddie could afford that."

"But that's more than twenty bucks. If I lose there's no ways I'll be able to pay you back."

"Then you had better make sure you win. Not so? Relax, it's only a game."

Michael starts dealing the cards.

"What you guys doing later?"

"Ag, nothing really," I lie. "We'll probably just take it easy."

"Boring. It's none of my business, but seriously, Nick, I don't know what you see in those two."

"What you mean?"

"What do I mean? I mean they're like yobos. Especially that Eddie. And as for cripple boy . . . He also seems a slice short of a sandwich."

"What does that make me then?"

"You've got a lot more going for you, but you're too stubborn to see it. It's like you've been brainwashed to believe otherwise. For Christ sake, you've got a brain in your head. Why do you think you and I are buddies? You really think I would be buddies with a loser?"

"Maybe you just haven't got to know them properly."

"Really? Tell me, where did Sean come in class last year? And don't lie."

"I don't know. Sean and Eddie are in the B class."

"Thank you. And you're in A?"

"Ja."

"And where did you come?"

"I think third."

"I rest my case."

"But what's that got to do with it? Sean and Eddie are the type of guys who would stand with you to the bitter end. Like, if you were fighting on the border, they're the guys you want in the bush next to you, watching your back . . ."

"Come on, get real, you've been watching too much *Rambo*," laughs Michael. "If Sean can't help you with the smallest thing like a pathetic birthday party, do you really think he's going to be there when you actually need him? As for Eddie, he would end up mistaking you for the enemy and shooting you in the back."

"Funny. Anyway, it's not that Sean doesn't want to help . . ."

"Don't stress over it, buddy, if you want to delude yourself that's your choice."

"I'm not deluding myself. Anyway, why are we talking about this?"

The more Michael talks, the more confused I get. And when I'm confused my head throbs, as if there's more blood going in than blood coming out.

"Just trying to show you the light. Geez, talk about being defensive. You would swear you've got a crush on the guy. It's Sean this, Sean that."

"I just respect him, that's all."

"Is that what you call it? Anyway, I don't need to hear anymore. Let's play cards."

"Fine by me."

I can't believe it, but I'm on a winning streak from word go. I win the first hand, with three Jacks, then the second with two Tens and two Kings. Michael must have total duds because he folds both times before I get to see his cards. In no time I'm up twelve rand and cruising on a high. Michael deals another hand.

I make a big show and dance of lifting my cards one by one. "Yeah, am I feeling lucky, or what!"

"You're slaughtering me, Nick. You must have played this before?"

"I swear I haven't, Michael. Sorry, but you're the one who wanted to play for real money. You're right, it's much more fun playing for real bucks."

I turn over my last card and break into an instant sweat.

"Shit."

"What?" says Michael, looking up from his hand. I can tell he doesn't look too chuffed.

"Nothing. You start."

"Okay, what the hell," he says. "I might as well be reckless. I'll open with five matches."

"You sure?"

"Why not? It's better to burn out than fade away."

"Neil Young. If that's the way you want it, Mikey, I will equal your five and raise you the same again."

My hands are clammy and I can feel Michael's eyes on me, searching for the cracks. But there aren't any.

"I'm impressed, Nick. You're braver than I thought. Okay, how about I equal your ten and raise you by another ten?"

I didn't expect him to do that. Suddenly I'm not so confident anymore. But I'm dead-cert he's bullshitting. It's obvious in the way he's pretending to be calm.

"Shit, Michael, that's a heap of money."

"Well, you're the one who wanted to raise the stakes?"

"Ja, but are you sure you can afford it?"

"I think I'll manage."

"Okay, if that's the way you want it, I'll match your ten and see you."

"Is that it? I thought you would push the envelope a bit further. You show your cards first."

"It's good you're sitting down. You sure you're ready for this?"

"Ready as I'll ever be. Let's see them, Nick Theron."

Acting the instant poker pro I am, I turn my cards over one by one. "Queen, Queen, Ace . . . I look up at Michael. "You hundred per cent sure you want to see my last card?"

"Come on, Nick, you're torturing me."

"Get a load of that!" I shout, and slap down the Ace of Spades.

"Fuck!" says Michael, throwing his cards down. "Fuck, fuck, fuck!"

"I swear, I knew you were bullshitting the whole time!" I'm dancing up and down, chuffed as anything. "Send those matches my way, if you don't mind."

I reach over to help myself to the heap in the middle. Michael grabs hold of my wrist.

"What?"

"Not so fast, cowboy. You haven't seen my cards yet."

"Okay, then, show them."

Michael turns his cards over, imitating me. "Ten, Ten, Queen, Five of Clubs."

"Big deal. And the last one?"

"Are you hundred per cent sure you want to see it? Your face is looking seriously anxious?"

"Yes, I want to see it. Show me."

Michael flicks the card across the floor. It lands face down. I reach across and turn it over. Ten.

"What are you going to do now?" asks Michael.

"Pay you back, I suppose."

"But you don't have the money."

"I'll make a plan."

"You want another loan?"

"And lose it all again?"

I won't lie, I've been waiting for Michael to come out and say, forget it, it was just a game, I don't need to pay him back. But he hasn't.

"I've got an idea."

"What's your idea?"

"Let's play another round, but this time you can use clothes instead of money."

"You mean strip poker."

"Call it what you want. And tell you what. I'll equal every item of clothing with five matches. How does that sound?"

"And if I lose?"

"No big deal. All you lose are your clothes. How bad is that? But if you win, think about it, you'll get your money back."

"Whatever. Let's play."

Half an hour later the rain is still lashing against the window and I'm sitting in my jocks. I'm kicking myself that I didn't make a run for it with Sean and Eddie. I'd be sitting at home now. Michael holds out the pack of cards.

"Your turn to deal."

"There's no ways I'm going starkers, Michael."

"But what if you win?"

"Oh ja. What if I win? How many times have I heard that today? I told you I never win anything."

Michael tosses the pack of cards across the floor.

"If that's the way you want it. Which I suppose means you will just have to pay me back."

"Like I said, Michael, I'll make a plan."

"But what if I need the money urgently, Nick?"

"What's urgently?"

"Let's say . . . by tomorrow, for instance."

"You know I can't pay you back by tomorrow."

I reach for my jeans because I'm starting to feel cold sitting in my jocks with the whole world watching me.

"What are you doing?"

"Getting dressed."

I can feel Michael's eyes on me as I sort through my clothes. It feels a bit weird.

"Maybe you can pay me back in some other way."

"Like what, for example?"

"I don't know. But I'm sure I can think of something."

I start pulling on my jeans, but my foot catches. Michael sticks out his hand for me to hold onto for balance.

"Thanks."

Before I know what's happened, I'm lying flat on my back, Michael on top of me. For a few seconds I lie there doing nothing; it must be the shock. I can hardly move. Michael has my arms pinned behind my head. His face is so close I can smell his Milo breath and Blue Stratos aftershave and his own smell under that. He's breathing hard and his mouth is half-open and I can see where his teeth meet his gums. I don't know why I notice all this; I just do.

"What are you going to do now?"

"What do you want me to do?" His full body weight is on me and I can hardly get air. I relax for a moment, then give it all I've got. It doesn't help – he's got me in one of those judo grips.

"You'll have to try harder than that."

"Okay, I give up."

"Say please."

"Please. Shit, you're squeezing my neck, Michael."

"Please, sir, would you mind getting off me?"

"Please, sir, would you mind getting off me? You happy now?"

"Please, sir, I would be very grateful if you removed yourself from me."

"Come on, Michael, it's not funny." I'm starting to feel desperate.

"Again. And louder."

So I say it, but I mess up the words, and he makes me say it again, twice, until I get it right.

"Please, sir, I would be truly grateful if you removed yourself from me."

"That's more like it." Michael pats my cheek and takes off the pressure. "Your turn now."

"To do what?"

"Put your hands around my neck."

"What?"

"I said put your hands around my neck. I'm giving you a chance to get back at me."

"I don't want to get back at you."

"Of course you do." Michael takes my hands and wraps my fingers around his neck. "Okay, squeeze."

"You not serious?"

"Harder."

I squeeze his neck again, this time harder. It's like squeezing one of those chewy sirloin steaks they serve at the Ranch.

"Come on, harder."

"Are you crazy?" It's as if he doesn't hear me. Instead he presses my fingers deeper into his flesh. "Like that. You do it now," he whispers. "I promise, It doesn't hurt." Although the whole thing's totally weird, I do as he says, pushing my thumb into the soft spot next to his jugular. "Harder, Nick."

"Michael, this is crazy."

"Don't stop."

I'm already squeezing so hard he can hardly get the words out. His lips are turning white like a dead person's and his eyes have this crazy blank stare. I'm scared I'm going to kill him or something. But he's gripping my hands tight and whispering, "Don't stop . . . Don't stop."

Just as I'm about rip my hands away, Michael's eyes roll back into his head and his body slips out of my grip and he collapses to the floor with a massive sigh. Now I'm seriously convinced he's about to die and I don't remember anything from the first-aid course we did in cadets. My body begins to shake.

I don't know how long Michael stays there on the ground but it feels like forever and a day. Time stands still while he lies there breathing heavily, in and out, in and out. He rolls over and stares up at the ceiling. At least he's not going to die. I know that. Michael lets out a funny giggle.

"Man, that was good."

"How can you call being choked to death good? Jissus, you had me seriously worried. I thought you were about to peg on me." Michael sits up and crosses his legs. He's completely normal again, like nothing's happened.

"You mean you've never done this before?"

"No."

"You're missing out big time, buddy. It's the best rush ever."

"I can think of much better ways to get a rush."

"Like what? A bottle of Old Brown with your buddies, Sean and Eddie."

"Well, at least Old Brown can't kill you."

"This can't kill you - unless you're stupid. Plus, there's no hangover the next day. You're so boring, Nick."

"Thanks a lot. Maybe I'm just not into sicko things like you are."

Michael stands up and walks to the window and stares out at the black afternoon, leaving me to get dressed. "Hey, looks like the sun might be coming out." He turns around. "Come on, don't look so serious. We were just having some fun."

"If you say so."

"Seriously, you don't have to pay me back."

"I'm going to pay you back. Every cent."
I tie my takkies and stand up. Michael holds out his hand.
"We still buddies? Come on, Nick, shake my hand."
I give Michael my hand.
"Ja, we're still buddies."

TWENTY - THREE

Even the tiniest platteland dorps get films before we do. And then by the time we get them they're scratched to hell and gone because they've already been shown a thousand times. It's no different this time. It's been forever and a day for *Rocky III* to arrive at The Phoenix.

I spot Sean and Eddie right near the front of the queue that's running halfway around the block. I lock my bike to the lamppost, do my Depeche Mode hair thing and navigate through the crowds hanging around on the pavement.

I tap Eddie on the back of the head and duck down to the ground. He looks around him, confused, before this idiot behind him spoils it all and points to me squatting below.

"What took you so long?" says Eddie. But him and Sean look

chuffed to see me.

"I don't want to talk about it, but I had a totally kak afternoon. I'm seriously glad to see you guys."

We shuffle a step closer to the ticket counter. "Apparently, the movie's totally brilliant," says Sean. He's wearing his Brut aftershave. Which spells SO – Special Occasion.

"Who says?"

"Russ. He saw it this arvie. He reckons it's Stallone's best ever."

"My boet also," Eddie says, digging into his pocket with that concentrated look on his face. Any second he's going to announce he forgot his wallet at home.

"I don't even care if it's crap. I'm deader than dead keen to see it," I say.

Eddie steps up to the guy behind the counter. "Give us three." He slides the full amount through the hole, then hands Sean and me our tickets.

"Here you go, Eddie." I hold out my two rand.

"Ag, keep it," Eddie says. "I'm sticking."

"Ja, right. Take it, Eddie."

Eddie pushes my hand away.

"You don't need to, Eddie. Seriously. You give it to him, Sean." Now I'm feeling bad Eddie won't take my money.

"Relax, man," says Sean. "If Eddie wants to stick you for your birthday, it's his choice. Let's head in before he changes his mind."

"Geez, thanks Eddie." And I really mean it because Eddie's mom hardly has a cent to her name.

"No problem," says Eddie. Maybe it's the neon light above, but I swear his bakore have turned pink. Now I feel totally bad for telling Eddie he must pay me back for that ice-cream at the pool.

Sean leads the way and hands our tickets to the frizzy-haired woman at the door. She's been tearing tickets for years, at least ever since we've been coming to The Phoenix. Sean and me hang around while Eddie goes off to buy something to eat from the tuckshop. There's a girl standing next to us with a bag of apples. This must be the only town on earth where people bring apples to the movies. She unties the knot and hands one to her brother. Sean looks up at the clock above the ingang door for the hundredth time. An hour later we spot Eddie pushing through the crowd, spilling Fanta behind him.

"Here's your change," he says to Sean and pours a handful of coins into his hand.

"Don't even try, Theron, I'm sticking this one," says Sean. Before I can say anything Eddie's handed me my Creme Soda.

The trailers have already started and we have to fumble our way in the dark. The Phoenix isn't one of those bioscopes where they give you special seat numbers and you have to sit there even if the guy in front is eight-foot tall and has an affro. You sit wherever you want at The Phoenix. But the place is so packed we don't exactly have much choice.

I spot three empty seats near the front. "How about there?" At least they aren't front row.

"Hey Scheepers, sit your fat arse down!" shouts someone from the back.

"Who said that?" Eddie shouts back. Like an idiot he keeps standing, staring into the dark.

"You're blocking the flippin' screen," says a woman behind us. It's true, Eddie's fat head has filled half the screen.

"Engelsman, sit jou moer neer!"

I yank on Eddie's sleeve. "Come on, Eddie, sit down!"

"Stuff you all," says Eddie, but he sits down and the row behind us starts clapping. It's always like this at The Phoenix. A total dog show. The matinees are even worse.

We settle down and start passing the popcorn back and forth, trying to keep up with each other. With Eddie you have to work at it or you get left behind. Even if you gobbed in the box it would makes no diffs.

"I'm seriously looking forward to this," says Sean. I know Sean would give his left ball to have a body like Sylvester. Maybe the right one as well.

"Me too."

"What did you guys do after we left? Jissus, but we got pissed down on big time."

"Got stuck at Michael's place."

"And did what?"

"Nothing much. But the guy's weird."

"Why you say that?"

"He just is."

"Did you tell him about us coming here?"

"Why should I? He doesn't need to know every move we make."

"Just wondered, that's all. Anyway, I'm glad it's just us."

"Me too."

Someone a few rows back lets out this massive burp, and for about ten seconds the advert for the new Toyota Cressida is drowned out.

"You must let me know if I must do anything for your party."

"Thanks, but it's mostly organisey."

"Seriously, I'm not just saying so."

"Thanks, Sean, I appreciate it. Eddie, pass the popcorn. Maybe we should go to Vegas after to grab something to chow?"

"No time."

"What you mean no time?"

"We've organised a birthday surprise."

"Who is we?"

"My boets and me."

"Like what type of surprise?"

"If we told you, it wouldn't be a surprise. Not so, Eddie?

"For sure. A lank big surprise."

"Ja, with the initials TR."

"What's TR?"

"Not what, who."

"You've got me seriously confused."

"Good."

Eddie leans over into the aisle. "Who's in the mood for a apple? There's a tree of them coming our way."

Eddie's not bullshitting, there is a whole bunch of apples rolling down the aisle. Eddie stretches his leg out and boots one of them to the front; it whacks the panel below the screen. The kid whose apples they are starts bawling a few rows behind. As the curtain opens all the way and the Lion roars, the girl we spotted outside the tuckshop comes sprinting past and begins collecting apples in the dark. Like I said, The Phoenix is a total circus.

But *Rocky* ends up being so brilliant I don't even notice the popcorn crunchers. Sylvester's body is ripped to perfection; he worked out non-stop getting ready for this film. By the end of it I would also give my left ball to look like him. Sean doesn't say a word the whole way through. He is transfixed, if that's the right word for it. So is Eddie, who is so transfixed I get to eat most of the popcorn.

TWENTY - FOUR

"Kief movie or what, hey?" says Sean.

"In the top ten of the century."

"It was okay."

"Listen to Nick. *It was okay.*"

"I'm only kidding. What I want to know is how does someone get ripped like that. I mean Stallone isn't even a pro bodybuilder. You reckon he was born like that, Seanie?"

"No ways, he worked out with a trainer for about a year before the movie. Same thing with John Travolta in *Saturday Night Fever*. And you remember how ripped he was?

"Ja, but he was more toned than ripped."

"Whatever. To get like that he worked out five hours a day and only ate lettuce and water."

"So what you're saying Sean is if we pumped weights all day and only ate lettuce we would look like that?"

"For sure, Nick. You've just got to want it bad enough."

"Maybe I do. But just not now. I would rather practise guitar five hours a day."

"Talking of which, what should we listen to?"

"How about Foreigner? The one with 'Urgent'. I love that song."

With the three of us parked off on the bed and Foreigner *Foreigner* playing in the background and the sound-to-light creating this atmosphere, it's another one of those moments you never want to let go of.

"The next few days are going to be a total jol. The fête, the party, camp straight after that, it's like someone's opened the floodgates."

"That's no lie, Eddie."

"And guess what?"

"What?"

"I've scored some zol for us to try."

"Like hell you did. From who?"

"Tony Romano's boet."

"You spoke to Tony Romano's boet?"

"No, to Tony. He said he'll speak to him.

"You're psycho, you know that, Eddie? What you think, Sean?"

"About what? Us trying it?"

"Ja."

"Why not? We're always gaaning on about it. Now's our chance."

"Okay, then, if you organise it, Eddie, we do it," I say. "Shit, I can't believe how it's all coming together."

"Told you having a party was a good idea."

"And for once, Seanie, you're right."

"Hey, chinas, someone's at the door!"

The door swings open before Sean gets to it. Russel. All breathless-like.

"She's here!"

"You serious?" says Sean.

"One-hundred per cent serious. But you okes better move it, otherwise you're gonna miss the show."

"Why, where are they now, Russ?"

"Checking out *Dallas* with Mom and Dad. Her and Vanessa just got back from playing tennis at Jamboree Park. Come, we're wasting time. Gary and me will meet you upstairs."

The air in Russel and Gary's bedroom is filled with this sweaty nervous tension, like we're preparing to go into battle. Gary comes back into the room.

"They're still watching TV."

"Let's do it, boet. Edward, you stand guard at the door. If you hear anything, I mean anything, you let us know."

"Ja, kaptein."

"What must I do, Russ?" I ask. I am jittery as all hell.

"You can help Sean and me move the bookshelf. Coast all clear, Eddie?"

Eddie gives a thumbs-up from the landing. JR's voice floats up the stairs. Sue Ellen is pissed again. Sean's dad coughs. A Benson & Hedges thirty-a-day cough.

I do as I'm told and grab a corner of the carpet. Sean and Russel take the other two corners.

"Okay, slowly now."

We drag the carpet carefully across the wooden floor, trying not to topple any books along the way.

"That's enough. Chips out the way, Nick."

I stand back so Gary can pass. He steps in behind the bookshelf with his screwdriver and starts levering away at the drywall. A second later he hands Russel a square of ceiling board the size of an apple box. Russel passes it to Sean. It's still covered in wallpaper. Gary steps out from behind the cupboard. Finally I understand what all the excitement is about.

"Bladdy hell!" says Eddie, who's abandoned his post.

We just stand staring at the hole in the wall. It's something out of *Escape from Alcatraz*.

"You like?"

"Jissus, I can't believe it," I tell Gary. "How long did this take you?"

"Quicksticks. Stuff's soft as cardboard. Go take a look. Sean, gooi us the torch."

I squeeze in behind the bookshelf with Gary. He also wears Brut, like Sean. He shines into the hole. This is the first time I've looked inside a double-storey roof. It's like looking into the guts of a whale, with the rafters forming the ribs and all the pipes and wires the guts and veins. Gary points the light on some rafters on the left. "That's where you're gonna go down."

"Me?"

"Ja, why not?"

"Hell, Gary, I don't know . . ."

"And there's the bathroom," says Gary, shining onto a patch of ceiling way below.

"Somebody's coming!" whispers Russel behind us. I leap out from behind the cupboard in a panic. "Only joking, Theron."

"You almost gave me a bladdy heart attack."

"What's it like?" says Eddie.

"Like something out of this world."

"Gary, I scheme she's already in there," says Russel.

"Tanya?"

"No, Mother Theresa, moegoe brain."

"How do you know?"

"Sean went to check and heard the bath water running."

"Okay, so who's first then?"

"Nick," says Sean and Gary at the same time.

"Why me? Why doesn't Eddie go first?"

"Because it's your birthday."

Now I'm really crapping myself.

"Don't you want to go first, Sean? Okay, okay, just checking, I'll do it. But what do I do if someone comes up here?"

"They won't."

"And you sure it's Tanya?"

"Hundred-and-ten percent sure."

"Maybe it's Tanya and Vanessa," says Eddie. "Two for the price of one."

"I'll shine for you," says Sean.

Russel slaps me on the back. "Enjoy, boet. You're in for a flipping birthday treat."

Sean and me move into position. This is more scary than anything I've done. More scary than the Octopus at the Rand Show. A thousand thoughts are running through my head. Like I'm going to fall through the ceiling. Or I'm going to have a sneeze attack because of my hayfever.

"What if it's your mom, Sean?"

"She only baths in the morning."

Not that I would mind checking out Sean's mom, varicose veins and all. I swallow this fat lump sticking in my throat. "Here goes."

Sean pats me on the back. "Wish I was you."

"I'm sure."

I squeeze through the hole and step onto the first rafter, gripping the beam for balance. So far so good.

Sean shines his torch onto the next rafter. Following his light I work my way slowly-slowly down this ladder of beams towards the ceiling miles below. My heart's pumping something crazy and I'm poep-scared I might lose my grip. The smell of damp and bat shit reminds me of that Drakensberg cave we once slept in.

I reach the bottom without landing on Sean's dad's lap. I look up; Sean and the hole in the bedroom wall are now miles away. Sean shines onto this straight beam on the left. Gripping the slope of the roof I follow the light, more relaxed now. This is like a dream. A wet dream. Tanya Reynolds is hotter than hot. She could easily be on the back page of the *Sunday Times*. Her and that yellow bikini thing she wears at the pool.

I spot the blanket a few meters ahead, an old brown army number. At the same time I can see Tanya and those long tanned hockey legs of hers that can wrap around the world and back, the shiny black hair that comes right down to her hips and those amazing lips and tits that Eddie talks about non-stop. Gavin Joubert swears he saw her tits when she dived into the pool and her costume came off.

Like Gary instructed me I carefully shift down onto my knees and listen. Nothing. No sound of running water or splashing. She must be just lying there relaxing after tennis with Vanessa. Lying there for ages, like girls do in the bath, her eyes closed, the water lapping against her skin. I'm now flat on the blanket, which honks like a wet dog, and "in position", as Gary called it. Like I said, this is something out of *Alcatraz*. I give Sean the thumbs up; he switches off the torch. And there it is: a pinprick of light coming through the bathroom ceiling. I inch myself a little closer so that I'm lying flat and more comfortable. Like the guy on the TV says, the moment has come, gentlemen. I put my eye over the hole and adjust to the light in the bathroom . . .

Later, when I describe it to Sean and Eddie, it's like being slapped on the back of the head with a cricket bat. Because, lying there in the apricot-pink bath with the chipped brown tiles and matching bathmat and toilet seat cover is not Tanya Reynolds and her amazing tits. Flipping hell, no. It's Russel, Gary, Sean and Eddie, all packed into the bath and giggling like schoolgirls, giving me the middle finger.

TWENTY - FIVE

There's only one thing worse than arriving too late at a fête. And that's arriving too early. And by the looks of it this year I'm way too early, with people wandering about like lost farts, not knowing what to do with themselves. Half the stalls are still setting up by the time I get there, so I take my time finding a place to lock my bike.

Same as last year, Rodney Meyer's dad is manning the secondhand table. Not my favourite - he's one of those types who think they're funny but they're not.

"Anything grab your fancy, pal?"

"I'm just looking, thanks. Is this tape recorder working?"

"Is my name Moses? For five bucks what do you think?" That's what I mean. I press the play button. Dead as a dodo. "Batteries not included," chirps Mr Meyer.

I dig out a flask with a leather strap around it. We could use it when we go fishing.

"How much is this?"

"Eight ront. Bargain of the century. You know what those things cost new?"

I screw open the lid and take a sniff. Rusty tea.

"Take the tape recorder also and you can have it for five."

I put it back on the table. "Thanks, I'll think about it. I just want to walk around a bit first."

"Suit yourself. You snooze, you lose. Hey, if you see Roddie tell him I want one of those pancakes and a coffee. Arthur! How things going, pal?"

The Allens. Another on my list of not-so-favourite people in the world. Not that Steven Allen is a bad guy or anything. I've just never clicked with him. It's hard to explain.

"Hey, Frankie boy, nice to see you!"

Rodney's dad gives Mr Allen a fat slap on the back, who then ambushes me as I'm about to sneak off.

"How you boy? I hear you guys have your own stall. What's it's all about?"

"Nothing much. Just a shooting range and that type of thing."

Maybe it's because Steven's brother Mark is one of those conscious objectors who are too chicken to go to the army that I don't go into the details.

Mr and Mrs Allen stand around making small talk with Rodney's dad, with me trapped between the table and Steven.

"What you been up to, Steven?"

"Nothing much."

"Ja, me too."

Talking to Steven Allen is like giving birth to barbed wire. He's a really quiet guy. Same as his mom, who hardly ever says a thing.

"Tell Nick about your trip to Kruger," cuts in Mr Allen. "Don't know when you were there last, Frank, but I'm telling you, what a place, hey. Five days, we ticked them all, except leopard and wild dog. God's gift to Africa, that's what Kruger is."

"Ja, but for how long?"

"True."

Mr Allen shoves the rest of the pancake into his mouth.

"How's your mom and dad, Nick?" asks Mrs Allen.

"They're fine, thanks." I make a big show of looking at my watch. "I better get going."

"No problem. You must come visit us sometime, hey. Stevie can show you the photos he took."

"Dad . . ."

"I'll check you later, Steven."

I walk away feeling a bit bad for Steven Allen. It must be hard being him, what with his brother and his dad, and his mom who hardly says a word. But I forget about feeling sorry for him the moment I spot our tent next to the bogs. Everything's set up and looking way more impressive than half the other crappy stalls around it. It's the genuine thing – an army tent that Mr Stevens organised through an officer buddy of his from Bloem. Sean and Eddie are stationed in front, handing out pamphlets.

"Hey, hey, hey, look who's finally decided to pitch," shouts Eddie when he spots me.

"Sorry, man, I got ambushed. How long you all been here?"

"Ages. We set the whole thing up already."

"Eddie's bullshitting. We've only been here a few minutes."

"Where's Angelo?"

"So called sick."

Mr Stevens and his friend Mr Alpert appear from under the tent flap. I hardly recognise them. They're both dressed in their old army uniforms, helmets, Nugget polish on their faces and all, ready for battle.

"Looks good, hey?" says Sean.

"Shit, ja, I hardly recognise you, Mr Stevens."

"Hell, I hardly recognise myself."

"Môre menere," says Mr Alpert, saluting. "From now on you will address us as Corporal Alpert and Corporal van Wyk."

Mr Stevens must have borrowed his uniform because that's what his badge says.

"Okay, guys, I think we're all set to go. Sean, you want to give Nick some brochures?"

Sean hands me a wad.

Come see the Youth Cadet Stall!!!
The Terrorist Tent – you will be blown away!!! Only R2!!!
Kill-A-Terr firing range – only R1 for five shots!!!
Amazing "Join ANC and Die" Tee-shirts!!! Only R10!!!
ALL PROCEEDS GO TO THE SAFE FUTURE OF
YOUR COUNTRY!!!

"Did you make these Mr Stevens?"

"Me and Keith did. You guys must hand them out to everyone who comes past."

Mr Alpert comes over. He's full on into this.

"Okay, we ready Vernie?"

"Ja, I reckon so, hey."

"Let's do it then."

Without any warning, Mr Alpert jumps straight into action.

"Hey, civvies! You English-speaking?"

It's Gavin and Chris Joubert, with that skinny friend of theirs from Gymnasium whose name I keep forgetting.

"Ja," says Gavin, wiping his mouth of candyfloss.

"And jy. Jy's Afrikaans, ne? Not a problem. I am tweetaalig. You gents want to test your shooting talents?"

"How much is it?"

Corporal Alpert gives us this wink and looks around, like to make sure nobody is listening. "Listen, for you three gents I will give the first round free."

"You serious?" says Gavin.

"No lies. You can go first, rooikop," he says to Chris and passes him the pellet gun. "Loaded and ready. You shoot at terrorist number one, jy nommer twee, and you number three. You each have five shots."

"He's good hey," says Sean.

"Oh, ja," says Mr Stevens.

Because there's only one pellet gun the guys have to wait to take turns to shoot. And while they wait Corporal Alpert makes small talk with them.

"Have you okies handled a rifle before?"

"I've only shot with a pellet gun and a Daisy," says Chris. "But Theo here has shot with real guns."

Theo. That's his name.

"Like what?"

"My pa se two-two. Hy het ook 'n thirty-eight, maar ek het nog nie met dit geskiet nie."

Corporal Alpert sucks air through his teeth. "Now that's a big bugger. It will make a hole this size in your head.

A few more guys have now gathered around, interested in what Mr Alpert has to say.

"Thanks for joining us, gentleman. Blondie, what have you handled?" he says to Eddie, like we're part of the crowd.

"Eddie's boet's a Recce," says Sean.

"Is that so?" says the corporal. "So you've handled his R1?"

"Ja, plenty of times." Eddie's such a bullshitter.

"I like what I'm hearing gentlemen. Corporal Van Wyk, please set up a new target for that guy. We need to be prepared, manne. And die eerste ding is to handle a rifle like a man. Let me ask you a question. Ja, you with the Volkskas . . . People's Cupboard T-shirt. How old are you?"

"Fifteen," Gavin says.

"Nice shooting, okie. En hoe oud is julle twee?"

"Also fifteen."

"I'm sixteen," says Theo.

"Perfect. So in two years from now you will be reporting for duty. Is this not the case?" They all nod, including the new guys watching from the back. Mr Alpert should have been a secondhand-car salesman. "So now is when you must start preparing. Getting your head and body into high alert."

"In high alert for what?" Chris Joubert asks.

Mr Alpert sucks in some more air. It's like a habit of his. Mr Lane our English teacher also does it.

"Jissis, maar jy is een vir a grap. Listen, you've all had a turn to shoot, so now Corporal Van Wyk is going to show you something very special in this tent."

"My brother hasn't had a turn yet," says Chris.

"You can have your turn after. But first pay the guy there your two ront and then follow Corporal van Wyk."

I stand at the door collecting money. In no time we've made ten rand. Just like that.

Mr Stevens holds the flap of the tent open and the guys squeeze into it, including Eddie and me because I haven't yet seen what's inside. It smells like a kaya, what with the paraffin lamps and all. The tent is kitted out with a camp bed in the corner, and an open trommel with stuff arranged inside. In the middle of the tent is a folding table with more things laid out on it.

"Please guys, don't be shy, take a look around. The South African Defence Force home is your home too . . ." Mr Stevens wouldn't be a good car salesman. "And, guys, when you're finished looking around we want to show you something special."

"What are these things here, sir?" asks Ron McKenzie. He's another of these weird guys from England whose parents came to work on the mine.

"Those, menere, are weapons of terrorist destruction," says Mr Alpert, ducking into the tent. "Corporal van Wyk, you want to carry on outside. Okay, from left to right, AK-47, limpet mine, hand grenade. All made where I ask you?"

"Taiwan?" I chirp.

"Russia! It is Russia and the communists who is using the blacks as their prawns to kill the whites."

"And what's that there?" asks Eddie pointing to a holey vest on a hanger.

"Looks like something you would wear, Eddie," I say. Mr Alpert holds it up so we can all see. "Are those genuine bullet holes?" For once I'm impressed.

"Made in RSA – one-hundred per cent R1. You want to join the ANC? This is what we give you. Luister, manne, there is other people queuing outside. So, any questions? Good, in that case, take for yourselves some pamflette and give them to your friends and those you care for."

We duck back into the light with our pamphlets, where already there's a new line of guys in front of Kill-a-Terr.

"What must we do now, Mr Stevens?"

"Go grab yourselves a boerie roll. You guys deserve it."

"How much you think we've made so far?"

"Dunno. We'll work it out later."

"Out the way," says Mr Alpert, pushing through us and ambushing a new group of guys. "More menere. You English-speaking?"

"They could have at least given us another serviette each. Now I've got bladdy tomato sauce all over me."

"Pretend it's blood, Eddie," I tell him.

"Ja, Swapo blood."

"Did you check that vest? I counted twenty holes," says Eddie, his mouth fat with meat. "We take no shit. I bet he hasn't even been to the border."

"Who?"

"Mr Alpert. Luke says he's just a big bullshitter."

"Who cares?" Sean says. "He's a bladdy good bullshitter. I reckon we're going to pull in at least three-hundred bucks."

"You think?"

"For sure." Sean wipes his hand across his mouth. "Now I'm vol."

Sean starts giggling.

"What's so funny?"

"Last night. Hell, but we nailed you good."

"Ja, ja. You don't believe me, but actually I smelt a rat."

"Like hell you did. Admit it, we got you. Hook, line and sinker."

"Ja, okay, I admit it. Happy now? But at least I got to see inside your roof. That was quite interesting."

Eddie presses his thumb and index finger together. "Imagine thinking you're this close to seeing Tanya Reynolds in the kaal."

"If I end up going bossies it's because of you guys."

Sean jumps up and wipes his hands on his shorts. "We better chuck. Mr Stevens is probably waiting for us."

We stand up and wipe the grass off our pants.

"You've got tomato sauce all over your crotch, Eddie."

"That's what I said."

"Are we still on for later?

"Of course."

"I've been having second thoughts about it. The guy's psycho, you know that?"

"That's why we're going together."

"Don't be chicken, Nick, we'll be out there chop-chop."

"Exactly, chop-chop like a slaughtered chicken. I'm not even that interested in trying the stuff."

"Now you say so. After I've organised it with Tony."

"Don't listen to him, Eddie. We're going," says Sean, like it's final.

"So how did we do, Mr Stevens?" asks Sean once we've packed the tent and everything back into Mr Alpert's bakkie.

"We did well guys. We did flipping well."

We hang around while Mr Stevens organises the coins and one-rand notes into separate piles. By the looks of it we've brought in a heap of cash. We're all pretty chuffed with ourselves, I'll say that much. Mr Stevens starts counting, writing in his black notebook, licking his pencil, writing in his notebook.

"How's it look, Vernie?"

"Almost there."

"You were bladdy good today, Mr Alpert. You brought in most of the money."

"Thanks boytjie. I enjoyed myself."

"Mr Alpert was a star, guys, that's for sure. Okay, let's see what we have here . . ."

Mr Stevens scoops the money back into the biscuit tin and stands up and stretches his sore back. For a grown man he looks like he can't contain himself. If my dad won the jackpot you wouldn't know.

"I have some good news and I have some bad news, guys."

"We didn't make enough?" says Sean.

"The good new is we did helluva well on the Kill-a-Terr. Two-hundred-and-twenty-four bucks, thirty-three cents."

"What's the bad news?"

"We didn't do well enough."

"Meaning we aren't going on camp," says Sean for all of us.

"But I guess we tried, hey."

"Don't look so depressed, guys. There's some more good news."

"Like what?"

"Like . . ." says Mr Alpert, ". . . we had an unexpected visitor while you guys were varking out on boerie rolls."

"Nothing in the bank yet but let's just say a certain someone was so impressed by the brilliant job you guys are doing that he's going to make us a donation."

"Meaning what, Mr Stevens?"

"Meaning you chappies better start packing for your team-build," says Mr Alpert, downing the last of his six-pack of Castle and letting out this long, slow, satisfied burp.

TWENTY - SIX

The Romanos live in this tiny flat above the old bakery, which went bankrupt after someone left a burning stompie behind. I've only been in their flat once and that was before Greg was sent back from the army. The place is a chicken coop, hardly big enough to kill a cat. I'm not lying, that's what they say Greg does. He kills cats for fun.

Their dad owns a radio repair shop near the mine compound, also a coop crammed with wire, old switches and broken radios. I don't know how he ever finds anything. Most of Mr Romano's customers are the blacks from the compound who hardly speak a word of English, never mind Italian. He must rip them off blind. Mr Romano's forever sitting behind this mountain of junk in his shop, with a soldering iron in one hand and a Lexington in the other. "*For after action satisfaction, ahhh, Lexington.*" After that ad came out everyone started smoking Lexington. Even us, until we discovered Dunhill.

All cocky-like, Eddie leads the way up the rusty metal stairs to the Romano's flat. I stick to Sean's back. When we get to the door Eddie bangs on it hard, which sends my heart racing. Sean points to a black rubbish bag on the ground and pinches his nose. There's a stench coming from it, like a cat has peed on it or something. More likely, there's something dead in it. Like Greg's latest victim. That's how jittery I am.

The door unlocks on the other side and a second later Greg Romano is standing in front of us in a white cut-off T-shirt.

"Hey, my chinas, how you keeping?" he says with this big smile, like we are long-lost buddies. I've never seen him this close up. He has a gap between his front teeth and a small scar running next to his eye. His hair is shiny and slicked back.

"We're keeping good," says Eddie, also acting like he's bumped into a long-lost friend. "Luke says howzit." Greg Romano shakes Eddie's hand and slaps him on the shoulder. He ignores Sean and me.

"Is it just the three of you?" he says, looking past us down the stairs. It's something out of *Miami Vice*.

Greg Romano locks the door behind us and starts singing that song, "Just the Two of Us", as we follow him down the passage into the lounge. To be honest, he doesn't have a bad voice. The lounge is a mess. All this electronic stuff from his dad's shop everywhere, dirty plates on the table and the TV on full blast. The Romanos' cat is lying on the couch licking itself. For a threatened species it actually looks quite healthy.

"Make yourselves at home, guys," he says and lifts the cat off the couch.

The three of us cram up onto the couch. Greg stays standing. He must work out because his arms are ripped.

"So, gentlemen, I understand you wish to make a small purchase."

Eddie nods and checks across to me and Sean for support, so we also nod.

"Excellent."

He gives us this evil smile, which sends my heart racing again. All I want to do is get the hell out before the cops break down the door. But Greg insists on dragging the whole thing out.

"Let me tell you guys something. I don't deal in crap. Because if that's what you want you can go buy it from the munts on the mine. You with me?"

All three of us nod. Greg stares at us for a bit, then reaches into his back pocket and takes out a bank envelope half-filled with brown stuff that looks like tea leaves. He tosses it onto the coffee table in front us, next to a plate smeared with dried scrambled egg and a white-bread crust.

"Get a whiff of that, guys. It's top drawer."

You would swear we do this everyday because Eddie opens the envelope and takes a sniff and nods his head up and down like he's impressed. He passes it to Sean and he does the same. Sean passes it to me and I take a sniff – it smells like wet leaves from a compost heap. I nod like I'm also seriously impressed. I hand the envelope back to Sean.

"How much do you want for it, Greg?" Sean says.

Greg goes down on his haunches.

"Because you're friends with Luke's boet, let's say fifteen for the full contents. Trust me, you're getting a bargain."

Eddie and me look at Sean, who scratches his chin. "Fifteen? Hell, Greg, I only have ten rand on me. We thought that would be enough."

"Ten? I told you, if you want crap you must go to the compound." Greg flashes me his evil grin. "What about you, Edwardo?"

"I swear, I don't have a cent on me, Greg."

I know Sean's got more money in his back pocket, but I just keep my mouth shut, praying he will give it all to Greg so we can get out of here before he decides to cut our throats. You never know with guys who've been sent back from the border and now torture animals for fun. Greg stands up and I'm thinking this is it, he's going to pull a knife on us.

"Okay, gentlemen. I'll give it to you for ten, but next time I'm not so generous. You with me?"

"We're with you, Greg. And we totally appreciate it," says

Sean and digs into his pocket and hands Greg a crumpled ten-rand note. Greg hands Eddie the bank envelope, who stuffs it into his rugby shorts.

"Okay gentlemen, anything else? Good, I think that concludes our business," Greg says, and points to the front door. He follows us down the passage. It seems like ages before he unlocks the door. But he's not finished with us yet. "One word to anyone . . ." And he drags his finger across his throat. I nod like there's no tomorrow. "Excellent, I'll see you around. Say howzit to your boet, Edward."

Greg Romano stands to one side and I'm sure he's still watching us as we take the metal stairs two at a time.

TWENTY - SEVEN

"Whoever wins the toss gets to choose, okay?"

"It's not fair, you always win," whines Simon. He's whinier than usual today.

"Nonsense. What do you want, heads or tails?"

Simon says tails. I toss the coin. It comes up heads.

"I'll take Dad's gun."

"You always get his gun."

"That's not true. I won it fair and square. Bladdy hell, if you carry on moaning Mom's going to be home before we've even started. I don't care, you can have Dad's gun, but then I get Bravo."

Before Simon comes up with another excuse I take my gun and empty a handful of pellets into my pocket and jog to the other side of the garden. Bravo Camp runs all the way along the wall between us and the Porra neighbours. The bushes in front have grown so thick we've got this tunnel running from one end to the other, which you can leopard-crawl without being spotted. It's brilliant.

I set up base under the low tree at the top end of the tunnel; it's also camouflaged by bush. I hang my dad's binocs on the branch – he'll kill us if he finds out – then arrange my pellets in a neat line next to the wall. The butterflies are already getting to work in my guts.

"Are you ready, Simon?" I shout.

Simon doesn't answer so I push the bush to one side and stick the binocs through the gap. You never know with Simon, it might be an ambush. But he's still farting around at Caprivi. His anorak is zipped to his neck and he's battling with the strap of his plastic bike helmet. He must be sweating like a pig because I'm lying in the shade and I'm already hot.

It's a bad thing to say, but ever since the funeral a black cloud has been lifting from our house. Like we are all recovering from a virus we didn't know we had in the first place. One of those viruses you only realise you had when you start getting better. Even my dad is in a better mood, now that it's behind us. Or he's just pretending for our sakes.

"Ready or not," I shout.

I crawl a few meters along the tunnel and move into sniper position, sticking the pellet gun through the bush. Not even a Swapo terr would spot me. I have the garden shed and upturned wheelbarrow in my sights, but there's no sign of Simon. I can't tell if he's behind the wheelbarrow. There's only one way to find out. I take aim and pull the trigger. *Twang!* The pellet slams into the wheelbarrow's belly.

"Hey, I'm not ready yet!" Simon yells.

"Too bad!" I reload and wait for the enemy to show himself. The seconds tick by. I start feeling fidgety. Simon's just sitting there, doing nothing. "Are you asleep or what?" I shout.

Still nothing. I'm about to tell Simon to get a move on when I spot a foot poking out the side. The adrenaline starts pumping big time, but I stay calm. You have to be calm in battle because if you panic you mess up. That's what Luke says. I shift my sights and then gently-gently squeeze the trigger. For a split-second I think I've missed because nothing happens. But then the foot disappears and the scream of a pig being slaughtered fills the sky.

"Yes!"

I stand up and sprint across to Caprivi to inspect the damage. Simon's rolling around the grass rubbing his ankle and bawling his eyes out all at the same time. The pig is dying a slow death so I pull out my Okapi and get ready to slash his throat. I swear, there's nothing like a kill to get the adrenaline pumping.

Simon calms down, but carries on rubbing his ankle.

"How was that for bulls-eye, hey, Simon? You've got to admit that was good."

"I don't want to play this game anymore," he says, and starts bawling again.

By now I'm feeling a bit bad. I kneel down on the grass next to him.

"Lemme see." But he won't let me touch his leg. "Come on, let me rub it for you, Simey. It will make it feel better."

"No, I don't want you to. I don't want to play this game ever again."

"I don't want to play this game ever again."

Simon and me look up. It's Michael, standing a few feet away, watching us with this smirk on his face.

"I don't want to play this game ever, ever again," he says again, in this squeaky baby voice.

"When did you get here?" I say.

Michael walks over to us.

"Ages ago. Come on, show us your injuries," he says to Simon. "Maybe we need to call a medic?"

Michael winks at me and I sort of wink back.

"Come, Simon, why don't you show us," I say.

Simon looks at Michael, then at me. He rolls down his sock. There's a blue bruise the size of a five-cent.

"Christ, the way you were carrying on I thought we would have to amputate your leg," says Michael.

I keep staring at the bruise. Michael plonks himself down on the grass next to us.

"What's this game you were playing? It looks like fun."

"Ag, we were just messing around," I say.

"You call trying to kill your brother messing around?"

"I wasn't trying to kill him. These pellet guns couldn't kill a fly . . ."

"What's it like having a brother who wants to kill you, Simon?"

Simon looks up from the ground.

"Not so nice."

"I wasn't trying to kill him. Simon and me always mess around."

"I bet you would like to get your own back, wouldn't you, Simon?"

"Suppose so."

Michael reaches into his pocket and hands Simon a pack of Beechies. It hasn't been opened yet.

"Help yourself. It's the new grape flavour." Michael and me watch Simon tear open the wrapper and stuff a Beechie into his mouth. He takes another one for later. "Maybe you want to play another game, Simon?"

"Like what?"

"How about hide-and-seek? I bet you like hide-and-seek?"

"Yes."

"But this hide-and-seek is more exciting."

"Like, how more exciting?"

"Much, much more exciting."

After Michael has explained the rules of his new game and he's given Simon two more Beechies, Simon is keen. Michael decides Simon can go first – as if it's a big treat. But I'm not so dumb. Especially after the thing with the barbel at the river.

"Right, buddy, you've got two minutes," says Michael. "If I was you I would make a move, unless you want to get slaughtered by the hunters."

There's a flash of panic across Simon's face and now he doesn't look so chuffed anymore with the idea.

"You better get going, Simon," I say.

"Okay, okay, I'm going," he says, and motors away down the side of the house. Michael sets his Casio G-Shock. There's a fat grin on his face.

"This is so childish. But what the hell, it should be fun. Just to be fair we'll give the little bugger an extra minute." According to the rules of the game we've got ten minutes to hunt the prey.

If we don't catch him by then, the hunters must let him go. "By the way, thanks for the invite."

"What invite?"

"Exactly. Was it a good movie?"

"Oh, that."

"Yes, that."

"It was okay."

"So why the hush-hush?"

"No hush-hush. I just didn't think you would be into the same movies as us . . ."

"Is that so? I love your thinking, Nick."

"I really didn't think . . ."

"That's your problem. But just forget it, okay?" Michael jumps to his feet. "What are you doing tonight?"

"Ag, nothing much. Probably take it easy at home . . ."

"Boring. My buddy from Joburg is coming to stay for the weekend. You should come hang with us."

"I wish I could, seriously. But my mom and dad are keen we spend time together. It's like this tradition . . ."

"Listen, forget it. I don't know why I bother making an effort." Michael jumps up onto his feet. It's like he's on this mission. "Okay, time's up for your brother. Let's go!"

Like a burning stompie tossed into a dry veld the morning explodes into life. Simon isn't hiding in any of the obvious places like I thought he would. I first check behind, and under, and in the caravan, but he's not there. I stand on Michael's shoulders and check the garage roof. We search the long grass running down the side of the garage. We race into the house, checking behind the doors, in all the cupboards and under the beds.

Michael and me stop to catch our breath.

"Shit, he's taking this seriously!" Michael says, breathing hard from excitement and the running around. "Seven minutes are already up. If he knows what's good for him, he better not be hiding outside the property."

"I'm sure he isn't." According to Michael's rules leaving the property is punishable by death. "Simon's not that dumb."

"Okay, let's not give up yet, he must be here somewhere. Nick, you check the back garden again, and I'll carry on searching the house."

Michael and me split up. Already I'm anxious we won't find Simon and it will be my turn next. I check my watch for the tenth time. Less than two minutes to go. I search the garden shed, this time turning the boxes and all the crap upside down in case Simon is hiding underneath. I race around under the fruit trees and stare hard into the branches. Only a minute left. I'm about to give up when an excited squeal comes from the house.

"I've got him, Nick!"

I don't need any encouragement. I'm back in the house like a shot. The squealing is coming from the laundry room.

Michael's got Simon with his arm twisted up behind his back. I'm so excited I hardly notice Simon's watery eyes.

"Where did you find him?" I'm still panting I'm so out of breath.

"In the laundry basket, under your mom's panties and bras! Can you fucking believe it?"

Simon is struggling to free himself from Michael's grip, but Michael's not messing around.

"What do you think we should do with him?" Michael doesn't wait for me to answer. "What did they do with perverts in the old days?"

Simon's face is looking scared and he's starting to snivel.

"Maybe we should let him go, Michael."

"They burnt them at the stake, that's what they did to perverts like you."

By now I have this giggle I can't control, a mixture of excitement and . . . I don't know . . . fear. But Michael's on a roll; he's a runaway train. Simon starts bawling big time.

"Seriously, Michael, I think we should let him go."

Michael lets go his grip and pushes Simon away from him. Simon flops to the ground.

"For fuck's sake. What's wrong with you? It's only a game." Michael turns to me. "Come, Nick, let's get out of here. We've got a party to organise."

"It's only a game, Simon," I say to him.

As I follow Michael out the kitchen door, I turn to check if my brother is okay. He hasn't moved or said a word. He's just sitting there on the heap of dirty laundry, staring at the ground in front of him.

TWENTY - EIGHT

The singing starts the second I walk into the lounge. My mom and Simon are still in their jammies; my mom must have been at it since sparrow fart because there's a tray on the coffee table piled high with my favourite donuts and other goodies from Athenia Bakery. There's also a heap of presents. Half the wrapping paper I recognise from Simon's birthday.

"Thanks Mom, thanks Dad," I say, when they've stopped singing and Simon's done his "*nog 'n hip hip*" for the tenth time. At least he's enthusiastic – I can say that for him. It's not even his birthday.

"So, pal, how is it to turn sixteen?" asks my dad. He's still sweating from his run. As usual my mom must have done all the work.

"The same as fifteen, I guess. Except for more pimples."

My mom gets up from the couch and wraps her arms around me. "You're growing up way too quickly for my liking."

"Come on, Mom. I'm not that old."

"Open your prezzies, Nick," says Simon, bouncing up and down the couch. There's a blob of cream stuck to his chin. I stretch over him for a donut.

"You guys didn't need to buy me so many presents."

"Maybe he's right," says my dad. "Why don't we keep some of them back for Christmas. What you say, Simey?"

"No! Nick must open them now."

"Actually, Dad, I'd say this looks like just the right amount. Can I go for this one first?"

"That's from me!" says Simon, real chuffed with himself. I know by the wrapping it's from him. Full of tears and he's used masking tape instead of Sellotape. "I bet you can't guess what it is."

"I bet I can." I know it's an LP, but I play along because Simon likes the game. I lift it to my ear and shake it.

"Sounds like . . ."

"You want me to open it for you?"

"I'm sure Nick can manage," says my mom.

The wrapping falls off the cover. "Wow, this is great." I'm genuinely chuffed. "How did you know I wanted Iron Maiden?"

"Don't look at me, I had nothing to do with it," says my mom.

"Thanks, Simon, it's a cool present."

"You call this music?" my dad says, holding up my record like it's a shitty nappy. "What's the world coming to, I ask?"

"Eugene!"

"I'm just saying . . ."

"Well, don't."

"It's okay, Mom. What can I open next?"

I shove in the rest of the donut and get going on the other presents. I don't deserve all this stuff. There's a denim jacket from my mom, which I really need, and a fishing box for my tackle, with two layers of compartments for different size hooks and sinkers. I also get a huge box of Quality Streets and the new Wilbur Smith book; I've read three of his already and they were all brilliant. My dad also gives me an envelope with a fifty-rand note folded up inside. Eventually there's only one present left, wrapped in gold paper, which I've been leaving until the end because I think I know what it is. I sit back and drink my lukewarm coffee, trying to make the moment last.

"Thanks Mom and Dad, you've totally spoilt me."

"Can I have another donut, Mom?" says Simon.

"You're going to make yourself ill. You've already had two."

"Ag, let him, Mom. It's my birthday."

"Thanks, Nick."

Simon stretches across me and helps himself to a donut and an éclair.

"Can I open this one now?"

But my dad is too busy trying on my new jacket over his running vest.

"How do I look?" he says, strutting across the lounge floor, pretending he's a model on a ramp. He hasn't joked around like this in ages.

"You look ridiculous, Dad," says Simon.

"What you mean, ridiculous? I'm a cool dude, man," says my dad in this American accent. The jacket sleeves are halfway up his arms. Simon's right, he looks totally ridiculous. I don't know why my mom lets him wear stokies. The only reason PW Botha doesn't ban them is because I bet he also has a pair.

"At least Dad doesn't look like those old guys who wear Woolworths jeans pulled up to their armpits and their shirts tucked in. All you need now, Dad, is one of those white imitation-snakeskin belts."

"I believe your sons are trying to tell you something."

"And I think I get the point."

"At least Dad's enjoying himself," I say.

"Philistines!" My dad plonks himself back on the couch. He's got seriously hairy legs.

"Open Dad's prezzie, Nick."

I pick up the small square box and take my time unwrapping it because I don't want to mess up the gold paper. Inside is a black box. I open the lid. My uncle's Omega. The one I learnt to tell the time on when I was a lightie.

"Dad, you can't give this to me. I'm serious."

"Jacques would have wanted you to have it."

The room has suddenly gone deathly quiet.

"It's okay," says my mom, and reaches over squeezes my dad's arm. My dad clears his throat. And then he clears it again.

"Sorry . . . I don't know where that came from. Sometimes it's just so hard . . ."

My mom passes him a serviette from the tray. My dad empties his head into it.

"I don't know what to say, Dad."

"Don't say anything. Try it on for size. I dunno if it's going to fit your skinny wrist. We may need to adjust the strap."

"Thanks, Mom."

"It's a pleasure."

"You sound like a foghorn when you blow your nose, Dad," says Simon. My dad snorts and drags Simon onto the couch next to him, and starts tickling him.

Sometimes I don't know what we would do without Simon in our family. One thing's for sure, we would be depressed half the time.

TWENTY - NINE

My mom and Simon stay in the car while I cart the last of the trays into the house. She really went to town on the snacks, with a whole bunch of different fillings for the sandwiches – tuna mayo, ham and cheese, you name it. And all of them cut into little triangles with parsley on top.

"Are you sure you don't want us to help?"

"I'm fine, Mom." Even though I'm not.

"Okay, we'll be off then. You must have a lovely time."

"Thanks again for everything, Mom." And I mean it.

I wait for my mom to reverse down the driveway. Simon is hanging out the back window, waving his arms about, navigating my mom into the street.

There's no sign of the flame torches that Michael said he would organise for the driveway. The front door is half-open so I don't bother putting down the tray and knocking. There's no sign of the BM either.

"Hey, Michael, I'm here!"

There's music coming from deep in the house. I lug the trays into the kitchen and drop them on the counter. Except for a packet of salt-and-vinegar that's been ripped open, the Checkers bags I dropped off earlier are still just lying there. I check my watch for the millionth time. I head through the sliding doors to see what's been done outside. The pool looks good, with the lights switched on, but there are none of the floating candles Michael promised to buy. A few normal candles and serviettes are laid out on the plastic table, but no paper plates or cups or anything else.

The music is coming from the TV lounge. I can hear Michael's voice and some other voice with one of those grating laughs. The door is slightly open, but I can't be bothered to say hi. Instead I just stand there, cemented to the floor, listening to Michael and his friend.

"Down the hatch, Jono!" Michael shouts.

Silence. Then the sound of a glass slamming onto the table, followed by a long burp and that grating laugh.

"Now your turn, boytjie!"

I head back to the kitchen.

By the time Sean and Eddie arrive for Michael's pre-party drinks I'm running around like a brommer on a camel turd in the Sahara.

"Am I glad to see you!" I'm so grateful to see them I hardly notice Eddie's outfit. "Where's Adele?"

"Her wanker of a dad changed his mind."

"Are you serious?"

If I had time I would ask Sean the hows and whys, but right now I can't focus on too much else but organising things. I point to the pile of unlit torches heaped on the veranda.

"Can I ask you guys to stick these things into the ground and light them? Michael was supposed to do it."

"Why, where's he?" asks Sean.

"Boozing it up inside with his friend from Joburg."

I hand Eddie the box of matches and race back inside to fill the bowls with chips and peanuts and all the other stuff I've set up on the outside table. I soon have everything out of the Checkers bags and arranged around the pool. It doesn't look the best, but will have to do. It's starting to get dark by the time I'm finished.

Sean is busy lighting the last torch and Eddie is going up and down making sure none of them fall over. It looks absolutely brilliant, something out of King Arthur, this avenue of flaming torches. I don't know what to say.

"Kief, hey?" says Eddie.

"Better than kief. I don't know what I would have done without you guys."

Of course I don't actually do it, but I feel like hugging Sean and Eddie right there on the spot. They must feel it too because we stand there for a few seconds, saying nothing, watching the torches burn and the day turn dark. I'm telling you, nothing, except maybe Eddie's orange shirt, will ever break the bond we have.

We head back inside. Michael and his friend are in the kitchen.

"Hey, the boys are here! How you doing? We ready to party, or are we ready to party? Jono, get your snout out of those chips. I want to introduce you."

Before I've even shaken Jono's hand I've made up my mind I don't like him. He's as tall as Michael and Italian or Jewish looking, with shiny black hair and this permanent smirk stuck to his lips.

"How you hanging, bud?"

"How am I hanging . . . ?"

"A turn of phrase, Nick. He means how is it going? Jono still thinks he's in Sandton."

"Sorry, boytjie, how thick of me to forget."

"What are we hanging around in the kitchen for? Let's head through to the lounge. Jono and I were just having a few pre-party toots."

"I don't know if we have time, Michael . . ."

"Relax. There's plenty of time. By the way, happy birthday, buddy. It's going to be a thrash."

"My turn next? But first, who's for another round?"
"What a kwessie?" says Eddie.
"*What a kwessie*," mimics Jono. "This is classic."
"I've still got, Michael," says Sean.
"Don't be a wuss, have another."
"Give the boytjie Esprit instead."
"*Touché*, Jono. Pear or peach, Seanie?"
"Sean, have another beer with us," says Eddie.
Sean just shrugs.
"If not, why not." Michael hands a Black Label to each of us.
"Thanks for the beers, Michael."
"No problemo, buddy. Cheers and all that crap. So, where were we now?"
"Your turn, boytjie!" shouts Jono, wiping his slobbery mouth.
"Okay, here goes." Michael leans across the carpet, takes hold of the empty Blackie and gives it a spin. It carries on forever, round and round the room, slower and slower. Nobody says anything; we are all too poep-scared it's going to land on us.
"It's you, Nick!"
"Crap, it's still moving."
"No ways, it's Esprit boy!"
"Shit!"
Sean can't believe it. The rest of us pack up. I'm slowly starting to get into this.
"Bad luck, buddy. You better down that beer cause you're gonna need it. So, boys and girls, help me here. What's my question to Sean going to be? Edward?"
"Alright, how about this . . . Seanie, how many times a week

do you trek draad?"

"You're sick, you know that?" says Sean, going red in the face. But the rest of us crack up. Michael clears his throat.

"I like. A classic or what, hey Jono? Nicolas, how about you?"

"Lemme think... Sean, remember that time in primary school when we came back from break and the overhead projector was lying smashed all over the floor. And Mrs Nel never found out who knocked it over."

"So, what's your question?" asks Michael.

"Was it you?"

"Lame question. You got one, Jono?"

"This one's easy. Boytjie, have you ever jerked off over the back page of the *Sunday Times*?"

"This game is bullshit. How can you ask questions like that?"

"Don't take it so personally, Sean. Let me think now whose question we are going to ask?"

"Mine's a kief one, Michael."

"What you say, Jono?"

Jono giggles. "I think I should leave the room. I'm starting to feel sorry for the boytjie."

"Don't feel sorry for him. It could be you next. Okay, after much thought and deliberation I have come to my decision." Michael does a PW Botha on Sean. "And remember, good sir, you've got to tell the truth and nothing but the truth."

"And if he doesn't? Nick, is this a kief game or what, hey?"

"He can opt for a dare. So, the question is, gentlemen... In any given week, Sir Sean, how often do you engage in blue vein solo? You know, throttle the chicken, as it were? Or, as Sir Edward here would say, trek draad."

"Told you mine was the best one! No lying, Sean, you have to tell the truth!"

Like vultures circling above a wildebeest with a broken leg we watch Sean, waiting for his answer.

"No rush, Seanie boy. Take your time, think carefully now." Michael says it in this calm, soothing voice. "And remember, you can always opt for the dare instead."

"Ja, but don't take all bladdy day, Sean."

"Don't rush the man, Edward. He's weighing up his options."

"I'll do the dare," says Sean out of the blue.

"Are you crazy, Sean?" I say. "If you answer the question it's over."

"I said I'll do the dare."

"Did you hear that, boys? Sean has opted for the big D. Are you sure about that?"

"Didn't you hear me the first time?"

"So what's it going to be, Mikey?" Jono is frothing at the mouth he's so excited.

"I'll have to think about it.

"I'm telling you, you're mad, Sean. You should have just answered the question." I can't believe Sean sometimes.

"You see the worry on my face?"

"Okay, but don't say I didn't warn you."

"Another Esprit, Sean? Sorry, beer. Help yourself boys, they're in the fridge. Right, who's next?"

"Shit, there's someone at the door!" I jump up. "Everyone's arriving."

"What about Sean's dare?" says Eddie.

"Don't you worry, we'll come up with something."

The moment everybody arrives they start tucking into the food as if there's no tomorrow. Especially the guys Eddie invited from his class. It's like this plague of locusts has dropped out of the sky and landed on the snack table; after a while all that's left are a few sausage rolls and chopped-up lettuce. You would swear half the people we invited haven't eaten for months.

Most of the girls Eddie and Sean invited haven't bothered to pitch. Or they didn't get the invite in the first place. So far it's only a few blorts and Natalie and her friend. Her name's Larissa or Melissa; Michael has turned the music up so loud I can't hear when she tells me. She's actually quite hot in her tight stonewashed jeans and black cut-off top with glitter down the front, and big dangly earrings. But when I try talk to her she acts totally not interested, so I don't bother.

After all the food has been polished off, everybody stands around the pool in these small groups, drinking what's left of the beers and blowing smoke rings and not saying much intelligent. Michael and Jono, who is apparently in the same class with him, are having their own private party on the deckchairs. It's weird, but it's like there are two parties going on at the same time, with a moat of crocodiles between the two. Every now and then Jono's grating laugh floats across the pool.

"This pozzie must have cost a fat whack-and-a-half. What you reckon they paid, Nick?" says Rodney, smoke pouring out his nose.

"What?"

"I said what you reckon they paid for this place?"

"I scheme at least a hundred Gs," says Gavin Joubert.

"I was asking Nick."

"I dunno. Something like that," I say.

"Did you okes see the size of that TV? I swear it's bigger than our lounge."

"We would have to watch *Dallas* in the garage."

"You can say that again."

"We would have to watch *Dallas* in the garage."

"You're such a wanker, Rodney, you know that? Where does your friend go to school, Nick?"

"St Johns."

"It's actually called St Andrews, Eddie."

"Same diffs? Same larney types."

"St Andrews. Is that a private school or something?"

"Don't you remember, dummie, they won interschools last year."

Gavin burps. "That's because they can afford the best coaches. If we didn't have Loch Ness for our coach we would also win."

"You talk such crap, Gav. Even if we had the best coach in the world . . ."

"You think Adele's not coming?" I ask Sean for what must be the tenth time.

"No."

"Maybe she'll come later."

"No, she won't."

Michael walks over to us. In his white Island Style pants and black cut-off T-shirt he's the best dressed of anyone here. By miles. He must think my friends are a bunch of skates. Especially Rodney Meyer. I don't know where he got that plastic leather jacket from.

"Is Nick looking after you dudes?" he says.

Maybe it's because Michael's standing and we're now sitting, or that he's from Joburg and we're not, or that it's his house and not mine, but suddenly nobody has much to say. My friends just sit there, staring into the bottom of their beer cans, this uncomfortable silence hanging in the air. They're a bunch of barbels out of water.

"I like your pozzie," Gavin says, and takes another swig of his Blackie.

"Thanks, buddy. As long as you guys are having a good time, that's all that counts. Nick, mind if I grab one or two of your beers?"

"Sure, I think there are still some in the fridge."

"Thanks buddy. Muchos appreciated."

Michael walks back to Jono. I turn back to my friends. Once again, as if by magic, they have heaps to say.

After two more beers I don't care anymore and the party starts to go better and a couple of our friends start shuffling their feet to the music. Sean's been chatting up Natalie and her friend, Melissa, or Larissa. That's one thing about Sean. He can talk to anyone. Even a girl he hasn't met before. I wait until he's finished talking before going up to him and tugging him on the arm.

"Should we do it?"

"Ja, let's. Eddie, come."

We drag Eddie away from the chip bowl and the three of us troop outside, me leading the way into the garden. We end up on the bench under the gazebo thing, far away from the house so nobody can see us.

"I love that song," says Eddie. He starts singing, "Forever young, I want to be forever young." He's completely out of tune. He would be even more out of tune if he wasn't so wasted.

"I also loved it until you opened your mouth. You got the matches, Sean? You can go first."

"You sure?"

"Hundred per cent."

Sean has to light three matches to get it going. He takes a few quick puffs. Every time he puffs his face lights up orange. It smells much sweeter than a cigarette and it makes tons more smoke. Eddie and me watch Sean's face, like we're watching the first man get ready to land on the moon; I've never smoked dagga before so it's quite a huge moment. Once it's lit up and going Sean takes a deep drag, coughs, and passes it to me. It's bent and lumpy. Sean coughs again and spits a greenie onto the ground.

"Tastes like bladdy peach leaves."

"Did you roll this, Eddie?"

"Ja. What you scheme?"

"Crap job."

"You must inhale deeply and then hold it there," Sean instructs Eddie and me, as if he's been doing it his whole life. My fingers tremble as I put it into my mouth. It's wet and woody, like something the garden boy would smoke. I do as Sean says – I take a big drag; too big because I have a coughing fit on the spot. Eddie thinks this is the funniest thing out. I spit out the bits that have ended up in my mouth.

"Fuck, you're right, it tastes like those peach leaves and BB tobacco we smoked when we were lighties. You have a go, Eddie."

Eddie takes a humungous puff that lights up the night sky, followed by an even worse coughing fit than mine.

We're too scared to have a second puff because of the stories we've heard about people going bossies who smoke too much dagga, so we stomp it into the ground and head back to the pool. When we get there Natalie and her friend have already left and it's just the dregs left. Michael and his friend are still sprawled out on the deck chairs, with a row of Lions lined up between them. Half of them mine and Sean's because when I open the fridge there's nothing left. I'm starting to feel quite out of it so I don't really care.

"Has it hit you yet?"

"Not yet."

"Me neither. It probably takes a while to kick in."

"You keen to go out somewhere after this?"

"Like where?"

"How about Turbo?"

"Now you're talking, Sean. Just say when."

Sean's been keen to leave the whole night. Not that he said anything. I just know Sean.

"How about now-now?"

"Okay, but I better tell Michael we're leaving. Where's Eddie?"

"Dossing in the flower bed. We'll wait for you in the car. Tell Michael thanks."

But in the end I don't tell Michael we're leaving. I don't know, maybe it's because I'm wasted, or maybe it's because Michael and his friend are so into their private party I just don't bother.

THIRTY

"What do you want to listen to?"

"I don't care, you choose." At this stage Sean can give me opera and I won't mind. He scratches around on the floor and finds a tape. I lean over into the back seat and give Eddie a poke in the ribs. "Eddie, wake up!" But he doesn't budge "Shit, I'm slaughtered from all that beer," I say, blinking my eyes. I can hardly see straight. I flip down the mirror and take a look. "Check my eyes, Seanie. Are they red yet? And you sure you okay to drive?"

"No, I'm fine."

"Me too. I reckon we didn't have enough of that stuff. We should have had another puff each."

"Unless it was just BB and leaves?"

"I wouldn't put it past Greg Romano. He's a slime ball deluxe."

"That's no lie. Are you having a good time?"

"I'm having a blast."

"That's all that counts."

I'm still staring into the mirror. "You sure my eyes aren't red?"

"No. How about some Van Halen?"

"Come on, Seanie, give me five." And Sean obliges and holds his hand out and we do a high-five. "How am I looking? Do you think I'll score?"

"With those dagga eyes, definitely."

"You bullshitting me, aren't you?" I say. And we give each other another round of high-fives.

"Okay, let's do like donkey shit and hit the road." Sean gives Russel's Fiat a rev like it's a Formula One Ferrari.

"Thanks, Sean."

"For what?"

"I dunno. For everything."

"No problem. That's what friends are for."

And Sean smiles at me and I smile back and I don't feel so pissed anymore. I lean forward and crank up the volume on the Hitachi, right up, until the speakers vibrate, and I push my seat back until I'm staring out the sunroof and watching the streetlights flash by.

"Come on, give it some stick, you're driving like an old man!" I scream above Eddie van Halen's solo. Van Halen must be the best guitarist in the world. He would beat Hendrix hands down. So Sean puts his foot flat and the Fiat nudges forward and by the time we hit Sand River Way we are doing over ninety.

"What a jol!" I scream, and slap Sean on the back of his head and he throws his head back and screams like a wild man. I pass him the bottle of rum and Coke he mixed earlier for the party, and he takes a swig and passes it back and I take a gulp, but not too big because I know I have to save myself. It's going to be a long night; I can feel it already. This sour beer-sausage-roll burp comes up and I hand the bottle back to Sean and he takes another swig. And we've got the windows wound right down and we're singing "You Really Got Me" at the top of our voices, and all the hassle that went into organising the party and the mixed-up feelings I've been having lately, they're already coughing in the dust behind us, and the only thing that matters is the high I'm having right now.

"Keep going straight. For old time's sake!" I shout, as Sean's about to take the turnoff to Turbo. So that's what he does. He keeps going straight until we hit the gravel road next to the graveyard and then he rams his foot into the floor.

We've done this a few times before, but only this time Sean really pushes the envelope. We must be doing at least a hundred when I give him the "Now!" and Sean takes his foot off the accelerator and I yank up the handbrake and the wheels lock and the Fiat begins to skid, but before it has a chance to lose control Sean pulls the steering wheel to one side and we start spinning. Round and round we go, three, four, maybe even five times before we come to a stop in this cloud of dust. For a couple of seconds we just sit there, too shocked to say anything, then we start giggling like schoolgirls, and then like crazies we start singing again at the top of our voices. It's finally turning out to be a brilliant night.

We pull into Turbo and by local standards the place is pumping because there are cars and bikes everywhere. It takes Sean a while to find a parking place; while he's manoeuvring into this tiny spot I have the mirror down, inspecting my eyes for the hundredth time.

"I bet there was also cat shit in that stuff Greg Romano sold us. There's no ways I'll score looking like this, Seanie."

Sean is too busy manoeuvring the Fiat back and forwards to agree or not agree.

"This bladdy parking space is tighter than a nun's doos." I crack up at that. Sean finally manages to squeeze in, cuts the engine and inspects himself in the mirror. "Let's do it! Eddie, you coming?" But Eddie's still fast asleep on the back seat. Typical. "Let's leave him." And we climb out the car and hit Turbo.

The place is pumping. Once we press past the bouncer, who

is seven foot-tall and about the same distance wide, straightaway we can tell it's not your the average night out in the sticks, where the guys outnumber the women two to one and the whole scene is more aggro. Sean gives the thumbs up, like we've struck oil, even though neither of us has ever scored at a disco. We have to inch our way up to the bar because there is such a crowd.

"What you want?" Sean shouts. "I'll get the first one."

I can hardly hear him the music is so loud. "I better take it easy," I scream back into his ear. So Sean orders two rum and Cokes and hands one to me. "Bastard!" And I pretend to head-butt him.

We find a spot against the wall where we can stand without getting shouldered. We sip our drinks and take in the scene. As usual the music is out of the Ark, but the sound system is good and it can handle the heavy bass being pumped out. Sean presses his mouth against my ear.

"Crap music," he shouts, as if he's just read my mind. "Check that girl dancing alone?" I look to where he's pointing, to a short tanned girl with black hair coming down to her shoulders. She's wearing a red mini-skirt and a matching top. Sean's mouth is back at my ear. "I'm gonna hit the floor."

"Go for it. I'll wait here."

To be honest, flapping my arms around with the whole world staring isn't my idea of fun. But Sean's got no problem with it. Even with his bad leg. Ever since he saw *Saturday Night Fever* and did that disco dancing class when he was on holiday in Margate, he's been fully into it. He's actually pretty good, working his John Travolta moves under the strobe light.

When the rockspiders and their girlfriends start looking like John Travolta and Olivia Newton-John, and every girl in Turbo looks like God's gift to mankind, I know I'm on my way to getting seriously wasted. Everything and everyone looks amazing and I don't care about a thing. I don't even care if this built guy next to me catches me staring at his girlfriend. I don't care about anything because I'm feeling invincible, like I've been given super-powers. I'm ready to take on the world. I'm even ready to hit the dance floor.

Sean's really getting into things, shaking his hips like a madman and going down to the ground and coming back up again and spinning around and almost losing his balance because he must be as gone as I am by now. He's dancing right next to this girl in the red mini-skirt. Next thing we are going crazy under the strobe light. Every five seconds he shouts into my ear, "You still having a good time!"

There's a break in the music and everyone stands around waiting for the next song. Sean starts chatting up the girl in the red skirt and she doesn't walk away like most of them do. When the music comes back on Sean is still talking to her and she's still acting interested. It's not that he's God's gift to women or anything, but Sean's got charisma – I think that's the word for it. He says something to her at the end of "Tainted Love" and she laughs like he's told her something really funny. Next thing, his mouth is back in my ear.

"Her name's Tracy! From Durban! Here for the weekend! Visiting her mom! Her toppies are divorced!"

The girl looks my way and smiles. I wave at her like an idiot.

Typical of Turbo, without any warning the music switches direction to Chris de Burgh. Sean says something in the ear of this Tracy girl and by the look on her face it's like he personally got the DJ to play "Lady in Red" for her. I can't believe it, but she lets him slow-dance with her, so I walk back to the bar. I need to sit down anyway. I find an empty chair and flop down, my head starting to spin big time. I light up our second-last Dunhill and stare at the dance floor, thinking how weird people and life are, that I'll never work it out no matter how long I live . . .

A hand grips my neck and squeezes; I twist round. Michael. Next to him, Jono. It's a total shock seeing them here.

"Thought you could sneak off without telling us?" says Michael.

"I wasn't sneaking off. I thought you saw us going . . ."

I'm suddenly stone-sober.

"I'm only kidding." Michael looks around the place. "So who you with?" I point to the dance floor where Sean's getting down on "Eye of the Tiger". "At least your boyfriend's having a good time."

The two dogs at the table next to us stand up and disappear into the crowd so Michael grabs their chairs and joins their table with mine.

"What you think, Jono?" shouts Michael across the table. "Not exactly Flashbacks, is it?" Jono curls his lip and rolls his eyes. I still don't like him one bit. "And you thought I was exaggerating?" Michael grabs onto his friend's arm, splashing my glass all over the table. "Please, I beg you, man, you've got to get me out of this town!"

"Christ almighty, get a hold of that one," says Jono, and he points to a chubby Afrikaner girl dancing just a few feet from us. Jono starts imitating her moves and they both crack up. I pretend I don't see her.

Michael points at Sean, who is still totally clueless. "Talk about moving the booty. John Travolta meets Elephant Man?" Jono leans across and says something in Michael's ear. Michael shakes his head and looks at me and winks. I reach for my glass, swirl it around and down what's left of it. An empty feeling has crept into my stomach, like I don't want to be here anymore.

The DJ decides it's time for some ABBA. I decide it's time for a slash. As I stand up I spot Sean heading our way, with this Tracy girl following behind. Sean's face drops the moment he sees Michael and Jono. This Tracy girl keeps walking.

"Thanks for the dance," she says to Sean.

"Hey, aren't you going to join us?" Jono shouts after the girl.

"Ja, come join the party," Michael shouts. "Seanie, organise the lady a chair."

Michael pushes the chair in the girl's direction.

"Ja, okay," says the girl and sits down.

"Pull up another chair, Sean."

Sean's not keen but sits down anyway.

Before Sean can do a thing about it, Michael and Jono are hogging this Tracy girl, chaffing her with this and that. I can only just make out what they're saying because the music is so loud and her words are slurred.

"I'm thinking of chucking," Sean says to me.

"Why? You were having a jol out there. Stay for a bit."

"No, I've done well. Club Duvet's calling. But you stay."

Michael says something to Tracy and she snorts and leans into him like she's battling to hold herself up. I can smell her perfume from where I'm sitting – apple flavour.

"How about we have one more drink and then we head out together?"

"Alright, sounds like a plan," says Sean. "I'll get the last one." He stands up. "Who wants something to drink?" Tracy asks for a Pepsi. I also want one. But Michael sticks his hand up.

"Hold up, cowboy, nobody's drinking Pepsi! My new friend here and Nick will have a Vodka Lime." Tracy looks at him and giggles some more. "And the same for us. In fact, Seanie boy, make it doubles all round. It's Nick's birthday, for Christ sake. Let's party!"

There's no point arguing because once Michael gets an idea in his head there's no stopping him. I push the last of my cash onto Sean, but he waves my hand away and works his way through to the bar.

"Thanks, buddy," shouts Michael behind him, then carries on chatting up Tracy, who is lapping him up big time.

"Okay, now I'm out of here for real," says Sean, after he's downed his Coke. "Okes, thanks for everything. It was a jol."

I stand up and also make to leave. I've hardly touched my glass. I don't know if I can face another drop.

"Hey, where do you think you're going?" says Michael.

"I'm catching a lift home with Sean. It's been great, Michael, thanks for everything, but I'm ready to crash."

"Sit down, Nicolas, you're not going anywhere." I look at Sean for support because I really wouldn't mind getting out of here.

Sean shrugs. "It's your choice."

"You heard the man, it's your choice," says Michael. "So what's it going to be, Nick? Are you going to be a total wet or will you stick around and enjoy yourself? What do you think, Jono?"

"Nah, he's gonna go," says Jono, his sarcastic sneer still plastered to his face.

"And what do you say, racy Tracy?"

"Come on, man, stay," she says in this slurry voice.

They are all staring at me waiting for my answer. There's nothing I can do but shrug my shoulders at Sean.

"Okay, I'll stay. But only for a bit longer."

Michael slaps the table, splashing Vodka all over the place. "That's our boytjie!"

Sean zips up his jacket. "I'll see you around, Nick."

He turns and leaves without saying bye to Michael or Jono. Or Tracy. When I sit down again Michael has this smug smile on his face; you would think he's just won the jackpot.

"We're going to get some fresh air. You coming?" shouts Michael in my ear, after him and Tracy have been dancing for about an hour; all this time Jono and me have been sitting at the table with nothing much to say to each other.

I follow them out. I'm seriously keen to get out of here.

Tracy and Michael are all over each other as we walk across the carpark. All the way down the grassy slope to the river she's making these drunk giggly sounds and holding onto Michael and bumping against Jono at the same time. She must be totally tanked after all those vodkas.

Outside, I feel I can breathe again. It's a perfect night, with the air so warm you just want to rip off your shirt. We make our way down to the river, where Michael and Tracy start pulling into each other. Michael gives Jono a thumbs-up behind her back. It's one big game for him.

Jono spots a pile of bricks that the municipality has been using to repair the pump station; he begins tossing them one by one into the water. I stand around like a lost fart, trying to get my head straight.

"You guys are bad," Tracy says every two minutes.

"Nick, how about you take us to your fishing spot?" says Michael, after a while.

"Now? It's after two in the morning, Michael." I can hardly stand anymore.

"Big deal. Hey, Jono, you keen?"

"I'm with you all the way, buddy." Jono picks up another brick and hurls it into the reeds. A duck explodes into the open and skims across the water, dragging a racket behind it.

"Geez, you guys are flipping bad," Tracy giggles for the hundredth time.

The whole way Tracy is moaning about her high-heel shoes getting messed up and telling us that we are flipping crazy. She's starting to get irritating, but as we trample our way through the long grass and mud she actually has a point; Michael just doesn't know when to stop. He's been on this mission from the moment him and Jono walked into Turbo.

"Christ, when are you going to stop your whining?" he says to Tracy as we come to our fishing spot. The way he says it puts an instant plug in her mouth.

"You guys are crazy," she says sulkily, more to me than Michael and Jono.

"I know, you've told us how many times already." Michael takes her wrist and pulls her back to him. "Give me a kiss."

"No."

"Come on, don't play hard to get."

Jono and me are watching to see what happens next. Michael holds her chin and turns her face up to him. She lets him kiss her on the lips, then pulls away again and walks off and sits down next to the river.

"Have you got a smoke for me?" she asks over her shoulder.

"Smoking's bad for you," Jono says, and laughs.

"They're finished," I say.

I walk a bit further along and squat down against the old willow. This is the first time I've been here so late at night, with the moon full and the water reflecting like polished metal. A duck flies past, almost skimming the water, the moonlight catching the tips of its wings. I close my eyes and begin to drift off, listening to the night sounds. Something is moving about in the reeds below, probably a frog or a snake on the hunt for bird's eggs. For a change the weaver nests above my head are dead quiet, but I bet they're on high alert, what with Jono's non-stop cackling down the way. Michael must have said something funny because Jono laughs. Tracy then says something; she doesn't sound too happy. Maybe she's just discovered she's sitting in a muddy patch. I could have told her.

It's too far away to see what they're doing, but Michael must be pulling in big time because she's doing her moaning and giggling thing again, like she's keen but at the same time she's not. When the moaning gets louder and higher pitched a funny prickle goes down my back.

"Nick!" shouts Michael, ripping me out of my dreamy state.

"What?"

"What the hell are you doing? Get your bony butt over here."

"Why?"

"Don't ask why. Just come."

I stand up and walk over towards them. I still can't make out what's going on, but it looks like Michael and Tracy are messing around on the ground, with Jono a few feet away, watching them get off.

"For fuck sakes!" says Michael into the dark.

"What happened?" says Jono.

"The bitch bit me! I swear the bitch bit me."

Next thing there's this slapping sound.

"Eina! Why did you do that?"

"That will teach you to bite me."

"Come on, lemme go," Tracy whimpers.

"Jono, don't just stand there, give me a hand," Michael hisses.

"Fuck, boytjie, what do you want me to do?" says Jono, laughing at the same time.

"Hold her!"

"What's going on?"

"Shut the fuck up, Nick. Jono!"

Next thing I know Jono is on his knees, holding Tracy's head back by her ponytail. She twists her head and tries to bite Jono's hand. This time Michael gives her a serious slap. Her squealing becomes a soft whimper.

"If she can't behave nicely, we will have to show her, won't we?" says Michael through his teeth. He looks up at me. I just stand there, paralysed. I might as well be watching a movie in slow motion. I can hear my teeth chattering in my skull. "Not so, Nick?" Michael gives this crazy laugh.

Tracy is now snivelling big time.

And Jono is still giggling non-stop.

"Christ, what's the matter with you? Calm the fuck down," Michael says to Tracy, stroking her face.

He stays where he is, pinning her arms under his knees. She's not struggling so much anymore. Everything slowly returns to calm. We've just come through a bad storm and it's going to be okay. I concentrate on the river, the water shimmering against the moonlight. Sean and me must come fishing at night sometime . . .

"Please . . ."

"Please what?"

"Get off me."

"First say you're sorry for biting me."

Jono giggles. She whimpers. She's also shaking like a leaf. And it's not even cold.

"I can't hear you."

"I'm sorry."

Tracy's mini-skirt is yanked up high. Her thighs are white in the moonlight.

"Shit, Michael. She said she's sorry."

"Did I ask for your opinion?"

"What are we going to do now, Mikey?" says Jono.

"I don't know. What you want to do?"

"I dunno. You decide . . ."

Michael looks up at Jono, then at me. "Maybe Nick wants a go with her. What you say, birthday boy?"

"Ja, I reckon she wants the boytjie," says Jono. "She's been checking him out the whole night."

Before I can see it coming Michael lunges forward and yanks my arm and pulls me to the ground. I nearly land on top of him and Tracy.

"Go for it, Nick," he whispers in my ear. "She's all yours."

I'm so close I can smell her apple-flavoured perfume, mixed in with the smell of grass and mud and sweat. She's staring at me with big eyes.

Michael takes my hand and shoves it between her legs. It's soft and warm. Michael starts moving my hand up and down. Up and down.

"See, she wants you, Nick," Michael whispers in my ear, his breath hot. "This is your chance, buddy. Don't be chicken."

"Ja, go for it, buddy," says Jono.

"Shut up, Jonathan." He shuts up. "Come on, what have you got to lose? You feel that?" Michael takes my fingers and presses them deeper between her legs. "Don't tell me you don't like that." My hand stays where it is. "Feels good, doesn't it?"

I have to swallow to get the word out. "Yes."

"So, go for it, Nick."

"Let me go," she whimpers again.

I rip my hand loose. "Please, Michael, I don't want to." I roll off Tracy and scramble to my feet.

"For fuck sakes, we don't have all night."

"Seriously, I don't want to, Michael. I want to go home."

"You hear that, Jono? Nick wants to go home to his mommy."

I don't wait to hear what Jono says. I turn and start running down the path alongside the river. Tripping and stumbling in the dark. Michael shouts my name. I don't look back. I just keep running.

THIRTY - ONE

The 1Time flight back to Cape Town is at two. Meaning I have to hit the road by eleven latest. It's now or never. I decide not to bother with breakfast; the last thing I feel like is eating. My back is so stiff I can't reach the tap with my mouth and I have to use a glass to rinse out the salt – what I would give right now for a tube of Mentadent P. The lump in my gut hasn't budged.

I pack my bags and tidy the bed and check the bathroom and all the cupboards and under the mattress to make sure I haven't forgotten anything. I walk down to reception to sort out my bill. The friendly Afrikaans woman isn't on duty. Instead it must be her husband who serves me and he acts like he's doing me a favour taking my money. I don't know what she sees in him.

While I'm arranging my stuff in the boot, I spot the madala shuffling down the path, waving his arms about. This is what I get for giving him a nice tip; now I bet he wants my arm.

I'm about to tell him I don't have any change when he hands me my credit card. Shit! He can hardly speak he's so out of breath. For the first time I notice the badge on his shirt.

"Hell, thanks, Jeremiah. You saved my life. Imagine if I forgot my bank card behind."

Not that he would know. I'm sure he doesn't even have a bank account. He tells me to have a safe journey and to come back soon. He starts walking back up the path.

"Hey, Jeremiah!"

Before I can change my mind I've pulled a hundred bucks from my wallet and handed it to him. The guy looks like he's about to keel over. But before he can thank me for the tenth time, I'm in the car and reversing out the parking lot.

It hits me as I'm driving down Voortrekker: God had it in for this place. You would have to be blind not to see it. The plummeting gold price. The mass retrenchments that came after. The miles of empty mine houses. Everything rusting and falling apart. Not a white man in sight. He might just as well have sent a plague of locusts.

The mine must still be operating because there's a cloud of steam gushing from one of the old ventilators. All this time I've been thinking the place has gone belly up. As I drive past I think back to the story I spun Simon, about this monster living underground and the steam coming up from its lungs. He actually bought it, hook, line and sinker, and for weeks after he took the long way round to school.

I decide to take a detour, past Sean's old house a bit further on. It's the same as Eddie's place, with grass pushing through the pavement, and the same ugly stoep at the front and the vibracrete wall and the cement driveway. Sean's mom always had flowers next to the driveway. Mostly pansies and daisies and daffodils. The pansies were my favourite. But now there's nothing but weeds and dust and a mongrel of a dog giving me the evil eye from the stoep. Even the upstairs window, Russel and Gary's room, is wrapped in burglar bars. A red Sierra is parked outside the house. Simon was right. This is where all Fords come home to die.

It's a pity Sean's folks no longer live here because I would visit them. I would pitch up at the front door and knock. It would be a hell of a shock, but they would be happy to see me. They're that type of people. And I would explain everything. Maybe one day I'll take a slow drive up the coast and visit them in Port Shepstone. Make things right with them. Maybe one day I will do that, when I've got some spare leave.

THIRTY - TWO

The sun is burning the back of our legs by the time Mr Stevens manages to squeeze the last things into the back of the Kombi. There is so much stuff to pack you would swear we are off to the North Pole. It's obvious Mr Stevens hasn't done this before, though he's acting like he has. It's total chaos. Eddie doesn't even have a sleeping bag; instead he's brought a pile of blankets and an old piece of sponge to sleep on. And Angelo has a brown suitcase that's from World War I, with locks and straps. Sean is the only one who's organised, with his own Badger backpack and tent.

"Right, guys, I think we're ready to rock and roll," says Mr Stevens. He looks at his watch for the hundredth time; we were supposed to be on the road hours ago.

The Kombi is from the Assembly of God church, with a cheesy *Jesus Doesn't Mind U-Turns* sticker splashed across the back window. We've already ching-chong-cha'd to decide who must sit in front with Mr Stevens, and Angelo lost. The rest of us pile into the back.

"Okie-dokie . . ." says Mr Stevens, polishing his Polaroids on the sleeve of his khaki shirt. He must have bought it especially for the weekend because the "S" sticker is still stuck on the collar. With his Polaroids and black moustache Mr Stevens looks a bit like Magnum. He seriously does.

He waits for Eddie to find the last of his NikNaks from under the seat. "You ready Eddie? Before we embark let's all close our eyes for a minute . . ."

Although we are running ten hours late Mr Stevens starts thanking Jesus for the good weather and the loan of the Kombi from the Assembly of God church. We could be halfway to Golden Gate by the time he asks the Lord to keep us safe on the road. And Eddie is already halfway through his litre Fanta.

Mr Stevens slides a tape into the deck. I bet some happy-clappy gospel band. Instead, John Denver comes blasting through the speakers. A minute later, as the mine dumps disappear into the horizon behind us and the speedo hits a hundred, Mr Stevens and the rest of the guys are belting out "Country Roads" at the top of their voices.

The landscape soon becomes less flat and there are more trees and less of those ugly thorn bushes. The veld isn't that dry white colour anymore, but soft and golden that you would actually want to lie down in it. That's what I could do right now. Just lie down and not think about things.

Mr Stevens holds the speedo at one-ten and fiddles non-stop with the different switches and dials and the tape deck equaliser. You would swear he's piloting a 747. Because we had to wake up at sparrow's fart I begin drifting in and out of my own world, taking in the scenery and Mr Stevens' music. This guy, Jim Croce, who I've never heard of, goes in next and he's really good, although his songs are quite sad. They're even sadder when Mr Stevens tells us from the cockpit that Jim Croce died really young in a plane crash.

Before I know it I'm half-asleep, my half-thoughts and half-dreams floating here, there and everywhere. My party and Turbo and what happened at the river – all one-minute miles away, the next sitting on the seat next to me, real and scary. I try force it away but it keeps creeping back up on me.

"Flipping hell!" blurts Sean, his eyes big as saucers and his face screwed up, as if he's dipped his head into hydrochloric acid. A second later it drifts over to my side of the Kombi, and it's a seriously bad one.

"Fuck, Eddie, you're disgusting."

"What?" says Eddie all innocent like. "It wasn't me."

"Swear on your dad's grave it wasn't you!" says Sean, and yanks the window open, letting in a gush of air. Eddie can deny it all he wants, but there's no two ways about it; it's an ESF deluxe – an Eddie Scheepers Fart. Sean tugs on my shorts and points to the front – Mr Stevens has wound down his window a few inches. Angelo hasn't noticed yet because of his snotty nose. The three of us pack up giggling until the tears are rolling down our faces and my stomach aches. Eddie lets rip again, only this time it's not funny.

We hit the N12 just after two and Mr Stevens announces we'll have a pitstop at a restaurant called the Golden Egg, which is next to the petrol station. While Mr Stevens stays behind to fill up the tank and make sure the guy doesn't mess up, the rest of us troop inside. I head straight to the bogs, with Eddie and Angelo in hot pursuit. The place stinks of sour piss. I freeze up if someone is standing next to me so I always pretend I need to make a number two. Angelo has the same genetic problem. Not so Eddie; even from inside the cubicle you can hear his fire hydrant.

Sean has organised a table at the front window. The chairs are covered in that plastic vinyl that tears the skin off the back of your legs if you try slide across it. We all squeeze in next to Sean so we can look out the window. Mr Stevens is still busy checking the tyres.

"I'm going to have the Morning Glory," says Sean. "What a

lag calling a breakfast a Morning Glory."

"Must be because it's so huge," chirps Angelo. He's actually not a bad guy when he comes out of his shell.

"That's no lie. Two fried eggs, pork or beef sausage, bacon, mushrooms, mini-juice, a free slice of toast. With a Mega-Coke or Bottomless Coffee," Sean reads.

"I'm having the cheese burger with bacon," says Eddie. "What you having, Nick?"

"Don't know. I'm not hungry."

"You sick or something? I bet it's your babelas from two nights ago."

"Look who's talking, Eddie. You passed out before the party was even over."

"I'm going to have the same as you, Sean," says Angelo. "Eddie, you want to swap your chips for my Coke?"

"No ways. I'm too Fanta'd out. Anyway, aren't you fat enough already?"

"Leave him alone, Eddie," says Sean. "Angelo can eat what he wants."

"Flip, I'm only joking."

"Is that what you call it?"

I'm in one of those moods where I can't decide what I want. While I'm going through the menu I'm busy scratching at something under the table. I sniff my fingers. Bubbleyum Grape.

A bakkie pulls up in front of us, towing a caravan that's ready for the scrapyard. A guy wearing blue rugby shorts and a short-sleeve khaki shirt with a collar steps out. His legs are thicker than tree trunks and he's barefoot. He bends over and checks under the bakkie, his hairy crack showing to the whole world.

"Why do okes always do that?" says Sean.

"What?" says Angelo.

"Check under their cars when they get to a petrol station."

"I know why," Eddie says.

"Why?"

"To make sure the houtie they knocked over on the highway isn't still stuck underneath."

A jet of Coke comes streaming out of Sean's nose. "I bet you got that from Luke?"

"Ja, how did you know?"

"Because I heard it before. It's one of those dumb army jokes. Except the guys in the Ratel don't bother stopping. And the so-called houtie is a Swapo terr."

"Imagine being married to that," says Angelo, as the rockspider's wife climbs out from the bakkie.

"I reckon she could kickstart a Jumbo, no problem."

"I bet her parents had to pay the lobola."

"What's lobola?" asks Eddie.

"Cows and sheep," says Angelo.

The guy is going around the bakkie kicking the tyres. The waitress comes back for my order. She's quite good-looking for a black. I order a Lime milkshake.

"To eat?"

"Nothing."

"Nick's on a diet. Seanie, I've got one for you. How do you pomp something like that?"

"Dunno, Eddie. Tell us."

"You cover her face with a flag . . ."

"And do it for your country," Sean says.

The guy and his wife climb back into their bakkie and pull off in a cloud of diesel.

"Angelo, pass the tomato sauce. You missed a lekker party. We all got totally vrot."

"I heard it wasn't so good."

"Who said?"

"Rodney Meyer and some of the other boys."

"That's because they left early. Why don't you have some burger with your tomato sauce, Eddie?"

"Eddie passed out he was so vrot."

"I didn't pass out. I was just resting. We even organised some dagga for the party. That's how big a jol we had, Angie. Not so, Nick?"

"Ja, I guess so." I'm actually feeling quite sick in my stomach suddenly. "Who wants the rest of my milkshake?" I shouldn't have asked because Eddie and Sean are on it like flies.

Mr Stevens blows his nose into the serviette and leans back against the vinyl. Already he's looking heaps more relaxed than a few hours ago.

"Now that's what I call a burger. How was your nosh?"

"Also lekker."

"I must tell you guys, it's really strange how life works . . . Tell me if this is amazing or not amazing . . . Ja, asseblief, another refill. Koue melk. Okay, remember how I was telling you about our surprise visitor at the fête?"

"And you said you would only tell us the details once the bucks came through."

"That's it. Imagine now . . . Just as Keith – Mr Alpert – and me were getting ready to pack up along comes this guy who we start getting into conversation with. We start chatting about this and that. Turns out he also plays club tennis and we're going to be in the same Round Robin tournament next month. I start telling him about our youth group and the team-build that we are raising funds for, and the old story of never enough bucks . . . What? Ja, hou die kleingeld. Anyway, here I'm gaaning on, blah, blah, blah, when this guy's son turns to him and tells him he's heard about our team-build from one of you guys and it's a good cause and his dad should help sponsor it."

"And what did he say, Mr Stevens?"

"I'm about to tell him, don't be bladdy crazy, you can't do that, when his dad says to me, 'How much do you still need, Vernon?' And I look him in the eyes and tell him straight. Adding on a few bucks for unexpected expenses. And he says, 'What do you think, Michael?' And Michael – that's the name of his son – Michael says, 'It's the least we can do for these people, Dad.'" Mr Stevens stands up and tucks his shirt into his belt. "You can ask Keith when we get back, those were his exact words: It's the least we can do for these people."

Because Mr Stevens misses the turn-off to the campsite and we end up doing an extra fifty kays, the sun is already melting behind the mountain as we drive through the boom. But it's really pretty, with the foothills of the Drakensberg washed in gold light and the poplar trees next to the river the colour of a dying fire. We slide open the Kombi door, while Mr Stevens cruises around looking for a good spot. The air smells of old wood-fire mixed with thatch and horses. There's no better smell in the world.

It's getting dark by the time we find a place close to the river, but also not too far from the bogs because anybody knows there's nothing more irritating than having to walk miles at night to park a coil.

We quickly discover it's not easy pitching a tent in the dark. Sean has his own tent and has it up in record time, but the other two Mr Stevens borrowed from the Assembly of God. It's chaos. If you saw us you would think we're trying to invent the atom bomb. It's embarrassing as anything because there's another cadet group going for it at the other end of the campsite and they look totally organised. Only after Sean steps in and helps Mr Stevens work out what fits with what do we get the tents up and our stuff organised for the night.

While we collect wood Mr Stevens goes off on a "fact-finding mission", as he calls it. It turns out the other group of cadets are from a rockspider school in Kroonstad. They've been here for three days already, but leaving at sparrow's fart tomorrow. Even Mr Stevens looks relieved about that – next thing they invite us for a joint exercise. What with their South African flag flying high above their army tents and the barefoot rugby types running around the campsite, they'd eat us for breakfast.

We build a huge bonfire under the stars and Mr Stevens turns out to be quite fun when he's relaxed. While Sean looks after the wors and chops he tells us about the time he studied something called theology in America, and why he and his wife got divorced after he got back. After supper we keep adding logs to the fire. Mr Stevens is a completely different guy to the one we know from home, playing his guitar and belting out campfire songs, which he knows most of the words to. I start feeling quite bad for him, after everything he's gone through since he discovered his wife was pomping one of the foremen at the mine while he was learning about God.

We are up at the crack of dawn and breakfast is a huge cook-up with burnt scrambled eggs and bacon and Ricoffy with condensed milk, before we leave on a "team-build exercise", as Mr Stevens likes to call it. It's actually just a hike up to Eagles Nest, which you can see from the campsite, but Mr Stevens likes to give technical names to everything. For example, we don't talk about something; we "debate" it. Or something is "up for discussion". Or, if we are about to do something he will give us a "briefing". And if it's past tense it's called a "debriefing".

Eddie and Angelo help Mr Stevens into his old army backpack. It weighs a ton. Sean leads the way out of the campsite, the rest of us following behind, and Mr Stevens bringing up the rear. We go down a path that tracks the river for a while, then breaks away and zigzags up the mountain. High up on the far side of the valley patches of wet rock catch the morning sun, but where we are the air is still so crisp you can cut it with a blunt bread knife. We pass two hadedas poking around for worms on the lawn; they don't even bother to fly away.

Sean and me are soon way up front, with Angelo and Eddie and Mr Stevens and his overloaded pack trailing behind. Every time I look back Mr Stevens has stopped to adjust the straps.

"Why've you been so quiet?" says Sean after we've been walking for a while.

"Who says I've been quiet?"

"What? You've hardly said a thing since we left yesterday morning."

"You reckon?"

"I don't reckon, I know."

"Whatever. Anyway, look who's talking. You've also been acting quiet since Mr Stevens told us about Michael's dad helping pay for us to be here."

"You blame me? I wouldn't have come if I knew." Sean carries on walking.

We come up to a ridge, where there's a view dropping off on all sides. The Free State isn't pancake-flat as most people think. There are parts that are actually really beautiful. Eddie and Angelo and Mr Stevens are way below us. Mr Stevens has his binoculars out and he's pointing at the sky. Sean drops his pack to the ground and flops down onto the long grass. I park off nearby, catching my breath.

"Angelo's actually not such a bad guy."

"Who said he was?"

"You know what I mean."

"I don't. He's a better oke than half the others at school. Just because his family is fat everyone's out to get him."

"Maybe you're right. I guess we better say thanks to Michael and his dad when we get back, don't you think, Sean?"

"Guess so."

"If it wasn't for him we wouldn't be sitting here checking out the view."

"And like I said, maybe now I don't want to be here checking out the view."

"You seriously don't like him, do you?"

Sean squints up at me. "What gives you that idea? Why, don't tell me you actually like him?"

"Ag, he's not so bad. You just got to get to know him. You've hardly given him a chance."

"No thanks to you," Sean says, and starts digging in his backpack.

"What you mean, no thanks to me?"

Sean fishes out his army water bottle and unscrews the cap. He doesn't offer me any. He screws the lid back on and leans over and picks up a pebble and flicks it over the edge. I follow its curve through the air. "You haven't exactly made an effort, have you now?" Before I have a chance to answer he carries on. "It's like when you are with Michael you don't care about anyone else."

"That's bullshit, Sean."

"No, it's not. It's forever Michael this, Michael that. It's like he's got control over you and you can't even see it. You're like this puppy dog. No matter how much you get kicked around you keep coming back for more."

"Oh, please, what crap. Anyway, you haven't exactly made things easy for me."

"What's that supposed to mean?"

"Ag, it doesn't matter, Sean. Let's change the subject."

It's too late. This heavy black cloud has appeared from nowhere and settled on the mountain. I stand up and walk over to the edge to see what's keeping the others. Now Eddie has the binocs and Mr Stevens is doing the pointing. I look up to where he's pointing and spot the pair of eagles pinned to the sky. They're hardly bigger than black dots. Right now I wish I was one of them.

"Why change the subject? You brought it up. You really want to know what I think of Michael? I think he's a doos. And I don't know what the bladdy hell you see in him."

"You think so? Maybe you're just jealous."

"Jealous? Oh, please. What would I be jealous of?"

"Jealous that you're not more like him, that you wish you had all the things and opportunities he has." And now I'm saying things I don't even believe. "You're jealous because he doesn't have a limp and you do!"

Sean shakes his head, but says nothing. He turns away and stares down the valley.

"I'm sorry, Sean, I didn't mean that. I swear I didn't. I don't know where it came from."

"A bit late for that. You've said it."

I stare at Eddie and Angelo and Mr Stevens making their way

across to us. Sean stands up and adjusts his pack.

"I swear, Nick, sometimes I think you've really lost the plot," Sean says, and walks away.

Time goes into slow motion after that and all I want is the team-build to be over with. But Sean acts like all's okay, although it's obvious he's avoiding me like the plague. I'm also okay with that because I don't exactly want to hang out with him. When Mr Stevens briefs us on another spanbou, this time where one guy gets blindfolded and the other one has to guide him through the poplar forest next to the campsite, he puts Sean and me together. It's weird because we act real polite towards each other and Sean makes sure I don't walk headfirst into a tree. If you saw us you would never think we had an argument in the first place, but underneath it all is this tension that makes everything heavy, even thinking. Schlepping a sack of lead around would be lighter.

For the rest of the weekend I'm a total zombie, going through the motions and pretending to have a good time. It's so bad that after our night patrol, when Eddie lets rip with a massive Bully Beef fart around the braai, I have to force myself to laugh. Even Mr Stevens has a good chuckle over it.

After we've packed up on Sunday afternoon and are getting ready to leave, Mr Stevens tells us to gather round for another of his "debriefing" sessions. We've only been here two days, but he's already brown from the sun and acts like he's personally conquered Everest. Blindfolded. In a wheelchair.

"Right, guys, I just want to say it's been a pleasure leading you on this team-build mission of ours. It's been brilliant. If this was the border you are the guys I would want to be with, watching my back." Mr Stevens looks at each of us and we nod solemnly.

"I'm telling you, if all the other cadet groups pull together like this one, then this beautiful country of ours is in safe hands. You guys were great."

"Thanks, Mr Stevens," says Sean, and walks up to Mr Stevens and puts out his hand. "Thanks for organising everything."

"Let's do it the proper way. Shaking hands is for civvies."

Mr Stevens steps back and salutes. Sean looks at us, then salutes back.

THIRTY - THREE

It's like I don't know what to do with myself since we got back from camp, except lie around the house, doing nothing. And don't ask me why I'm reading *Tight Lines*. It's filled with nothing but photos of fat crunchies in tight rugby shorts and dirty T-shirts, holding up dead fish. Mostly salt-water fish. Cob, leervis, galjoen, that type of thing. I would be much more into fishing if we lived at the coast. Sean and me would go fishing every day. Not that that's ever going to happen now.

I flip forward to the fresh-water section. The pictures are now of muddy dams and rivers and ugly fish. There's a photo of a guy with a scary-looking forty-five-kilo barbel, caught at Hartebees. The photo could have been taken next to the Sand River. There's even a big willow tree just like ours in one of the photos.

"Knock, knock." My mom pokes her head around the door. "You ready to go?"

"Guess so."

"Don't sound too enthusiastic."

"I'm not in the mood, Mom."

"Tell you what. After we've popped in at the home and bought your blazer, we'll go to the mine club. What you say to that?"

"And Simon? Is he also coming?"

"No, just you and me. Come on, we haven't done anything together for ages."

I don't know if it's Dries Vermeulen's massive grunter caught off Gericke's Point on eight-kilo tackle or the stuff that's swimming around my head, or my guitar staring at me from the corner. Whatever it is I don't want to think about it. I roll off the bed and dig out my slops.

"Can we go now?"

"The thing I want to know is why they give these places such rosy names. I mean, when you think about it, there's no difference between an old age home and a mortuary."

"That's a depressing thought."

"Well, it's true. The one is just a departure lounge for the other. *Sonskyn?* What a bullshit name, Mom. And that place gran stayed at, what was that called?"

"*Village of Happiness*."

"You see what I mean? That's also a bullshit name."

"Language, Nick."

"Sorry. But why can't they just say it like it is?"

"What do you mean?"

"Chips that mine truck, Mom, he's not indicating. Okay, how about . . . *Death's Door?* That's a good name. Or what about, *Home for the Nearly Dead?* Or *Stairway to Heaven?*"

"Geez, but you are in a cynical mood today," says my mom, but trying not to smile.

We pass by The Phoenix – *Rocky* is still showing – then swing a left into De La Rey and then a right at the NG church, and then out of town down the long road towards the industrial area and the prison.

Huis Sonskyn vir Swart Bejaardes, as it's called, sticks out like a sore thumb; you would have to be blind to miss it. It's a long brown block of a building with tiny windows at the front and a high wire fence running right around to keep the old fogies in. The place is real depressing.

The bored-looking black guy at the gate lifts the boom and waves us through – if we were on a kidnap mission he would still wave us through. The only patches of shade have been hogged by white Datsuns with G number plates. The idea of waiting in the blazing sun doesn't exactly appeal so I have no choice but to join my mom. I help her carry the basket of stuff she's baked, all of it stuff you don't need teeth for. The first time my mom came here she baked crunchies and the nurses ended up eating them.

I've never been inside before and it's worse than I thought. I don't even know if my dad knows my mom comes here. He wouldn't be seen dead in a place like this. So it's like her and my secret. There's a waiting room with plastic chairs and old salt and pepper wall-to-wall carpets and a pile of *Readers Digest* that's at least a hundred years old. On the wall there's a faded poster of a tropical island with palm trees. A fat woman in a nurse outfit is standing behind the counter. Her badge says M *Masebe*. She's got a huge smile and perfect white teeth.

My mom and the nurse woman chat for a while, like they're old buddies. I'm not exactly keen to hang around the dingy waiting room so I follow my mom through the door marked A-Section. We walk down a long dark passage smelling of Jik and old age. At the end of the passage the door opens to a stoep and a quad area covered in moth-eaten brown grass. There's a fountain or some other water feature in the middle that's bone-dry.

The stoep is lined up with ancient blacks on white plastic chairs. A few of them are in wheelchairs. They don't look in a good way. Some of them don't even look human. They're mostly bags of skin and bone dressed in old rags, staring at the ground and scratching at their paper-thin skin.

My mom looks back to check that I haven't fainted. She stops at this shrivelled old man with snow-white hair, and puts her basket down. He must be at least two-hundred years old. He's so tiny his stick legs don't touch the ground. He's wearing Bata school shoes, but no laces and socks.

"Hullo, Mr Mafokeng!" my mom shouts into his ear. "How are you today?"

I look around, but nobody seems to be paying much notice. Mr Mafokeng's tiny head looks up at my mom and flashes this toothless smile, and his eyes sparkle like he's just come back from the dead.

My mom and Mr Mafokeng are soon chatting away about the weather and Mr Mafokeng's children, Dumisani and Harriet, who haven't visited him in ages by the sounds of it. The old people in their plastic chairs begin to stir and look more alive. When Mr Mafokeng gets revved up about the families never visiting, an old woman in a rusty wheelchair rolls her head from side to side and claps her hands. He's a total character, this Mr Mafokeng, with a laugh that's way too big for his body.

My chest wants to burst as I watch my mom go around greeting the old people by their names and handing out biscuits, and before I know it I've forgotten the things that have been bugging me and start helping her hand out the rest of the stuff she's baked.

The mine tea garden must be the most underrated spot on earth. Most times we come here we have the place to ourselves and the menu has just about everything it says it has. The only other people who come here are oldies with purple hair and moms with young kids who want to feed the ducks.

We find a shady spot near the pond and wait for the waitress to serve us. To kill time we watch a skinny kid with red hair tearing chunks from a loaf of white bread and squeezing it through the chicken wire. The ducks are going psycho for it. They're the type of ducks that would kill their own mother for a few crumbs.

My mom breaks the silence. "This is nice, don't you think?"

"Guess so."

"What are you going to have?"

"The usual."

"Float and chocolate cake?"

"Yip."

"I might try the scones for a change. And a Nescafe."

My mom's been trying to make small talk all afternoon. I don't want to sound ungrateful and all, but I'm really not in the mood for talking. Which isn't like me.

The waitress takes our order and we sit watching the redhead for a while. The kid's mother is sitting alone at a table, watching him start a duck riot. She's looking more stressed by the minute.

"Is everything okay?" my mom asks out of the blue. I keep staring at the kid, feeling her eyes drill into me.

"Ja, why shouldn't everything be okay?"

"Well, you don't seem to be your usual self since you've got back from camp."

"What's my usual self?"

"For starters, you are usually a lot more talkative."

"Maybe I just feel like being quiet for a change. I can't be on stage twenty-four seven, you know."

"Nobody is saying you have to be on stage. We are just a little worried something may be wrong and you're not telling us.

"Who is we?"

"Your dad and I."

"That's a first. Since when is Dad worried about me?"

"He's got his own way of showing it, Nick."

"That's no lie. I must be blind."

"You mustn't talk about him like that. He's been through a difficult time. We all have. Anyway we're talking about you right now, not Dad. You've hardly been eating."

"I've ordered chocolate cake, haven't I?"

"I'm talking proper food."

While the waitress is arranging everything on the table I ask for extra ice-cream to prove my mom wrong about my eating. I scoop the whole lot into my float and make a big show of eating it.

"How's your cake?"

"Nice. You want some?"

"I'm fine, thanks."

I stuff a chunk of cake into my mouth. They've used Stork,

not real margarine.

"Thanks for the clothes, Mom."

"Pleasure. I'm relieved we could find you some school shoes at the same time."

"Me too. I was getting ready to go back to school barefoot. You should try some of this float, Mom. It's much better with extra ice-cream."

My mom takes a small, delicate sip. Everything she does is delicate. That's what I like about her. That she's delicate and strong at the same time. She hands the glass back.

"I'm harping on, but you would tell me if there's something wrong, wouldn't you?"

"There's nothing wrong, Mom. I told you already. Can we change the subject?"

"Okay, fine. There's something else I have to tell you. Dad's been called up for a camp."

"Another one?"

"Ja."

"But he's only been back a few months."

"I know."

"How long this time?"

"The form said two months. But we hope it only be a month like last time. Maybe you can say something nice to him when we get home."

My mom's near to tears, I can see that, but I don't know what to say. I just stare at the kid on the other side, who is busy trying to unhook himself from the fence.

Not that anyone would, but if they ever made a statue of my dad it would be of him on his La-Z-Boy, his shoes off, his *Castle* in his left hand and his *Citizen* open on his right. Today's front page has a kief photo of a burning bakery van, with rioters going berserk in front of it.

"Hi Dad."

"Howzit, my boy. How was the day?"

"Good."

"Glad to hear. Your mate called."

"Who?"

"Whatsisname . . . Mark, Mike, you know, the Dempsey chappie?"

"Michael?"

"That's the one. Called twice, in fact."

The afternoon with my mom instantly vaporises into thin air.

"What did he want?"

"Who knows? By the sounds of it he wants to talk to you about something. Said I must tell you to swing by. You must introduce us sometime. He seems like a decent chappie."

"Did he say what it's about?"

"Nope. Why, is there a problem?"

"No problem."

"You sure?"

"Ja, I'm sure. Mom says you've been called up for a camp?"

"Yip. Your dad hit the jackpot again."

"When do you have to go?"

"Soon. End of the month." My dad flips to the sports section. "Now, that's what I like to see. Free State back in the running."

"Dad?"

"Ja? Always knew the boys had it in them. We could even get to the semis at this rate . . ."

"I wish you didn't have to go."

My dad stops reading and looks up. For once our eyes meet.

"Thanks, Nick. Can't say I'm really in the mood for it, but listen, if I don't go who's going to protect you lot. Not so?"

THIRTY - FOUR

It's getting dark by the time I pedal up to Michael's front door. Sucking in a deep breath, I knock. Nothing. So I knock again, harder this time. I'm getting my hopes up when a door slams deep in the house. Next thing a light goes on and there are footsteps coming down the passage. The front door scrapes open and Michael's standing in front of me in his black Adidas tracksuit, barefoot, his hair wet and slicked back.

"Hey, look what the cat dragged in. Nick, my buddy! Good to see you."

"Hi, Michael."

"Where have you been? I've been trying to get hold of you for days."

"I was away . . ."

"I know that. I mean since then."

"Busy, I guess."

"Shit, I thought maybe there was something wrong. What have you been so busy with?"

"This and that. Getting organised for school, that type of thing. And you?"

"This and that, too. We've also been away for a few days."

"Where to?"

"Sun City. Pity you were so occupied. I was going to invite you."

"To Sun City?"

"More like Sin City. You ever been there?"

"No."

"In that case you missed out big time. We had a total blast. Gambling, non-stop eating, blue movies, you name it."

"Blue movies?"

"Oh ja, plenty. There's a whole TV channel dedicated to them. You would have creamed yourself wet. And I got myself the new Sony when I was in Joeys."

"I thought you already had one."

"I do, but I couldn't resist. You must see the features on the latest one. I'll give you a demo sometime. Hey, what are we standing around for? Come inside."

I follow Michael into the house. The lights in the lounge are dimmed low. There's classical or opera music playing. The stuff my mom listens to. Michael walks across the room and turns the volume down.

"My dad said there was something you wanted to talk to me about?"

"Oh, so you got my messages?"

"Why do you think I'm here?"

"I don't know. Maybe you were being spontaneous for a change? No worries, I'm glad you pitched."

"Why wouldn't I pitch?"

"You know. Not getting back to me when I phone. Leaving the party without telling us. Anyway, what can I get you?"

"I'm fine."

"Come on, have something. You want a Coke?"

"Okay, I won't say no. Where are your mom and dad?"

"At some meeting, as per usual. Here you go. Cheers, Nick. To good friends and all that jazz."

We clink bottles.

"What is it you wanted to talk about?"

"Jesus, why so jumpy?" Michael points to the leather couch.

"Sit, Fido, sit!"

I do as he says. I sit. Michael stays standing, leaning against the fireplace, acting cool.

"Seriously, it's good to see you, Nick. It seems ages since you were here last."

"It was the night of the party."

"I know that. Wasn't a bad party, don't you think?"

"It was okay."

"'It was okay', he says! Jesus, I'm surprised you remember any of it. You were drunk as a skunk."

"I wasn't that drunk."

"You were man down, Nick. I thought we would have to carry you home from that dive. By the way, how did you get home?"

"I walked. You make it sound like I was paralytic."

"Deny it all you want," laughs Michael. "It doesn't change the facts: you were motherless, my buddy. And we won't even talk about old Edward. Jono and I had a good chuckle about it afterwards. You want a glass for that?"

"I'm fine, thanks."

I wish Michael would also sit. My dad also does it – hovers over you.

"Deep down you're actually quite the animal, you know that?"

"Why you say that?"

"What? The way you were all over that bird. You were savage, buddy!"

My skin goes prickly when Michael says this.

"All over her! What you mean?"

"Come on, Nick, we know you were wasted, but surely you remember that? Oh, or maybe it was the dope you guys smoked on our property."

"Who told you about that?"

"Your buddy Edward. Who else?"

"I hardly had any . . ."

"Hey, don't worry about it. Besides we were talking about something else."

"You were all over her, Michael, not me."

"That's not the way Jono and I saw it. Feeling her up and all, what do you call that?"

I just sit there, saying nothing, my insides getting colder by the second. Michael walks over to the hi-fi system and adjusts the graphic equaliser.

"I love this part," he says, and cranks up the volume and stands there with his eyes closed, listening to the music. At the end of the part he loves he opens his eyes and turns the volume right down. "She wants to lay a charge against us."

"Charge? What type of charge?"

"You tell me."

"Seriously, I don't know what you're talking about."

Michael places his Coke on the mantelpiece.

"She says we tried to rape her."

"This is crazy, Michael. I can't believe what you've just told me."

"You're telling me. But don't panic. I'm sure we can work something out."

"How can I not panic? But we didn't do anything . . ."

"Just calm down, okay?"

I breathe in deeply, trying to pull myself together. "This is seriously crazy . . ."

"We've got to stick together on this, Nick." I nod. "Because if we don't, I can't help you . . ."

"Why do you keep saying *me*, Michael? You guys were also there. You were also all over her."

"Says who?"

"It was obvious. You can't deny that . . ."

"Obvious to who, Nick? It's not obvious to Jono and I."

"And what about after I left? You haven't even told me what happened after I left."

"There's nothing to tell, that's why. We all had a bit of fun with her. You had a bit of fun with her. She was wasted. She freaked out. You had a panic attack and ran away. Jono and I got bored and went home. Finito. End of story."

"And you just left her there?"

"Of course we just left her there. What were we supposed to do? Lift her onto our shoulders and carry her home?"

"I mean, you didn't do anything to her?"

"Fuck no. Even if we wanted to, which we didn't, she was so legless there was no ways she was up for anything. Anyway, what are you saying?"

"Nothing. It's just that you were the last ones with her."

"And, the conclusion you're drawing is?"

"I'm not drawing any conclusion. I'm just saying . . ."

Michael slaps his forehead and laughs. "Duh! I get it. Nick here thinks Jonathan and Michael screwed that dumb chick's brains out after he ran home to his mommy. Why didn't you just say so in the first place, instead of beating around the bush?"

"I'm not saying that. I'm just saying . . . I don't know what I'm saying. I'm so confused, Michael."

Michael walks over and finally sits himself down on the couch, but right up next to me.

"I want to say something, Nick. You listening? Good, because I'm going to say this once and once only. After you left Jonathan and I did nothing with that chick. You got me? Christ, for all we know maybe you hung around and came back for seconds."

"That's so crazy . . ."

"Why is it so crazy? According to you, you did nothing? But she wants to lay a charge against all of us. Explain that to me."

"I can't. What are we going to do, Michael?"

"I dunno. But I'm working on it."

"Working on it how?"

"Well, let's just say we all had a little chat."

"Who is we?"

"Tracy, her mom, my dad and me."

"You serious? You told your dad?"

"I didn't have any choice, buddy."

"And what did they all say?"

"We explained to them that it's all one big misunderstanding."

"And they believe you?"

"Like I said, we're working on it," says Michael, rubbing his fingers together.

"You gave them money? So they won't lay a charge?"

"That's what we're hoping."

"How much do you have to give them?"

"Way more than you can afford."

"What ever it is, Michael, I swear I'll pay you back. I can't believe you did all this for me?"

"I know you would do the same."

I stare dumbly at Michael. "But still . . ."

"We've got to put this behind us, Nick. How were we supposed to know she's a gold-digging slut. That's all there's to it."

"This whole thing has been worrying me. Ever since that night . . ."

"You think it hasn't been worrying me? You won't believe it, but I honestly thought maybe you had gone back after we left. I thought that's why you've been avoiding my phone calls. And meanwhile you're thinking the same bad things about me. Crazy, hey? I swear, this is what happens when buddies don't trust each other."

I manage to squeeze out a pathetic laugh. "It is crazy. So are you saying I don't have to worry? It's all over?"

"Sort of. She could change her mind any minute."

"But you gave them money?"

"I said we offered them money. We're still waiting to hear. By the way, you haven't blabbed off to Sean, have you?

"Why would I do that?"

"He is your best buddy."

"I'm not sure about that anymore."

"How so?"

"Just stuff that's happened between us lately."

"Seriously, you can't squeak a word to him. If he finds out he'll cause shit. That I promise you."

"Why do you say that?"

"Because he has something against me. He's jealous of our friendship."

"That's what I told him."

"Really?"

"Ja."

"That must be it then. You get people like that in this world. Seriously, Nick, can I trust you to keep this secret?"

"Of course you can."

"Say it."

"What?"

"That you promise you won't say anything."

"I promise I won't say anything."

Michael takes hold of my hand, holds it to his chest and looks me straight in the eyes.

"And I swear, I will do whatever it takes to get us out of this mess."

247

THIRTY - FIVE

The Phoenix looks like it has always looked. A leprosy victim. The plaster on the high side wall is peeling off; they never did invent a ladder long enough to paint that wall. The front of the building doesn't look much better; that's what happens if you don't prep properly. The glass doors where we used to queue up, they've been plastered over with God-squad posters. There are torn and scraped-off bits where someone's tried to remove them. The windows of the Romanos' old flat have been smashed. The metal staircase is still there.

Who would have thought, old Tony Romano making a success of his life? And from what I heard from Simon, all above board and legal. The one guy you're dead-cert will end up behind bars like his brother instead ends up a Catholic priest in a township outside Joburg, setting up feeding schemes and doing good work among the poor. Like I always maintain, what you see is never what you get.

I leave the throbbing CBD behind and cross over the bridge. No matter what time of the year, before or after the rains, the river stays the colour of brown mud. No wonder Retief or whoever it was motoring past in their ox wagon named it the Sand. It's actually quite pretty if you stop and think about it, what with the willow trees and the weaver birds and the reflections on the water and the secret patches of soft green grass for fishing.

I make my way towards the industrial area. Because it's been so long and so much has changed, I end up driving round in circles before I find the place. But eventually I stumble on it at the end of a potholed gravel road that used to be a tar road, surrounded on all sides by rusty mine buildings.

The pine trees are much taller than I remember. Razor wire runs all the way round from either side of the iron gates. I didn't know there was a market for second-hand coffins and tombstones; or maybe it's the body parts they're after.

I park the Kia a little way from the iron gates. Apart from me there is one other car. Good. The last thing I need now is to be accompanied by a full-blown funeral procession.

I sit for a while, fighting off these waves of dread and some other emotion I can't put my finger on. I've been putting this off for thirty years, so you must understand it's not easy for me. I was hoping I would feel numb by the time I got here, that opposite emotions would cancel each other out. I light a cigarette, take a drag, then toss it out the window.

I'm not out the car and he's already there, a brommer to a freshly-laid turd, taking his first drag. A black guy in a beanie, a scar running down his check, looking chuffed with his score. He must have spotted me coming, seen the GP number plate coming from a mile away.

"Thank you, Captain. I like this Rothmans. You mustn't worry, I look nicely after your car." He's not asking me; he's telling me. "Too many skollies here. No work on the mines," he says, pointing to the sky.

"Your choice, china."

He can do what he wants; I've got more important things on my mind.

The gates and the pine trees and the crunching gravel under my feet are weirdly familiar. As if it's last night, Michael and me taking our midnight stroll.

I haven't counted on the fact that people also die like flies in small towns, because when I push open the gate I discover mile upon mile of graves stretching in every direction. For the next fifteen, twenty minutes I wander the narrow gravel pathways, becoming more and more desperate. There's no order to the place; the 1970s are mixed in with the 1990s and 2000s.

But then I see the pattern; I've just been going about it back to front. In no time I've narrowed my search to the '84s to '86s. I'm now off the gravel path, stepping between the graves. Next to a fading photo of a girl with blonde pigtails I find what I came for.

THIRTY - SIX

This thing with Michael, it's a tapeworm with a thousand heads. You chop off one and another ten grow in its place. And just when you think it can't get worse it does . . .

Because we've hardly sat down for supper when the doorbell goes. Simon sprints off to answer it. He's back a second later, but says nothing.

"So, who was it?"

"That guy . . ."

"Evening all." Again, it's like being whacked on the back of the head with a cricket bat. This time for a six. "I hope I'm not interrupting."

My dad wipes his mouth and leaps up and walks round the table.

"Not at all."

"Hi, Mr Theron, I'm Michael Dempsey."

"Ja, of course, Michael. Lekker to finally meet you." My dad shakes Michael's hand. "You're just in time for some graze."

"I don't want to impose or anything . . ."

"Nonsense. Grab a seat. There's plenty to go round. You like macaroni and cheese?"

"What a question, Mr Theron."

"Well then, grab a seat, pal."

And my dad pulls out a chair at the head of the table and Michael slides into it.

"You sure I'm not imposing?"

"A hundred-and-ten per cent sure."

"Hullo, Nick," says Michael.

"Hi."

"So . . ." My dad's the only one chuffed to have an uninvited guest for supper. For once Simon and me feel the same way; you would swear Michael's got fangs he's moved up so close to my dad. "You'll be interested to know we sat next to your folks at the mine dinner."

"Yes, they mentioned it, Mr Theron. Apparently it was quite a blast."

"Ja, it was good. I'll tell you one thing. Your mom and dad know how to have a skop."

"That they do. They also really enjoyed meeting you and Mrs Theron."

"They did? Nice to hear."

Before Michael has a chance to lay it on any thicker, my mom walks in, carrying the tray with the macaroni and cheese. Michael jumps up.

"Hi, Mrs Theron. Let me help you with that."

My mom's done this a thousand times before but she hands the tray to Michael.

"Mind moving that jug of orange juice, Nick. Thanks, buddy."

"It's Oros, not orange juice," says Simon.

"Ja, just put it there, Michael," my dad says, looking impressed. "Isabel, this is Michael Dempsey."

"Of course, nice to meet you, Michael. We met your parents just the other day."

"Dad's already told him," says Simon.

"I hope you're staying for a bite to eat."

"I've already twisted the guy's arm. Told him your MC is the best thing this side of Italy," says my dad, and winks at Michael, who winks back.

"That's if you don't mind, Mrs Theron?"

"Of course not. I can't believe we haven't met before. Nick's told us a lot about you."

"Hopefully not all bad."

"Quite the opposite. Nick, why don't you fetch an extra plate and cutlery for your friend?"

"Thanks, Nick, you're a star," says Michael, as I walk past him.

I take my time in the kitchen because I need to get my head straight. It's like being eaten from the inside out. While I'm digging around for a clean knife and fork my dad and mom are cackling over something Michael's said. I move closer to the door and stand there listening.

"I don't know what my dad was thinking, but he leaned over

to pay the gondolier and the next thing we hear is this massive splash. We turn around and there's my dad treading water and looking like a drowned rat."

"Goodness me," says my mom, her hand still over her mouth as I walk back into the room. "He must have been so embarrassed."

"Thanks, Nick," says Michael. "That wasn't the half of it. He had his wallet and passport on him at the time."

"Hell," my dad says, shaking his head. Even Simon is interested in Michael's story. "And? Did the old man manage to save them in the end?"

"Lucky for my dad he didn't spend too much time in the water. But to cut a long story short we spent the rest of the day in the hotel room blow-drying my dad's passport and a wad of traveller's cheques."

"That's really funny," says my mom. "You tell a good story."

My dad gives the sign. We close our eyes. "For what we are about to receive, may the Lord make us truly thankful. Amen. Tuck in, pal. What you think, Simon? Quite a story, hey? Blow-drying traveller's cheques. I like that."

"It's funny, Dad."

"This macaroni is really tasty, Mrs Theron. It beats anything my mom's ever made."

"Told you it's the best thing this side of Italy."

"I'm sure your mom is an excellent cook, Michael."

"No, seriously. My mom's not one for the kitchen. What with my parents' careers and all we don't get to spend much quality time sitting around the table like this. It's really great. Again, thanks for having me."

"Try telling these two here that mealtimes are quality times," says my dad, waving his fork in our direction. "You're spot on, we're blessed."

"I suppose you only miss something when you no longer have it," says Michael.

"That's no lie." My dad gives my mom a look across the table. "You guys should take a page out of Michael's book."

"Can I have another roll, Mom?"

"Perhaps first ask Michael if he wants one, Simey."

"Do you want a roll?"

"I'm fine for now." Simon stretches across. "Maybe a little later," says Michael.

"Wait a little while, sweetie," my mom says.

"But I want one."

"Simon! So, Michael, what do you plan to do after school?"

My dad's favourite topic.

"I'm thinking of going into law. Or maybe medicine at UCT. I still need to decide."

"I can see you doing both."

"You really think so?"

"Ja, I do. If you want my opinion, I'd go the law route. Much more dosh in it. Unless you're a plastic surgeon or something like that."

"I suppose I want to help people. That's why I thought medicine. But you're right, with law one can also do good."

"That's a nice thought, Michael," says my mom.

"No really, I know it sounds stupid, but I have this need to give something back."

I can't believe my mom and dad are lapping up Michael's every word.

"It's not stupid at all. It's very mature. Have some dressing."

"Thanks, Mrs Theron. I just don't think people appreciate what they have. I'm not even talking materialistic things. Like, what you guys have here, most people take it for granted. But it's only when you don't have it that you realise how important it is."

"You're spot on the button there, Michael. It's the small things . . ."

"Exactly, Mr Theron, that's what I'm trying to say. I mean, take one's friendships . . . Maybe it's old fashioned, but things like loyalty and honesty and standing up for each other. Things like that mean a lot to me."

"They mean a lot to me too, Michael." I can't help myself, it just comes out.

"That's not old-fashioned, pal," continues my dad as if I'm not there. "What you're talking there is real values. Not throwaway values. That's the problem with this country . . ."

"I like that, Mr Theron. 'Throwaway values'. That's a good word for it."

"Twenty bucks and it's yours. Only kidding." My dad stretches over me for the salt. "Well, all I can say, Michael, with values like that you've got a future ahead of you."

"Thanks, sir, I appreciate it. By the way, the dressing was really good, Mrs Theron. You must give the recipe to my mom." Michael pierces a baby tomato onto his fork. My mom stands up to clear the plates. I watch Michael chew slowly on his last mouthful. He swallows, then winks at me across the table.

A month later we get up from the table.

"Michael," my dad says. "A pleasure meeting you. I'll be honest, Nick is privileged to have a friend like you."

"Thanks, Mr Theron. Nick and Simon here are privileged to have you as parents. And thanks again for dinner – it was excellent."

After my dad and Michael have shaken hands and told each other how great they are, blah, blah, blah, I lead the way to the front door.

"You want to walk with me part of the way?" he says.

"Didn't you come by car?"

"No. We need to talk."

"Can't we talk now?"

Michael looks past me. "As long you don't mind your brother listening in."

I turn around. Simon, standing a few meters away, watching us.

"What do you want, Simon?"

"Nothing."

"In that case, scram! Okay, then, I'll walk with you to the end of the road."

Michael makes small talk all the way to the bus shelter on the corner of Hibiscus Avenue. Someone's carved *PFP se Moer* in fat letters along the one side.

"I'm going back to school on Sunday."

"I didn't know that."

"That's why I'm telling you now. And it doesn't look like I'll be coming back."

"What, not even for holidays?"

"Definitely not for holidays. My dad's been offered his old job back and chances are they'll be long gone from here before our next school break."

"But what about this thing? Have you heard anything more from them?"

"No, nothing."

"It's still really worrying me, Michael. What must we do now?"

"I don't know. We just have to wait."

"You act so relaxed about it. What if they change their minds and go to the police? Then what?"

"Guess we'll just have to face the music. Not so, Nick? I've done everything I can. What more do you want?"

"I don't know . . . Can't you maybe speak to them again to make sure everything is okay?"

"Listen, why don't you speak to them?"

"Me?"

"Ja, why not? I'll give you the phone number."

"You know I can't do that, Michael. Sorry, I'm just worried, that's all."

"And you think I'm not? If only you knew what I've been going through. I just don't show it, that's all."

"I said I'm sorry."

"It's okay. Shit, you guys weren't kidding about those ears in the shoebox."

"You saw them? Who showed you?"

"Old Edward himself. Talk about gross. Especially that necklace."

"You speak like Eddie and you have become big buddies?"

"The boy's a hoot. I like him."

"Eddie didn't say anything to me."

"Since when must Eddie report to you?"

"I just like to know what's going on."

"Now you know. The whole time you've been saying Sean would take a bullet for you. You're wrong. Eddie's the one who would actually do it. But you're right about his brother. He's a total psycho."

"You met Luke?"

"Oh, yes."

"Like, when?"

"Let me think now . . . Must have been when you were on your boy scout outing. Which reminds me, you still haven't thanked my dad for helping you out."

"We're still going to. We just haven't got round to it . . ."

"Don't go to too much trouble."

"I promise we will do it before you guys leave . . ."

"Forget it, this is getting boring. I was just thinking, now that I'm leaving and all we should do something together. You know, like my way of saying sorry for the all the crap I've caused you."

"That's no lie."

"You won't believe me, Nick, but I feel bad about the way things have turned out. I want us to end on a good note. I feel I owe you guys. You and Sean especially."

"You don't owe us anything."

"No, but I do. Do you want to hear my idea?"

"If you insist."

"Okay, you know my dad brought his boat down from the Vaal?"

"You told me."

"So I thought why don't we hang out for the day at the dam? It will be a total blast. Imagine – we can cruise up and down, drink a couple of frosties, a braai afterwards . . . What you think?"

"I don't know if Sean will be so keen."

"Of course he will be. Especially when you tell him about the boat. You must see this thing, Nick. It's a beast. What's more, none of you have to lift a finger. I'll organise the whole tootie. What you say?"

"I'll think about it."

"And you'll also talk to Sean? We can do it day after tomorrow."

"I'll try. But I can't promise."

Michael looks at his watch.

"I had better get moving. I told the folks I would be back ages ago. So I'll see you boys on Thursday?"

"I said I'll try."

"And I know you won't let me down. You're a good guy, Nick. You know that?"

"Sometimes I wonder."

"You are. You mustn't forget it."

And Michael turns and walks away.

THIRTY - SEVEN

Eddie's gate has been like this since day dot. I would have gone crazy ages ago because chalk scraping on a black board is nothing compared to metal on cement. The rottweiler-cross-pavement-special next door goes ballistic every time someone opens the gate, so he must feel the same as I do. Lucky he's kept chained to the washing line.

I bang on the door, ready to give it to Eddie for not telling me about Michael, but it's Luke who opens. All this time I've been thinking he's gone back to the border by now.

"Howzit, boet," Luke says in that deep voice of his. "You

looking for Edward?"

"Ja, is he in?"

"Dunno. I've just woken up from a kip."

"Sorry."

"No worries. I had to get up for the door, anyway. Come inside."

I follow Luke's shoulders into the house. He's wearing a pair of black PT shorts, nothing else. Not even jocks, by the looks of it.

"Edwardo!"

I trail after Luke into the kitchen and its usual mess of breadcrumbs and an open tin of Bully Beef on the table, and the dishes piled up to the ceiling. I would go nuts living here. We head down the passage to Eddie's room, neither of us saying anything. I never know what to say to Luke and he's hardly ever in the mood to talk. There's no sign of Eddie. I could have told Luke he's not here, but I go through the motions so he doesn't think I'm impolite.

"Doesn't look like Eddie's here, Luke."

"I scheme you're right. You want to wait for him? Maybe he'll be back soon."

"Ja, okay. I'll wait a couple of minutes."

"Lekker."

I follow Luke back down the passage, kicking myself for saying I'll wait because now I have no choice in the matter.

"Come park off in the lounge."

"Ja, okay." I'm feeling as awkward as all hell now.

Luke walks over and switches on the TV. He flicks over to TV1. "Same old kak." I'm praying he keeps the TV on so we have something to distract us. Luke falls onto the couch with a heavy sigh. "Gooi my smokes this end, wont you?" I reach over and pass him his Texans. "Only four left. Must send my boet to get me some more. You want one?"

"I'm fine, thanks."

"Good choice. These things are bad news." Luke lights up and lets out a cloud of smoke through his nose. He must have lungs of steel. We both stare at the TV. Me and Luke Scheepers watching *Liewe Heksie* together. "Hey, did you already get a load of my boet's new Walkman?" Luke aims his toe at the dining room table. "Check it out. Apparently it's last year's model. Dolby stereo, techno crap like that. It's got the works."

"Can I have a look?"

"Sure thing. You must have seen my boet's face. Chuffed as all hell, I'm telling you."

The Walkman is still in a box. I slide it out. It's almost brand new. "It's even smaller than I thought."

"Kief, hey. How those headphones?" It is kief. More kief than anything I've seen in a long time. And I'm not exaggerating. "I swear, you need a fokken diploma in rocket science to understand all the functions. You must get Edward to give you a demonstration."

"Has Sean seen it?"

"Nah, Eddie just got it. Lucky poes or what?"

I turn the Walkman over in my hands. "How much does something like this cost, Luke?"

"You asking me?"

"Didn't you buy it for Eddie?"

"You mad? Not on my army packet. That new chommie of yours . . . He's the one who gave it to my boet. Just like that." Luke snaps his fingers.

"Who?" Now I'm seriously confused.

"That tall oke, man. The kaaskop . . . ?"

"You mean Michael Dempsey?"

"Ja, Michael, that's his name. Nice oke or what, hey? Don't worry, I also couldn't believe it."

I stare dumbly as Luke lights up another Texan plain.

THIRTY - EIGHT

There's a photo in one of our albums, of Sean and me standing together in one of those blow-up swimming pools with fish swimming around the bottom. You would think we were twins, both with the same straight white hair and podgy legs and baby boeps. Sean is holding the fish net and I'm holding the bucket for the imaginary fish we are catching. The photo was taken in the front yard of our old house. Sean and me have been best friends since we were this high and that's all that matters. If you can't tell your best friend stuff, who can you tell? At least that's how I see it.

I find Sean sitting at his workbench, with a soldering iron in his hand. Sean will die with a soldering iron in his hand.

"Hi, Sean."

Sean stops what he's doing and turns around.

"Oh, it's you."

I can tell by his face I'm the last person he expected to see.

"Who did you think it was?"

"I don't know. Just not you."

"Thanks a lot."

"I didn't mean it like that." Sean unplugs the soldering iron and stands up. "You want to sit?"

"I'm okay." I stay standing at the door. Maybe this wasn't such a great idea.

"I was actually thinking of phoning you," he says.

He must see the doubt on my face.

"I was. I've been feeling crap about all the stuff we said to each other on the team-build."

When Sean says this and he smiles his gap-tooth smile, the heavy load I've been lugging around evaporates.

"I've also been feeling crap about it, Sean."

"Seriously?"

"Seriously. I've been acting like a doos. I don't blame you for not wanting to speak to me."

"That's not it. I've been wanting to speak to you. It's just that I'm confused lately. I can't get my head straight."

"Tell me about it. But I'm the doos."

"No, you're not, I am."

"No, I am."

For the next ten minutes Sean and me argue who's the biggest doos: him or me.

"Do me a favour, won't you?"

"Anything Sean."

"Hold this wire for me while I quickly finish soldering."

"Like this?"

"Ja. But not too close or you'll bugger up the circuit board."

"What you making?"

"A remote control for the garage. I don't know if it will work."

"It will work, Seanie."

"You scheme?"

"Definitely. You're the one making it."

"More to the left. You're breathing down my neck."

"Sorry."

"It's okay."

"What's this playing?"

"The new Bad Company. I bought it yesterday. What you think?"

"Very kief. Where did you buy if from?"

"Manos. They've got some good stuff in. You can let go now."

I watch Sean blowing the wire for a while.

"I've just had a brainwave."

"What?"

"Are you hungry?"

"Is a pancake flat? Why you ask?"

"Why don't we hit the Ranch for a burger? I'm sticking."

"You serious? With what?"

"My birthday money. I got fifty bucks."

"I can do this later. What are we waiting for?"

All the way to the Ranch, with Sean pedalling and me on the back with my takkies dragging along the dirt and rocking the bike from side to side, we debate what we're going to eat and who's going to stick who. And it's like old times again when it was just Sean and me and we could mess around and say what we wanted to each other and not care. Sean will think I want something if I tell him, but there's no denying it: I don't know what I would do if he wasn't in my life.

The Ranch is a total dump, but the burgers are brilliant. Everything in the place is imitation Wild West, including the owner, Johnnie Silver, whose real name is Johan Da Silva. The waiters have to wear paper cowboy hats and speak in an American accent, which sounds dumb because most of them are rockspiders. It's the cheesiest restaurant in the world.

"Howdy folks, what can we do you for?" says the bored-looking waitress after we've sat down and looked at the menu. Because it's four o' clock in the afternoon we have the place to ourselves. Sean and me know already what we are going to have. Bounty Hunters, with extra chips on the side. "Anything to drink with that, folks?"

Sean asks for a Tarbrush Soda and I order a Slime Creek, which are just other words for Coke and Creme Soda floats. Like I said, the place is totally over the top.

We talk about this and that, about the camp with Mr Stevens, about school starting next week, something I don't want to think about right now, about the garage remote-control thing Sean's busy building.

When the burgers arrive Sean takes a massive bite, dislocating his jaw in the process and squirting tomato sauce down his chin. He wipes his hand across his mouth.

"This was one of your better ideas."

"Definitely."

"I spoke to Adele on the phone."

"Is it? I thought she was on netball camp."

"She is. She phoned me from a tikkie box at the hostel."

"What did she have to say?"

"Send the tomato sauce this way, won't you? We couldn't speak long because the phone kept chowing her money. She said she misses me. How's that, hey? And here I am thinking she never wants to see my face again."

"That's great, Sean."

"Ja, and we've organised to do something when she gets back on the weekend. It's like I've been on this high ever since. It's going to be so lekker to see her again."

"That's so great."

"She also said she wants to talk to me about something important."

"Like what?"

"I don't know. She just said it's lank important. I don't want to get my hopes up but maybe she wants to go steady."

"Sounds like it."

"I should buy her a gold chain or something? What you reckon?"

"Ja, why not?"

"You don't think it will make me look desperate?"

"No ways. You should do it."

"Okay, maybe I will then."

"I'm chuffed for you, Sean. I can see you and Adele together."

"Me too."

"Everything good with you, folks?" interrupts the bored-looking waitress. She's been working at the Ranch for years. Eddie once tried to get a job here so he could eat as many free burgers as he wanted, but they fired him after one day because he messed up the orders so bad.

"Sean, there's something I need to talk to you about."

"I know."

"How did you know?"

"Dunno. Just did. You not eating those chips?" I slide the plate across the table. "Okay, I'm ready."

I take a deep breath. I hardly know where to begin.

"Something happened after the party . . ."

And so I start giving Sean the details, starting from the moment he left Turbo.

"Shit, I wish you hadn't told me this," says Sean, once I've gone over the whole story for the second time.

"I'm sorry, but I just didn't know what else to do. Michael said I must promise not to tell you."

"Why?"

"I don't know. He thinks you will cause shit for him or something like that."

"Maybe I should."

"Please, Sean, you mustn't do that. Michael's doing everything he can."

"I wasn't serious. So what are you guys going to do?"

"Michael says he's working on it. He says we just have to sit tight and not panic."

"Have you told Eddie?"

"No."

I've already decided not to tell Sean about the Walkman. It will just confuse matters.

A mom and dad and two kids enter the Ranch and start walking around the place trying to make up their minds where to sit. The youngest kid is trailing after them and picking his nose at the same time. They circle around for five hours before plonking themselves in the booth next to us. That's how people are in this town. No idea.

"Michael wants to treat us."

"Treat us? Why would he want to do that?"

"He's going back to school on Sunday and says he wants to end off on a good note. Apparently he's not coming back."

"At last some good news."

"For once you're right. His dad's accepted some other job and they're going to move in a few months time."

"But they just got here."

"I know. Crazy, hey? That's how they are."

"How does he so-called want to treat us?"

"He's going to take us out on his dad's boat. You must see this thing, Sean. It's got twin engines . . ."

"Have you seen it?"

"Not yet, but Michael's says it's a beast. He says you'll go crazy for it."

"Does he now?"

"Ja. And he said he'll organise the whole thing, including a braai for after. All we have to do is pitch up at the dam, that's it. It could be quite fun, don't you think?"

"I don't know . . ."

"I say we just do it, Sean, and then we put everything behind us and start fresh. I swear, I just want things to be normal again, like they were before Michael pitched on the scene. Like you, Eddie and me used to be. I know you also want that?"

"You really know how to choose them, Nick."

"Thanks a lot."

"Pleasure."

"So will you come?"

"I'll think about it. You want anything more or should we make like Norris and chuck."

Sean looks around for the waitress. She's behind the counter, chatting up the griller. Sean catches her eye and she makes her way slowly towards us. You would swear she's doing us a huge favour.

"So, have you thought about it?"

"Okay, I'll come. But . . ."

"What?"

"I swear to God, this is the last time I'm doing anything with you guys."

THIRTY - NINE

We see the boat before we see Michael. He wasn't lying – it's a beast of a thing, with chrome railings and white leather seats and two mean black Mercury engines sticking out the back. *Annabelle* is splashed in red down the side.

"Did I tell you or did I tell you!"

We work our way through the tangle of yachts parked on the grass, down to the water.

"This way, dudes!"

Michael jogs up the jetty to greet us.

What with the boat and the morning sun reflecting off the dam, and Michael in his khaki baggies and cut-off T-shirt and cap turned back to front, it's something out of a Stuyvesant advert. That's until Eddie steps in front of the camera.

"Kief boat, china!"

"Glad you like it. So how are the lads doing? It's great to see you, really great." Michael goes around shaking our hands, first Sean, then Eddie, then me. He's in a seriously good mood. "I'm chuffed you could make it, Sean."

"Thanks for inviting me."

"And how's this weather? To think in a few days I'll be back in the smog of Joburg. You boys have something really good here."

"I told you it's not so bad, Michael."

"And you were right, Nick. So, are we ready to hit the water? Fantasimo, it's going to be fun. I've planned a big day for us. But, first things first. Eddie!"

"Ja, Kaptein!"

"Can I ask to you carry that fuel tank?" Eddie leaps at the opportunity to rip off his T-shirt. Michael points to another heap of stuff on the grass. "And Sean, mind loading the skis and harness? Nick, you can bring the cool box and braai goodies."

"Geez, when did you organise all this, Michael? You're making us feel bad."

"Like I told you, my treat. Okay, I think we have everything. Let's do it!"

Eddie climbs on first. "Check this thing out, kêrels."

"It's something from *Star Trek*, hey Sean? Must we take our slops off, Michael?"

"Don't worry, whatever. Just make yourselves at home."

"We don't even have a bladdy couch like this at home."

"Hey, Eddie, pack the beers in the fridge, won't you?"

"Ja, like this boat has a fridge."

"Michael's not bullshitting, Eddie. There, under the steering wheel. Where do you want us to sit, Michael?"

"Wherever you want, but try spread the load. Maybe you sit this side, Sean." Michael rips off his T-shirt and tosses it to the front. He's seriously ripped. Much more than Sean who is more chunky-like. And he hardly works out. "Okay, let's fire up this baby."

The Dempseys' boat isn't one of those putt-putt lawnmowers where you have to pull the rope for hours to get it started. Michael turns the key and a split-second later the Mercury engines kick into life. He guns the throttle, blasting a cloud of oily blue smoke across the water. We haven't even left the jetty and Sean and me are already gripping the handrail.

"Impressive or what, hey, Seanie?" Sean nods. "Eddie, you better move it."

"No rush, Edward," says Michael, idling the engines.

Eddie unpacks the last of the beers into the fridge, then grabs a seat at the front of the boat.

"I still can't believe your dad lets you take this thing out on your own."

"S'true. My toppie never even let me use his pliers without holding the other end."

Michael manoeuvres the boat away from the jetty, and then turns the nose until it's nothing but us and open water, with the mine dumps and old Number Three shaft way in the distance. Only when you're on the water do you realise how big Flamingo Dam is. It's the only decent thing about this town. Besides the river, that is.

Michael pulls back on the throttle and a second later we're flying across the water.

I swear, it's like sitting on a rocket. I'm crapping myself and it's the most amazing feeling ever. We're soon going so fast the only things in the water are the Mercuries. Michael gets into it big time, throwing moves, carving into the corners and giving it stick on the straights. Up front, Eddie's hair is standing up straight and his knuckles are white from gripping so tight – he could be an advert for the electric chair. One second I'm praying we're not going to die, the next I'm screaming at Michael to go faster. I look across at Sean; he's smiling into the wind and his teeth are clenched like that *Life* magazine photo of the guy in a wind tunnel.

Michael seems to know what he's doing; the speedboat handles everything he throws at it. In no time we're at the other end of the dam and Michael cuts back on the power.

"How was that?"

"That was flipping incredible, Michael! What you reckon, Seanie?"

"Ja, it was amazing. How many horsepower are in those things?"

"One-fifty in total."

"Shit, that's huge. We must have been going at least a hundred kays."

"Feels like it, doesn't it? What you boys say we cruise around some more and then stop off somewhere for an early braai? Don't know about you but I'm starving." We all agree it's a plan. We're so fired up with adrenaline that even Sean's starting to have a good time. "Sean, why don't you have a go at the wheel?"

"You mean it?"

"Why wouldn't I mean it? It's all yours."

"Go for it, Sean." I'm chuffed for Sean, because I know he can do it.

"I won't say no, Michael."

While Michael shows Sean the ropes I pull off my T-shirt and lie back, taking in the morning sun on my face, the water gently slapping the side of the boat. This is exactly the fresh start I was telling Sean about.

Sean gets the hang of it in no time and we're soon cruising at a rate again. I chuck Sean the thumbs-up. He's totally in his element, his hair wild in the wind, this fat smile plastered across his face.

"Where we gonna braai?" Eddie shouts across to Michael.

"How about we head for that island?"

"I thought speed boats aren't allowed there."

"I don't see anyone to stop us. Hey, Captain, head yonder."

Sean brings the boat round in a long slow arc and heads towards the bird reserve. It's this real Robinson Crusoe island with its own little beach and all. As we pull up close a flock of flamingos scatter in all directions; they don't know what's hit them. Michael takes over from Sean and cuts the engine. We drift towards the beach, known as the Blue Lagoon ever since that movie with that superhot actress Brooke Shields. Michael tosses Eddie the mooring rope.

"You do the honours, Edward."

Eddie dives into the water, not even bothering to check if it's deep enough. He swims the rope to shore and makes a big Camel man show of wrapping it around a thorn tree.

"Nice one, boytjie! Right, let's get ourselves sorted."

Michael has come fully organised, right down to the matches and braai grid. We unload the stuff and set up camp on the sand and go around collecting rocks for the braai, which Sean packs into a circle.

"Who's for a frostie?"

"What a kwessie?"

Michael hands out two beers each.

"Jissus, my hands will get frostbite if I stand here holding mine too long."

We wait for Michael to get back from the boat and open his first.

"Well, lads . . . What can I say, except that it's been great knowing you all. Even you, Seanie." Michael winks at Sean, who gives him this lame smile back. "Only kidding. No really, it's been a blast. I'm actually quite sorry to be leaving."

"Then you should stay, man."

"Thanks, but no thanks. It's been a bit of a weird holiday . . ."

"That's no lie," I say, and we all laugh about that because it's true.

"And I know you probably think I'm a wanker. Especially Sean here."

"I never said that."

"You don't have to say it. But it doesn't matter because past is past. What do you say?"

"I'll drink to that."

"Me too."

"What about you, Sean?"

"No problem this side."

"Glad to hear." It's quite a sombre moment, us four guys standing on the island, staring at the sand, not knowing what to say, the flamingos checking us out from a distance. All I know is my mouth feels like a parrot cage because I haven't drunk a thing since waking up. "Well then, let's enjoy ourselves!"

We down our first beer at a rate and switch over to the second. We're on the third before the fire's even lit. Michael puts Sean and Eddie in charge of the braai and they're soon chirping happily away. In no time I'm also floating around in this fuzzy space, the sun and the beer getting to me. Everything will end up okay; Sean, Eddie and me can start fresh when Michael leaves for Joburg. I'm not even going to mention the word "Walkman" to Eddie. From this second past is past.

Sean and Eddie go off to find more wood.

"Thanks for organising all this, Michael."

"For you, buddy, anything. All's well that ends well."

"I hope so."

"You don't sound convinced?"

"I'm fine. Even though this thing's still worrying me."

"What thing?"

"You know, what happened with that girl and all."

"Oh that."

"Have you heard anything more?"

"Not a thing."

"And you're not worried? What happens if you leave and they suddenly decide to change their minds? What do we do then?"

"Drink another beer."

"Shit, I can't believe you can act so relaxed."

"Nick."

I sit up, the flies getting to me now.

"What?"

"Can I tell you something?"

"Sure."

"I was pulling your leg."

"About what?"

"The whole thing. The charge, the meeting, the money."

"Sorry, I don't know what you mean."

"I was having you on. Kidding, bullshitting, pulling your leg, arsing around . . ."

"You telling me none of it is true?"

"That's what I'm saying, buddy."

"Hang on, I'm confused here. Are you're saying she never wanted to lay a charge against us in the first place? That you made it all up?"

"Hey, finally, you've got it. If only you could see your face right now. Seriously confused. Come on, at least I told you. You have to admit, I got you good and proper!"

"You're such a bastard, Michael. I just can't believe you would do something like that. It's not bladdy funny!"

"I think it's hilarious."

"Of course you do. Meantime I can't even sleep at night I'm so worried."

"Not my problem you take things so seriously."

"I swear, you're something else, you know that? I'm really glad you're leaving. There, I've said it, and I won't take it back."

"You don't need to. I'm also glad to be leaving. Oh, come on, stop being such a wet. You must learn to laugh at yourself once in a while."

"All I want to know is why me, Michael? Why us?"

"What you mean?"

"Don't act so innocent. Why did you choose me to be friends with?"

"Because I liked the look of you, that's why? I thought you were different to the rest of them. Believe it or not."

"You just see everyone as a puppet. You don't even know what a real friend is . . ."

Right now, I could vomit. I seriously could. My head is pounding like crazy and I feel naar to my stomach.

"Come now, don't get all heavy on me. Anyway, here they come. Hey, guys! I see you had some luck?"

Sean and Eddie appear from out the bush, dragging a massive dead branch behind them.

"Ja, we scored big time."

Eddie tosses the branch down and knocks over my beer in

the process.

"Now, why the fuck did you have to do that, Eddie!"

"Sorry, china. I didn't see it."

"Is that all you can say? Sorry? Why don't you just look for a change? There's beer all over the place now."

"Nick, Eddie said he's sorry. What's been going on here?"

"You're such a moegoe, Eddie. Nothing's been going on, Sean."

"I said I'm sorry, Nick."

"Here, you can have mine."

"I don't want yours, Sean."

"Hey, guys, there's plenty more where they came from."

"That's not the point, Michael. Ag, just forget it."

Sean squats down and pokes at the fire, shifting the coals around.

"Edward, fetch Nick another beer."

"He can fetch it himself."

"And make sure it's a cold one."

Eddie takes his time walking over to the boat. Sean carries on poking at the coals.

"The fire looks ready. Michael, can I put your meat on?"

"You're braai master. Do as you please."

"What's the story, Nick?"

"There's no story, Sean."

"Doesn't look that way to me."

"Nick's peeved off with me. And just when we were starting to have a good time."

"Why, what happened?"

"Sean, I really don't feel like talking about it."

"In that case pass the grid."

"Whatever."

"Come on, Nick, stop acting like a doos. Careful with the grid, man. You're going to drop the wors in the sand."

"As if I care."

"Here's your beer, Nick," says Eddie.

"I don't want it."

"He doesn't want it, Michael."

"In that case, I'll have it," says Michael. "Cheers, guys. To our futures and all that." Sean, Eddie and Michael clink bottles over the fire. "Who knows what they're going to bring."

"Lekker stuff, I scheme. I'm going to be rich and famous."

"Doing what, Eddie?"

"I dunno. I'll think of something. You watch."

"Like robbing a bank? That's the only way you'll get rich and famous."

"*Touché*, Sean. Talking of the future, I just remembered something."

"What?"

"You still owe us a dare."

"No, I don't."

"Oh yes you do."

"It's true, Seanie, you do. From that night of the party."

"Thank you, Edward."

"It's too late now."

"It's never too late. Don't you remember my words?"

"Ja, you said you will think of something later."

"Exactly. And I reckon now is a good time as any. What do you say, Nick?"

"It's up to Sean." It's like that day with Simon all over again. I can just feel it coming, a black cloud building in the air.

"It's not up to Sean. It's up to us, the committee."

"You can't force him to do something he doesn't want to."

"Maybe so. Then again, where there's a will there's a way."

"Whatever that means. Eddie, can I have one of your smokes?"

Eddie tosses his box of Gunston my way. I don't feel so pissed off with him anymore. Not when he offers the whole box.

"You want one, Sean?"

"Thanks."

I hold the match to Sean and wait for him to light up, before lighting my own. It's not Dunhill but it's better than nothing. I hand Eddie his box.

"I'd say Sean doesn't have much choice in the matter. We all agreed on that?"

"Maybe it depends on the dare, Michael. It can't be something ridiculous."

"What's the dare going to be, Michael?" says Eddie. "Like a down-down or something?"

"This is bullshit."

"Why's it bullshit, Sean? You're a good sport, aren't you? Youth group leader, school colours in fishing, a shining example to others, etcetera, etcetera. If anyone is up for a dare, it should be you."

"Come on, Sean, don't be a wuss. Fair is fair, you took the dare."

"Jissus, Eddie, you're a poet and you don't even know it."

Eddie chucks me a zap sign, but a friendly one, and shoves a piece of raw wors into his mouth.

"So we all agree then?"

"I didn't say I agree. I said it's Sean's choice."

"I agree," says Eddie. "As long as it's something Sean can do."

Michael wipes the top of his beer and takes a slow sip.

"Right. What we've decided, Sean . . ."

"I like the 'we' bit."

"For your dare the jury has decided that after our braai . . ." Michael levels the sand and places his beer carefully down next to him. The guy loves dragging things out. "You will swim back to shore."

Eddie punches the sand.

"Swim back to shore. I like that! Time to bring out the flippers, china."

"You're not serious, Michael?"

"Of course I'm serious, Nick. Why, is there a problem?"

"The shore is miles away."

"Nonsense, it's not that far. Well, Sean, are you up for it?"

"Michael's bullshitting. You don't have to do it."

"Christ, can't you let the guy speak for himself?"

I see Eddie's full on into the idea. "You going to do it, Sean? I reckon you can do it easy."

Maybe Eddie's right. Sean can do it, no problem. So far he hasn't said a word. Just has that blank look on his face, the one he has when he goes into himself.

"If Sean does the dare, we'll follow him all the way in the boat, hey Michael?"

"Of course, Edward."

"In that case it's not such a bad dare, Sean. I also reckon you can easily do it."

"There we go, for once even Nick agrees."

Sean turns the grid over.

"Meat's ready."

"Do we take that as a yes?"

Sean looks up. He looks straight into Michael's eyes.

"I'll do it."

The breeze has picked up by the time we've polished off the

wors and the breadrolls and packed the stuff into the boat. I'm feeling a bit calmer, now that we're going back and I won't ever have to see Michael again after today.

"Is that everything?" Michael shouts from the boat. "In that case, *on y va*. Seanie boy, you ready?"

Sean's standing at the edge of the water, hugging himself to keep warm. He's stripped down to his rugby shorts and is pumped from all the weights he's been doing. I'm telling you, Sean's a brilliant guy.

"Go for it, Sean," shouts Eddie. "We'll be right behind you." He's also proud, even though he has a weird way of showing it.

"Good luck, Seanie."

Sean gives me a thumbs-up and before I have a chance to return the favour he's hit the water. He comes up and kicks straightaway into crawl, his favourite stroke, cutting through the water like it's no effort.

"I'm impressed. The guy has some backbone after all."

"Sean has more backbone than all of us put together, Michael."

Michael starts the engines. Eddie and me move to the front of the boat so we can see better.

"How long you think it will take him?"

"Ag, half an hour max."

"I scheme so too . . . Now what's wrong? Michael, why did you cut the engines?"

"Sorry, boys, I forgot my slops."

"I'll go get them."

"Not to worry, Nick. I also need to pee."

By the time Michael dawdles his way back and we finally get moving again the wind's kicking up white horses and slapping spray up the side of the boat.

"Now I feel naar," Eddie says. "I can't handle when a boat's like this."

"Blame Michael for taking so long. Anyway, serves you right for scoffing all the wors."

"I swear, Nick, I think I'm going to puke."

"Whatever you do make sure you don't puke on me." Just to be safe I move across to the other side. Eddie leans over the edge.

"What's the matter with him?"

"Says he wants to puke."

Come to think of it, I'm not feeling so good myself now.

"Edward! You hurl in this boat and I kill you. You understand?"

"He's fine, Michael. Please, let's just get going."

"Whatever you say, sire!"

Michael restarts the engines, reverses slowly and turns the boat around. It feels like forever and a day before we leave the island behind.

Eddie's now got his head between his knees. He looks up at me. He's not bullshitting; his face is albino white. I can't help laughing, even though my guts are turning to mush by the minute.

"Oh fok!" You would think Eddie's been stung by a wasp; he spins round and gets his head over the side of the boat without a split-second to spare. The puke comes out in a fat gush, not just once but three times. Beer mixed with chunks of wors, then a gallon of yellow liquid, and then just spit and air. The puke slick hangs around in our wake for a while, before disintegrating in the choppy water. Eddie sits up and wipes his mouth with the back of his hand.

"Now I feel lekker again."

"A waste of good beer, Edward. I should charge you for it."

We've been so caught up with Eddie's puking we've clean forgotten about Sean.

"Eddie, I can't see him. Michael, can you see Sean?"

"Not yet, buddy. He must be way ahead by now."

"You sure we haven't passed him already?"

"Hundred per cent. If you two clowns would get your act together maybe we can get going. What you say to that idea?"

"Ja, please, Michael, let's."

I try stand up to see better, but easier said than done, what with the choppy water and the boat rocking from side to side and the light drizzle that's come out of nowhere.

"Eddie, you must tell me if you see anything. You think he's in front of us?"

"I scheme so. We would have spotted him already."

Eddie's right – we would have spotted Sean already if we had passed him. It feels better if I tell myself that.

"Maybe we should go back just to make sure, Michael?"

Michael yanks the throttle, sending me flying.

"That's not funny, man."

And now the rain hits the dam big time, slapping the water with golf balls. Eddie dives for his vest. It's like being sandblasted alive.

"I say we vote to head back to shore," Michael shouts above the racket. "What you say, Edward?"

Eddie looks over at me. We're both crouching over by this time. "The oke's right, Nick. There's no point of sitting here getting pissed on. I bet Sean's long back and freezing his ballas off."

Michael guns the engine. "What's it going to be?"

"But what if he isn't, Eddie?"

"Then we'll pick him up on the way. Fok, but this rain stings!"

I look up at Michael, leaning into the rain, water streaming down his face, his mouth hanging half open, waiting for us to make a decision.

"You really think Sean's back already?"

"How can he not be, Nick? It's been ages."

"You're right."

"Of course I'm right. I reckon we gooi."

I look up at Michael.

"Let's go back!"

I don't remember much after that.

Except there's no Sean waiting on the jetty.

Except Michael takes his time parking the boat.

I hit the jetty running, chased by the pounding of loose planks, shouting Sean's name into the rain before I've reached the grass.

Eddie right behind me now as I slow up at the boat shed, checking between, under the boats. Nothing.

I look back at Eddie. Catch my fear in his eyes.

Past the clubhouse, the braai area, to the end of the yacht club, up to the razor-wire fence. No Sean.

"Carpark!" I follow Eddie, tracking the razor-wire, up and around the clubhouse, past the girls' bogs.

Mrs Dempsey's silver Ballade 105i parked on its lonesome in the gravel yard.

"Eddie, let's go back to the boats. Sean *has* to be there."

Eddie goes one way, me the other. Moving slower this time, bending down under the trailers, making double sure.

And then . . . something in the corner of my eye down near the water – Sean's head poking out from a canvas boat cover!

Sean spots me and shouts against the wind, "Hey, moegoe!

What flippin' kept you so long?"

Sprinting down the grass now, tripping over my own feet, dodging between the yachts, tears of rain and relief pouring down my cheeks.

I grab hold of Sean, catch him off balance, and give him this massive bear hug. We stand back from each other and swap high-fives. Over and over and over I tell him how good it is to see him . . .

But there's no Sean when I get there. Only a loose cover flapping in the wind.

I just stand there, the cold in my legs spreading slowly upwards, Eddie's shouting coming closer, the vibrating cables, masts, rain against zinc answering back.

FORTY

When I finally come around I'm lying curled up on Sean's grave, my cheek plastered in snot and gravel. Lucky there is nobody to witness the spectacle; if there was they would get on their cell and call Lifeline. I don't know how long I've been lying here. It could be minutes; it could be hours. My tears have dried and the autumn sun feels warm against my back.

Sean's grave is a nice simple one, nothing grand. A white marble tombstone with simple words from our favourite song. Someone has placed a small vase of daisies on the grave. They're still quite fresh. I'm half trying to work out who could have left them. After the mine crashed I thought everyone had left.

There is so much I want to tell Sean. About my life. My half-life. About dropping out of Tech and ending up a pen pusher in the army. About my messed up marriage to Andrea. About my divorce. About meeting Jenny last year at a battle of the bands. About my two kids, who I only get to see once a week if I'm lucky; they would have got on like a house on fire. Like a madman, out comes my wallet and the photos I carry of Josh and Mia, and I'm asking Sean doesn't he think they're cute, and when is he going to come visit us. You won't believe it, but now I start giggling like a village idiot. I tell him about Jen and her heart of gold, that she's a total hippie, and I don't know where I would be if I hadn't met her. And out comes the picture of us on honeymoon in the bush.

Of course, there's no answer, only this lonely silence coming from Sean's grave. My heart feels like it's being ripped in two.

But I'm not done yet. I haven't come all this way to talk about my family. The waterworks open up again and I have to really work hard to keep myself under control. I take another deep breath and carry on.

I tell Sean I wrote a long letter to his mom and dad apologising for not coming to his funeral, but I ended up not posting it. I want him to know this isn't about excuses. I don't want to be excused. There's no excuse for missing your best friend's funeral. It's just that after that day at the dam, I could hardly move. And that's how things have been for the last thirty years.

I've lost track of time sitting with Sean in this peaceful place. I don't want to leave. But eventually I sit up and look at my watch. It's getting late. I tell Sean I'm sorry, but I have to go because I have a plane to catch and I only took two days' leave and I have a sales meeting first thing tomorrow morning. I promise him I'll come back soon and this time I'm going to bring Jen and the kids, which I should have done in the first place with Andrea. I stand up and clean myself up. I must look a state. I walk slowly back towards the car, forcing myself to look straight ahead.

So that's how things end – six feet under a Syringa tree, at the arse end of the world.

There's no sign of my car guard. I soon work out the reason why: PG confetti scattered across the back seat.

It's weird; it's like I don't care, like brain and body are disconnected, like I'm watching myself go through the motions of what next: Report it. Get a case number. Claim the insurance when I get home. Problem solved.

My hand's on the ignition but it doesn't want to turn. Who was I kidding all these years? Believing it will, it must, eventually go away. But how can it when your soul is buried between a mine dump called Everust and a river called the Sand?

Way after the '94 elections I decided to visit Sean's parents in Shepstone. I went as far as booking the flight and hiring the car. Had it all worked out. I would kill two birds with one stone. Overlap it with a sales trip. Anyway, as my big date with Fate approaches, this fantasy of mine – I swear, that's what it was all along, nothing but a dumb fantasy – begins to fall apart. Who am I to offload onto two old fogies who've spent all these years trying to forget? An upcoming star in my own episode of the TRC? Besides, what was I going to say when the door to 104 Earl's Court opened? "Morning, Mr and Mrs Daniels. It's been a long time. I'm here to ask your forgiveness."

I cancelled the car and lost what I paid on the SAA ticket. And that's where I left it. Until that night at the Holiday Inn.

I had seriously better get moving now because I've been sitting here for ages, staring through the windscreen at this couple who've been here before me organising their flowers and pulling up the weeds and trimming the grass around the grave with pruners they've brought specially for the job. It must be a son or daughter. Maybe an only child. Who else would you put in so much effort for, besides your own kid?

About that night at the Holiday Inn . . . So here I am settling into Room 608, enjoying the Inn's facilities, taking a slow wallow after a day on the road, trying the different soaps and lotions, getting my money's worth. I don't know if they designed it that way, but with the bathroom door open I could watch TV at the same time – the Holiday Inn should advertise it on their brochure.

The Deluxe rooms have DSTV Compact, so I'm busy flicking through the channels, trying to keep the remote dry, and I end up at this program about a massive development going down in the Transkei, with Deborah Patta or some other bulldog presenter travelling up and down the coast interviewing stakeholders, those for and against progress.

I'm about to climb out the bath when who do I spot being interviewed? Ladies and gentlemen, the one and only . . . Michael Dempsey. I know straightaway it's him. Okay, he's put on about ten kilos and his cheeks are fatter and that chiselled look is long gone. But it's the same Michael alright. His face is tanned, from all the time he spends on the golf course and Tiffindell ski slopes. He still has some of his blonde hair, cut in with grey, and the Michael smile and Colgate teeth. And he's charming the panties off Deborah or whoever, telling her how much employment is going to be created by his golf estate and casino. How he's donating money from his own pocket to the local communities. When he turns to the camera and tells the world his vision for the Eastern Cape, it's typical Michael. At one point he's looking straight at me.

When I eventually lifted myself out of the bath the water was lukewarm and my skin grey and wrinkly and the sales convention dinner I was looking forward to the furthest thing from my mind. I've gone back in time and Michael is there with me, real and alive as anything I've ever known.

A couple of cop vans are parked in front of the police station. There's no visitors' parking. Or, at least I don't see one. Just a long yellow line running for miles in front of the station: official police vehicles only. I have no choice but to cross over and jump the pavement and park halfway in the veld.

Before I go in there's something I've got to do. I unlock the cubbyhole; more dedication and my car guard would have scored a cellphone. I dial the number. Eddie's mom answers. I haven't heard her voice in three decades. It's the Rod Stewart voice of the dying. Emphysema. Two packs a day. How many years. That's a double highway running through the lungs.

"Can I speak to Eddie please?" She doesn't recognise my voice. She doesn't have time to. A second later Eddie's on the phone. "Hey, Edward, it's me."

"I thought you left already."

"I'm just about to. Listen, Eddie, I just want to say . . . I just want to say it was really good to see you again. Seriously. I've really missed you."

"Good seeing you too, Nick."

Silence.

"There's something I want to ask you, Eddie."

"Like what?"

"The flowers on Sean's grave . . . Do you know who put them there?"

Another long silence. And then . . .

"Who do you think, Nick? Who do you think, man?"

And for the second time in one day my heart feels like it's being ripped in two.

I lock the Kia, walk round the back and make a quick damage assessment. I've been in insurance – I know what to look for. It's only the glass; the frame is still fine. Don't know why I'm even bothering to report it: not worth the hassle, but if you don't they take you to the cleaners.

The cop station is as sad as the rest of this town. I push past the battered wives and their six-pack of babies in crusty nappies and a dronkie with a vuil bandage wrapped around his head, a patch of yellow oozing through. I climb the cement stairs and walk into the station. Three bored-looking cops look up from their KFC takeaways. They look at each other, deciding whose turn it is next to serve the public. One of them eventually stands up, wipes his mouth with the back of his hand and waddles over to the counter.

"Ja, meneer?"

"I need to lay a charge."

The cop reaches under the counter and lifts out a dog's breakfast of an A4 book and opens it slowly. He licks his fingers until he finds a blank page. If he carries on at this rate I'm going to miss my plane. And you never know with Jap crap.

"In what matter do you want to lay a charge?"

I look him straight in the eye.

And now I see it. For the first time in thirty years I see it clear as day in those yellow cop eyes. It wasn't and it never will be like they said – *accidental drowning*. Not to me. Not to Eddie.

"Meneer, in what matter do you want to lay a charge?"

I'm still looking at him. And he's looking at me, thinking maybe he should reach slowly for his gun. I take a deep breath. It's crazy, I know it's fucking crazy and will go nowhere, but for once in my life, just this once, I'm going to do the right thing. I'm going to let Michael and the world know that I, Nicolas Eugene Theron, won't let this end six feet under a Syringa tree.

"I want to report a murder."